Fragments of a Mortal Mind

Fragments of a Mortal Mind

A Nonfiction Novel

DONALD ANDERSON

UNIVERSITY OF NEVADA PRESS *Reno & Las Vegas*

University of Nevada Press, Reno, Nevada 89557 USA
Copyright © 2021 by Donald Anderson
All rights reserved
Interior design by John McKercher

LIBRARY OF CONGRESS CATALOGING-IN-PUBLICATION DATA

Names: Anderson, Donald, 1946 July 9– author.

Title: Fragments of a mortal mind : a nonfiction novel / Donald Anderson.

Description: Reno ; Las Vegas : University of Nevada Press, [2021] |
Includes bibliographical references. | Summary: "Fragments of a mortal
   mind : a nonfiction novel shows us how the disparate elements of our
   lives gather into the construction of our deepest selves. The author
   describes how the world we take in becomes us as we metabolize it.
   This quasi-memoir novel is a meditation on living in America"
   — Provided by publisher.

Identifiers: LCCN 2020045105 (print) | LCCN 2020045106 (ebook) |
   ISBN 9781948908788 (paperback) | ISBN 9781948908795 (ebook)

Subjects: LCSH: Anderson, Donald, 1946 July 9– | Autobiographical memory.

Classification: LCC PS3601.N54 F73 2021 (print) | 3601.N54 (ebook) |
   DDC 818/.607—dc23

LC record available at https://lccn.loc.gov/2020045105
LC ebook record available at https://lccn.loc.gov/2020045106

The paper used in this book is a recycled stock made from
30 percent post-consumer waste materials, certified by FSC,
and meets the requirements of American National Standard
for Information Sciences—Permanence of Paper for Printed
Library Materials, ANSI/NISO Z39.48-1992 (R2002).
Binding materials were selected for strength and durability.

First Printing
Manufactured in the United States of America

25 24 23 22 21   5 4 3 2 1

*Words are properties of thoughts,
and thoughts cannot be thought without them.*

—WILLIAM GASS

Author's Note

My gratitude to the writers I quote, especially Eduardo Galeano and David Markson, toward whose lifework I offer a full tip of the hat.

May the enclosed short quotations nudge readers toward the full texts. We are, after all—aren't we—where we've been and what we've read?

I reiterate here some facts and attitudes and words (often altered or amended) appearing in previous work— in particular *Fire Road*, *Gathering Noise from My Life*, *When War Becomes Personal*, and *Aftermath*, from the University of Iowa Press and Henry Holt. I am indebted to these publishers.

I offer a dance of gratitude to the University of Nevada Press and to my excellent readers Brian Turner and Sara Nović.

PART I

That is how we writers all started: by reading.
We heard the voice of a book speaking to us.

—Margaret Atwood

Who are we—any of us—to slip the summons of time? To slip the summons of failure, tribe, success, panic, decent want, insanity, death, fashion, entitlement, lucidity, quiddity, impotence, license, humility, blood, shame, arrival, unsettled grief, vision, terror, perfidy, loss, pity, art, error, heaven, truth—*mutinous* truth—sympathy, surrender, avoidance, damage, history, sperm, agency, tallying competition, self-pitying self-importance, glamour, turbulence, egg, chaos, inaction, imploration, tyranny, defiance, mask, horror, intention, invention, rites, discovery, recovery, sweet order, troth, ire, murk, pox, sorrow, clemency, inoculation, vicissitude, love? The frustration with time and reality? The fluid fruitfulness of memory?

. . .

Jean Piaget, the esteemed child psychologist, claimed that his earliest memory was of nearly being kidnapped at the age of two. He remembered sitting in his baby carriage, from where he watched his nurse defend herself against the kidnapper. He recalled scratches on the nurse's face and a police officer with a short cloak chasing the kidnapper off. The policeman swung a white baton. The rub against Piaget's recollection is that the event had not occurred. Years later, Piaget's nurse confessed that she'd fabricated the event. Piaget subsequently wrote that he must have heard, as a child, the account of this fabrication and projected it into the past in the form of a visual memory. It was, then, a memory of a memory, constructed falsely.

. . .

Mind and brain studies agree on one thing: there is no agreed-on model of how memory works. The experts tell us we can trust, though, that a good model for how memory works must be consistent with the notion that memories are made in accordance with current needs, desires, influences...

. . .

It struck me today that I am four years older than each of my grandfathers at the age they died.

. . .

How about the studies that show there is no correlation between the subjective feeling a person has about a memory and that memory being accurate?

. . .

The ones his age who shook my hand
on their way out sent fear along
my arm like heroin. These weren't
men mute about their feelings,
or what's a body language for?
        —William Matthews, from "Men at My Father's Funeral"

. . .

Why do I remember, sixty years after, the mugs bought for someone's birthday party? There were seven kids in our house, and every birthday we got to choose the birthday meal and dessert, but we got to have only one birthday party to which we could invite outsiders. We got to choose what year we wanted to do that. Most of us were probably in grade school when we made that decision. The mugs were brown, white foam glazed into the cup's lip and dripping down the sides. My mother filled the cups with hot chocolate and miniature orange marshmallows. The cake was an angel food that had been hollowed and filled with berries and whipped cream. I can see the mugs now.

. . .

I see my grandfathers and my father in suits, which is not at all accurate except in the case of my father. He wore suits in the conduct of his job as a Mormon bishop following his daily labor in the Butte, Montana, Anaconda Company's copper mines. My grandfathers wore bib overalls—not suits—in the conduct of their affairs: my father's father for his treks to the twenty-four-hour miners' bars and my mother's father for his carpentering. That grandfather had taught himself to build houses by way of a correspondence course when the Goodyear Tire Company pulled out of Lincoln, Nebraska, and he moved his family to a small city in Montana: Deer Lodge.

. . .

Home of the Montana State Prison, Deer Lodge today hardly numbers more than three thousand, many of whom are employed at the prison. We made a point to attend each year the prison rodeo. The highlight is when at the rodeo's end, four prisoners set up a card table in the center of the arena. The four then sit to "play" cards. A bull is let in. In time, the bull charges the table. The last prisoner to vacate his seat is crowned victor. Of what?

. . .

A prison rodeo clown settling down an agitated horse by taking a bite of the horse's ear, then spitting out the chunk...Does writing it make the incident true?

. . .

Sitting in the driver's seat of my ten-year-old Toyota Highlander, 130,000 miles on the odometer, I think: "There's a good year or two in this heap." Then: I climb out of the Highlander (we've always owned Toyotas) to reenter the house: "I'm buying a car."

"Are you?" says Ellen. "What car?"

"One the kids will fight over at the funeral."

The mix of rain and snow may explain why there is no one in the Porsche showroom, save a Honduran or Peruvian swiping at vehicles with a feather duster and a single salesman at his desk in the southernmost corner.

The salesman rises. He looks about fourteen. He's wearing a tie. After the test drive, we return to his desk. We'd had to use the heater and defogger. Costs have not been discussed nor are now displayed on any visible paperwork. It is a restaurant with no prices on the menu.

"Will this be cash?" the fourteen-year-old asks.

We conclude the necessary transactions. As a joke to myself, I ask before I leave: "Is there anything I need to know?"

"Don't drive over 150 miles per hour." The kid is straight-faced.

"Why is that?"

"You'd need different tires." He means it.

When I was a kid, my father constructed a truck out of a 1949 Hudson Hornet sedan. It was two-tone black-and-white and looked like an elongated vw Beetle.

My father formed the "truck" with an axe and a hacksaw. After he removed the back seat to connect the space with the trunk, he cut and folded the roof to contain the front seat. He bent the roof by ramming it like a fullback, a pulling guard. I was upright in what had been the back seat. *You helping?* he asked. We rammed the roof.

He hacked a hole for a Plexiglas rear window and metal-screwed everything as tight as he could. During winter, the heater had to hump to keep the cab heated. The finishing touch was quarter-inch sheet metal welded to the frame for the truck bed. There was no tailgate.

Things in the Porsche are meticulously fitted. It talks to me. "Mind your remaining miles," it will announce in a suggestive British accent when I have what the car thinks is eighty miles left of gasoline in the tank.

. . .

In the scientific literature, a confabulation is a fantasy that has unconsciously emerged as a factual account in memory. A confabulation may be based partly on fact or be a complete construction of the imagination. But confabulation is not just a deficit of memory. It is something anyone might do—*need* to do—and *does.* Experiments suggest that confabulation may be a routine activity for healthy people—the manner in which we justify our everyday choices.

. . .

I made up the part about the British accent.

. . .

My grandfather claimed that he trained with Jack Dempsey—in fact, helped him prep for his 1919 championship fight with Jess Willard. My grandfather stated that he'd cracked Jack Dempsey's ribs in training—that Dempsey fought and won that championship fight thus damaged. My grandfather *was* the right age—in fact, the exact age as the world champ. The two of them were both residing in Colorado at the time of the training. Finally, my grandfather was the amateur middleweight champion of Colorado, Utah, Arizona, and Nevada while attending the Colorado School of Mines in Golden, Colorado. He was not as big as Dempsey, but Dempsey was a small heavyweight, tipping the scales at only 185 pounds, unlike the giant he defeated or the taller and heavier heavyweights of today.

. . .

My grandfather produced six teeth that he had kept and claimed that Dempsey had broken them, snapped them at the gum line. I cupped the six brown and dried teeth—*relics*—as my grandfather recounted Jess Willard's own broken teeth, smashed ribs and jaw, broken nose, and crushed cheekbone. My grandfather died when I was sixteen. If his story wasn't true, I knew then, as I know now, that it most certainly should be.

. . .

If I were to remember different things, I should be someone else.

—N. Scott Momaday

. . .

Reading: a form of eavesdropping?

. . .

I lived on nothing but dreams and train smoke…

—Tom Waits

. . .

Memory provides double perspective, enabling us to know our earlier selves in a way that may have eluded us at the time.

. . .

When you are old enough to have a drink with your grandfather, he will have been dead for ten years.

. . .

I remember making shadow figures of animals on my bedroom wall—crocodiles and rabbits. Who first showed me?

. . .

Here is the church and here is the steeple. Open the doors and see all the people.

. . .

We know people by what they say and do, and pile up in their grocery cart. Have you noticed?

Entr'acte

The day my father retired, he dubbed it a *privilege*. The man worked on his vocabulary, memorized poems. He could quote by heart long sections of "The Song of Hiawatha" and the entirety of "The Cremation of Sam McGee." He dodged games like Scrabble or Boggle and puzzles of the crossword sort, as if these were trivial means to acquiring language. Context was his game. Though, in contradiction, when he procured library books for me to read—Edgar Rice Burroughs (Tarzan and Mars), James Oliver Curwood (grizzlies and *Canucks*), Booth Tarkington (Penrod and friends)—he advised that should I come upon a word I didn't know to just go ahead and skip it. I don't recall a dictionary in the house.

There were two bookcases in my childhood home. Waist high and constructed of pine, they flanked the front door to the house that had jammed and that no one used. Except for a partial set of Wonder Books, there were no children's resources on those varnished shelves, dedicated as they were to volumes of Reader's Digest Condensed Books and religious tomes like *Ben-Hur* and *The Robe* and a blue-bound, thumb-indexed *Complete Works of William Shakespeare* that seemed fancy to me.

One Christmas, with the miners on strike, I unwrapped a complete set of the Bomba the Jungle Boy series. My father had received the set from a friend whose children were grown and gone. My siblings unwrapped books too. We all got oranges. Forty years my father drudged in mines and smelters, arriving each day, he said, to an *unswept* room where he changed into *corroded* clothes and *slimed* boots, descending to work beneath the earth's seemingly hard surface. He wore an abused hard hat. Upon retirement, he purchased a shotgun he'd heft, sight, and hand about. It was an expensive Browning he termed *consistent* and *reliable*. He knew how to talk about the shotgun's construction: *close-radius pistol grip, ventilated-rib barrel,* etc. He kept the weapon clean and oiled. He didn't hunt. He'd always owned chainsaws, but, upon retirement, bought a new one. Kept it oiled. When my father died, my younger brother stole both tools right after the funeral, backing his truck up under the carport, then sliding off before eating what the church had brought (casseroles and JELL-O).

A venison man, Jim owned numerous firearms, but as a family, we sensed, without proof, that he'd used Dad's over/under when he shot himself seven years after our father had passed. James II, as it turned out, was a welcoming site for both booze and cancer. A mechanic and master welder, he was a high-functioning drunk who also broke horses. He blamed what happened to his pancreas on diesel and solvents. On the day Jim died, he'd received his second supply—we were later told—of morphine patches he decided not to use.

An unfulfilled goal for Jim was to write the definitive text on how to hunt, prepare, and cook up duck. Jim is buried in Idaho. My father rests some four hours north in Montana. An adjacent plot had been allocated for my mother, who, when she swiftly remarried, taught me all I'd never quite processed when I'd first read *Hamlet* (yes, in my mother's blue-bound edition!). Despite the remarriage, she now rests beside my father, reinstated. He'd had the stone prepared before his own death. All that had to be added was the death date, to follow the hyphen from the birth date: *1925–*. *Beloved Wife and Mother*. I've not been back to see if 2009 has been added.

A sweet-voiced alto, my mother was the typing champion of her high school. She played clarinet and, late in life, taught herself piano on a secondhand upright that she had tuned once a month. A thin bent man, known in our house only as *The German*, came with a bag of silver tuning forks and the sour smell of cabbage. He'd fought in the Great War for the United States and marched in the Fourth of July parades wearing his olive wool uniform and Doughboy steel helmet. He threw paper poppies at the crowd. Besides tuning pianos, The German painted houses and one summer my then teenaged brother helped him paint a porch and garage.

When Jim drove up for our father's funeral, he loitered outside, where he nipped whiskey and smoked and wailed. The service was a Mormon affair. Despite my father's high church standing and his belief, he displayed patience with drunks as if he saw earnest virtue in such focus.

Proud of my four years of college, my father'd often ask, before *he* retired, what *my* salary came to. I'd been promoted to major after eleven years in the U.S. Air Force the summer my parents visited in Washington, DC. When he saw the new rank, my father asked what a major collected. His term was *compensation*. When I announced the amount,

I realized I'd named a figure that exceeded his after all the years he'd humped in the mines and smelters for the Anaconda Company, above or below ground. No words were exchanged to confirm the amounts. I was twenty-five years younger than my father at the time and wore clean clothes to my workplace. He never again inquired as to what I was paid in the Air Force or out.

After the shotgun and chainsaw, my father sprang for a car. He'd long craved a luxury Buick, so he bought one. When he detected that the GM engine was a brother Chevy, he felt duped, or, in his word, *snookered*—the alien motor lodged, as he said, *in his craw thereafter*. He'd paid cash for the *bogus* sedan. He took a loss when he traded the canary Park Avenue in.

My father sought and used words like *metanoia, kerfuffle, swill*. And would go out of his way to throw in something foreign. *Verboten*. When I was very young we were driving for some reason through Texas. In El Paso we tripped over into Mexico. At a fruit stand, my father raised two fingers on his left hand and pointed to the cluster of bananas with his right. When he pronounced *Dos*, I was amazed that he spoke Spanish.

I claim no weapons. I've owned a chainsaw, but it was a mini-electric, hardly an instrument to haul to the woods. Past seventy, and a decade beyond my father when he retired, I still work, and am not thinking of calling it quits. I went back to school for two more degrees after I'd finished the first and still come home in clean clothes after finishing my shift teaching college, no need for safety glasses or gloves. Always the day shift. No steel-toed boots.

I worked in the mines the summer between high school and college. I understand that a dollar's value was different in 1964, but I also realize today that the amount normally carried in my checking account triples what my father paid for the family abode. I pay more in annual taxes than my father ever earned in a year. The house we lived in—all nine of us—had one bathroom. My house now, for the two of us, contains five. What is it I feel? *Shame?* Why is that?

. . .

When your father dies, you will be clobbered by the fact that you can't ask him something only he would know. You have no idea how much you will miss him.

. . .

What history proves is that if you don't create your own personal versions of the past, someone else will do this for you. How many books, for instance, seek to refute the fact of the Holocaust, complete with footnotes? And who can forget the opening pages of Milan Kundera's novel *The Book of Laughter and Forgetting*, which describe a photograph from which a party official has been airbrushed from history?

. . .

There is a conjunction between memory and reflection (imagination) that becomes the story you star in. *You write your life to have a life.*

. . .

My rides have always been red or black or gray, my lifetime three choices of car color. The Porsche, it dawns on me, is the color of the birthday mugs: a rich coffee brown.

· · ·

Orange…seems to be the only basic color word for which no other word exists in English. There is only orange, and the name comes from the fruit. Tangerine doesn't really count. Its name also comes from a fruit, a variety of the orange, but it wasn't until 1899 that "tangerine" appears in print as the name of a color—and it isn't clear why we require a new word for it. This seems no less true for persimmon and for pumpkin. There is just orange.

But there was no orange, at least before oranges came to Europe. This is not to say that no one recognized the color, only that there was no specific name for it. In Geoffrey Chaucer's "Nun's Priest's Tale," the rooster Chaunticleer dreams of a threatening fox invading the barnyard, whose "color was betwixe yelow and reed." The fox was orange, but in the 1390s Chaucer didn't have a word for it. He had to mix it verbally. He wasn't the first to do so. In Old English, the form of the language spoken between the fifth and twelfth centuries, well before Chaucer's Middle English, there was a word *geoluhread* (yellow-red). Orange could be seen, but the compound was the only word there was for it in English for almost a thousand years.

—David Scott Kastan, with Stephen Farthing, from *On Color*

· · ·

A favorite professor, a little Scotsman, elfish, repeated that imagination was rightfully seen as the creative power to link disparate materials together in a search for form that satisfies a personal sense of truth.

. . .

Personal writing is art, not a legal document.

. . .

To write something down is to make a fossil record of a mind.

—Jill Lepore

. . .

The acknowledgment of doubt is precisely what allows us to suspend it.

—Michael Pollan

. . .

If all we wanted from one another was information, then all we'd need to do is exchange our driver's licenses. It's something else we're after. What is it?

. . .

In the nineteenth century, commonplace books were the thing. Readers hand-copied into personal books—"scrap" books if you will—passages from poems, newspaper stories, science fact, memorable weather, city politics, Bible verses, family myths and histories, an assembling, by hand, of what a person valued or thought about, a kind of diary—secret or not—of thought.

. . .

The man who does not read good books has no advantage over the man who cannot read at all.

—Mark Twain

. . .

In fewer words, your commonplace book should be such as to be evaluated positively for *quality of mind*, whether anyone else flips through its pages or not.

. . .

James Baldwin wrote that no one can argue with another's experience or decision or belief.

. . .

Please try to be clear, dear James, through the storm which rages about your youthful head today, about the reality which lies behind the words *acceptance* and *integration*. There is no reason for you to try to become like white people and there is no basis whatever for their impertinent assumption that *they* must accept *you*. The really terrible thing, old buddy, is that *you* must accept *them*.

—Baldwin in a letter to his nephew

. . .

...snowflakes the storm brings are shelter from its cold.
—William Stafford, from *Sound of the Ax*

. . .

My father called, deeply pleased, to be able to inform me that the leadership of the Mormon Church had received a "revelation" that they were called on, of a sudden, to *accept* African Americans as *full* members into the Mormon faith.

This is 1978 and the Mormons (officially the Church of Jesus Christ of Latter-day Saints) was disavowing itself of its policy (since 1849) of prohibiting black men from being ordained into the priesthood and black men and women from taking part in ceremonies conducted in Mormon temples. For a long time, African Americans had been invited to be second-class Mormons, a status from which they could be baptized and pay tithing, yet not be integrated into full-standing membership.

What was pleasing my father, I think, was that he thought this newfound acceptance of blacks would convince me to return to the fold, the church's long-standing position on blacks having been a sticking point. I don't believe he understood me when I said this new stance only made the whole thing worse. "You're not happy?" he asked. "I'm happy," I said, "now BYU can get some running backs." I was ashamed the minute I said this. I wasn't going to point out that allowing blacks full status would open up whole continents to proselytizing—the more members, the more lucre flowing into the coffers. To this day, however, the church's presiding presidency and Quorum of, yes, Twelve Apostles are all light-skinned men. And so it goes. I suspect now that as a kid I was being taught a kind of gentrified white supremacy. There wasn't a sense of physically harming dark-skinned people so much as cultivating a sense of pity for them, which is also harm.

. . .

Lynching, the first scholar of the subject determined, is an American invention. Lynching from bridges, from arches, from trees standing alone in fields, from trees in front of the county courthouse, from trees used as public billboards, from trees barely able to support the weight of a man, from telephone poles, from streetlamps, and from poles erected solely for that purpose…. The [telephone] poles, of course, were not to blame. It was only coincidence that they became convenient as gallows, because they were tall and straight, with a crossbar, and because they stood in public places. And it was only coincidence that the telephone poles so closely resembled crucifixes.

—Eula Biss, from *Notes from No Man's Land*

. . .

According to the 1860 Census, one in eight Americans was considered property.

. . .

When I was growing up, I understood Mormon doctrine to be that blacks were black as a consequence of God's curse on Cain. Having murdered his brother Abel, Cain was then struck with a blackened skin. One of Noah's sons, Ham, married a daughter of Cain. From that marriage sprang, in Joseph Smith's words, "a race which preserved the curse in the land."

. . .

"And the sins of the fathers shall be
visited upon the heads of the children,
even unto the third and fourth
generation of them that hate me."

Well, then, I hate thee, unrighteous picture;
Wicked image, I hate thee;

So strike with Thy vengeance
The heads of those little men
Who come blindly.
It will be a brave thing.

        —Stephen Crane, from *The Black Riders and Other Lines*

. . .

The Mormons pushed the notion of white-skin supremacy onto Native Americans as well. Spencer W. Kimball, the Mormon "prophet" on watch when blacks were enfranchised, was, as well, a booster of the Indian Placement Program, wherein "Indians" from reservations were placed into white Mormon foster homes. "I saw," he pronounced from the pulpit, "a striking contrast in the progress of the Indian people today as against that of only fifteen years ago. Truly the scales of darkness are falling from their eyes, and they are fast becoming a white and delightsome people." What was that supposed to mean?

. . .

The T-shirt featuring head-dressed warriors astride ponies and clutching spears that reads: HOMELAND SECURITY— *Fighting Terrorism Since 1492.*

. . .

The book about Columbus titled *What It Feels Like to Be Discovered.*

. . .

About 123 million people died in all wars of the twentieth century (37 million military deaths, 27 million collateral civilian deaths, 41 million victims (genocide and other mass murder), and 18 million victims of famine.

.   .   .

We're forever reading atrocities as mere omens; anything to do nothing a little while longer.

—Don Paterson, from *The Book of Shadows*

.   .   .

Who but Mandela would have said, *Resentment is like drinking poison and then hoping it will kill your enemies*?

.   .   .

Adolf Eichmann read *Lolita* while awaiting trial in Jerusalem. And was indignant over what he termed its unwholesomeness.

—David Markson, from *Vanishing Point*

.   .   .

One of my daughters lived in South Africa during Mandela's presidency. Mandela was so beloved as his nation's leader that his constituents commonly referred to him as "Papa."

When my daughter and husband returned to the States, my grandsons, still in grade school, had two questions: (1) What happened to all the black people? (2) Why do we have to wear shoes to school?

And then, snow surprised them.

.   .   .

And here comes the snow, a language
in which no word is ever repeated.

> —William Matthews, from "Spring Snow"

. . .

Today's newspaper: *Wilfred Owen died on Armistice Day 1918, the last day of the war.*

Actually, Owen's parents were informed of his death *on* Armistice Day. Owen had died the week before.

The newspaper is running the story in commemoration of the one-hundredth anniversary of the assassination of Archduke Franz Ferdinand of Austria—the act that starts the war.

Turns out that the assassin is one of nine children, six of whom had died in infancy. The newspaper reports a celebration in Sarajevo where the assassin, Gavrilo Princip, is treated as hero.

In truth, it was Princip's accomplice who first tosses the bomb—a kind of grenade—at the motorcade. The bomb is deflected by the Archduke—hitting him in the arm. The Archduke is in an open car, so as to wave at his non-Austrian minions. The deflected bomb explodes late, missing the Archduke's car altogether. Hard not to see it as a kind of cartoon: the Duke in a tallish hat with a lavender plume and the bomb a black ball with a visible fuse lit. Right? So here's the rest: the bomb thrower swallows a cyanide pill, then leaps into the nearby river. The cyanide pill, though, is expired, and the river that time of year is four inches deep.

The Duke—ever paternal—drives to the hospital to visit the injured victims of the car that actually caught the bomb. *Mistake*, because Princip happens to be on the sidewalk when the Duke's driver takes a wrong turn. The Serb had been in a sandwich shop. While the driver is backing up, Princip shoots the Duke and then the wife when she tries to shield her royal hubby.

What if the Serb hadn't been hungry?

So what starts the war?—a misthrown bomb, a wrong turn in a car, bad cyanide, child non-mortality, lunchtime? Austria takes a hard line against Serbia, and other powers in Europe choose sides. Within thirty days, a half-assed squabble between Austria and Serbia transforms into the first great modern war.

At the hundred-year assassination site celebration, someone calculated that to hold a second of silence for every person killed in World War I in Europe the attendees would have to stand mute for about two years.

Princip's cyanide pill was expired too.

For World War II, you'd be standing around quiet for a dozen years or so.

· · ·

My freshman year of college, my math profs was a drunk who'd worked on the Manhattan Project. He spoke as if he knew them all—Teller, Fermi, Oppenheimer...

So: he shows up late for class, soused, stares at us from the door, then approaches the board to pick up chalk. He draws a line across the board and then continues all around the room, across the windows and walls, dragging the chalk, until he's back at the door. He gives us another look—like he feels sorry for us or something. Then clears his throat, saying, *teaching*: "Even-That's-Not-Infinity…"

. . .

The United States entered World War II late, but still suffered a million military casualties.

. . .

What notion do we have of what Europe experienced? In World War I, a total of 6.7 million nonmilitary people were killed. In World War II some 40 million killed. As for soldiers, the Soviets themselves lost 8 million or so. Both world wars combined cost 80 million Europeans their lives.

. . .

More soldiers dead in the American Civil War than in *all* our other wars *combined*. The only real war on our home soil.

. . .

The trouble with the Civil War is that it is like a Turner Classic Movie. Too long ago and has been made too theatrical. It's all Noble Causes, and movie stars. Not much grapeshot. When have you seen a movie about dysentery and field amputations? The real Civil War is a lot of dead, empty sleeves, orphans, and crutches. Where's the movie about Sherman's March?

. . .

On 9-11, we lose three thousand in the Towers. How many Iraqis and Afghanis since? A half million or more?

. . .

Most know the number fifty-eight thousand, but what of the three million Vietnamese we killed? In their own country, we killed them, then left. Left behind poisoned water and soil. Unexploded ordnance. At one time there were more prosthetics per capita in Vietnam than anywhere else in the world.

. . .

To talk about Vietnam is to talk about POWs. When you spout words like POW *courage* and POW *honor*, you don't have to bring up that thing about what we were doing in Southeast Asia in the first place. You don't have to talk about bombing a nation that if it had decent highways you could drive the length of in ten hours, the width of in three. You don't have to mention that George Kennan, the architect of the domino theory, had refuted his own notions before Congress almost before the war began. You can pretend that the POWs were poor misunderstood nice guys who were kidnapped by pirates.

. . .

Four times the ordnance was dropped on Vietnam than was dropped in *all* of World War II, worldwide.

. . .

re: What to Worry About
Armed drones. Then see how many citizens want tickets to the Super Bowl or the World Series.

. . .

Climate change…has brought longer, hotter summers and a series of devastating droughts, priming landscapes to burn. Tree-killing insects such as the mountain pine beetle thrive in droughts and closely packed forests. The most recent outbreak of bark-beetle infestation, the largest ever recorded, has destroyed billions of trees in fourteen western states and much of western Canada. Dead trees make fine kindling for a megafire.

—William Finnegan, from "California Burning"

. . .

In 1874 America, Rocky Mountain locusts
rushed up from the ground
like struck oil. The rasping clouds
of their bodies sawed shadows
into every seam and clod of entire states.
They ate the wool from living sheep,
the wooden hafts of axes. They collected
in drifts against fences,
blew and banged and clattered
on slats like thrown gravel.
It must have felt like the end
of the world then, every tender shoot
raptured into insectoid jaws.
. . . .

Do you know the differences
between a grasshopper
and a locust? Taxonomically, none.
The distinction is mathematical:
A grasshopper is a single digit
that hangs and vanishes in the heat-warped summer air,
and a locust is a particle in a swarm

that divides as it multiplies
like cancer, division
after division of advancing hunger
until one gaunt morning
the meal is finished
and the bones preside.

—Greg Larson, from "Plague"

. . .

Remember in *The Deer Hunter* when De Niro, all eager to get to Nam, kept asking the Green Beret at the bar what the war was like, and the only answer the Beret kept giving was *Fuck It*? Remember?

. . .

A Secret Service agent told me he only worried about the three B's: Booze, Broads, and Bullets. In that order, he said.

. . .

I live in a country where one party wants to impeach a president for lying about a blow job and then calls for nothing against a president who lies to start two wars. Help me here.

. . .

You have a bucket list? A friend of mine does: medical marijuana and gay marriage. Maybe it's a joke. Could be a joke. Can't tell.

. . .

On the same page in the paper talking about World War I is the article about some guy who got caught on video kicking a squirrel into the Grand Canyon from one of the overlooks. It's gone viral on YouTube—a million views, like ten times the number of U.S. deaths in World War I. More interest in an airborne squirrel than in the anniversary of the planet's first modern war?

. . .

The piece about the state-of-the-art solar plant in the Mojave Desert? More than 300,000 mirrors, each the size of a garage door, reflect sunshine onto three boiler towers forty stories high. The water inside is heated past boiling to produce steam to generate enough electricity for 140,000 homes. The problem is that birds flying through the concentrated sun rays ignite and burn. Some estimates are as high as 28,000 a year. The solar company says it's only 1,000.

. . .

They call the burning birds *streamers*.

. . .

re: (Overheard at a writing conference, recorded on an iPhone, later transcribed into my commonplace book)
Couple of gay dudes moved in on our block. Immediately planted roses.

Ever notice that grown queers dress like nine-year-old boys? You know, the cocked baseball cap, loud socks…

My little brother's gay. Doesn't cock his cap.

No, just the opposite.

That's beneath even you, Fuckhead.

Just saying.

Brother did tell me that Subaru is a lesbian car.

Oh?

Pay attention for a week, then tell me.

MORE:

My wife's great uncle—actually her step-great uncle—graduated from the Naval Academy in the twenties. First guy to land a jet on a slant-deck carrier or something. Famous. Commanded a carrier himself, knew Eisenhower. Shot down over Midway. Spent a week in the water. Said he punched sharks. Showed me his Academy ring. Said he was wearing it when he punched sharks. I have the ring.

MORE:

My hearing's starting to go. She said "teak oil"; I thought she said "tin foil." She said, "I'm a little off kilter"; I thought she said, "a moth killed her." Do you think this is serious?

I don't know. A writer always fills in, doesn't he? Whether he can hear or not.

AND:

Been reading a biography of Buzz Aldrin. He was military, graduated West Point, but cross-commissioned into the Air Force, fought in Korea, shot down two MIGs—so, you know? *Cred.* What he said about war was that from the distance of space war had a "benign" quality—that, intellectually, he could realize that wars could be under way (of course Vietnam was) but that, emotionally, from that distance, it was impossible to understand such things.

Tell you what? I wasn't viewing Iraq from space, OK? I was in Ramadi. It looked different from there.

Did you know that Aldrin's mother's maiden name was Moon?

It was not. You're lying.

It was. Look it up. Do it on your phone. Go ahead. I mean, it's cool in its own way, OK? *Moon.*

Either cool or fucked. Beats me.

It's cool. Admit it. If you're Buzz Aldrin, your mother's maiden name should be Moon.

It's like something out of Dickens. It's something Dickens would have done.

Tell me something I actually need to know. Give me news for my world. Tell me something to use.

If nine Russians tell you you're drunk, lie down.

We are temporary motherfuckers. Everybody keeps talking about surviving. But we aren't meant to *survive*, only to *live*. That's it.

AND:

Reread the fucking *Faerie Queene*. I don't care.

OR:

In the end, he married the ugly one with money. Broke his cute little girlfriend's heart. She had a kid. Maybe that was it. It could have been that.

AND THESE:

Read *Middlemarch*. You'll stop wondering where Henry James got his syntax.

What is Life but guarding your small fire against winds?

Our emotional lives are the only substantial plot in our lives. Otherwise, all to report is you're born and then you die…

The cause of Death *is* Life.

We are the only society that sues for spilling coffee on ourselves.

We're doomed. Now what?

If you are deciding to give a beggar money, first check out his smart phone and shoes.

If you are black and drive a luxury car, the police will stop you.

The dandruff on her shoulders looks like flour.

I'm too pretty to work.

If you die, that's one thing; if your brother dies, quite another.

She spends her time reading magazines devoted almost entirely to hairdos.

Motive? More often than not, people don't know why they do things.

When the governor in my state closed liquor stores during the coronavirus panic, there was such an outcry that he reopened them by labeling them "essential." In addition to meeting regular customers' needs, hospitals, worried about having enough beds for any virus victims, stated that the reopenings would help them avoid a flooding of alcoholics needing medical detox.

AND:
I'm talking to this guy I know who's just *concluded* a divorce. Says he lost everything. Not just some things: *Everything.* I said a divorce lawyer friend of mine said that after the best

divorces, *both* parties should feel screwed. *In my case*, my guy says, *my ex-wife does* not *feel screwed*. Then he tells me what he did. He charters a plane, one of these planes with a big side door for, like, you know, skydivers. But instead of skydivers, the guy loads up a washer—a clothes washer, a Maytag—not full-size, *apartment* size, a *stackable*, but *still*. Has the pilot fly over his ex-wife's cul-de-sac, drops the washer onto the ex-wife's new car, a Buick LaSabre parked on the street. People don't look up, he says. It's why snipers position themselves in trees. It's why they hide in trees.

THEN:
Do you know Jesus, Bob?

. . .

This morning when I walked, the sun just risen, the sand from the snowplows, now blown by traffic to the edges of the road, cast shadows disproportionate to their heights. The shadows looked like stalagmites or little armies.

. . .

What is a novel but a cautionary reminder of the ways things can go wrong?

. . .

The information that Eldridge Cleaver, the fiery Black Panther leader, later renounced his past and became a Mormon and a Republican?

. . .

Or that Donald Trump and Mike Pence, who ran for election on more guns and more guns, which, they claimed, meant more protection, have demanded a ban on firearms during the forum at which they are slated to speak at, yes, the annual meeting of the NRA?

. . .

The second before the sun went out we saw a wall of dark shadow come speeding at us. We no longer saw it than it was upon us, like thunder. It roared up the valley. It slammed our hill and knocked us out. It was the monstrous swift shadow cone of the moon. I have since read that this wave of shadow moves 1,800 miles an hour. Language can give no sense of this sort of speed—1,800 miles an hour. It was 195 miles wide. No end was in sight—you saw only the edge. It rolled at you across the land at 1,800 miles an hour, hauling darkness like a plague behind it. Seeing it, and knowing it was coming straight for you, was like feeling a slug of anesthetic shoot up your arm. If you think very fast, you may have time to think, "Soon it will hit my brain." You can feel the deadness race up your arm; you can feel the appalling, inhuman speed of your own blood. We saw the wall of shadow coming, and screamed before it hit.

Less than two minutes later, when the sun emerged, the trailing edge of the shadow cone sped away. It coursed down our hill and raced eastward over the plain, faster than the eye could believe; it swept over the plain and dropped over the planet's rim in a twinkling. It had clobbered us, and now it roared away. We blinked in the light. It was as though an enormous, loping god in the sky had reached down and slapped the earth's face.

—Annie Dillard, from "Total Eclipse"

. . .

The influenza epidemic of 1918–19 killed at least 650,000 Americans, four times the number of U.S. troops who died in World War I. As many as 60 million people on the planet died. Dubbed the "Spanish flu," the onslaught of illness disappeared as puzzlingly as it had first emerged.

. . .

We are food.
The rest is mystery.

—Alison Sean, from "Sand Key"

. . .

Although writing about war in *The Things They Carried*, Tim O'Brien was also writing about story—pursued and usable "truth." *The Things They Carried* is a testament to the power of story while it is, at the same time, a meditation on the elusiveness of truth and the shiftiness of memory. O'Brien instructs:

> In any war story, but especially a true one, it's difficult to separate what happened from what seemed to happen. What seems to happen becomes its own happening and has to be told that way. The angles of vision are skewed. When a booby trap explodes, you close your eyes and duck and float outside yourself. When a guy dies, like Curt Lemon, you look away and then look back for a moment and then look away again. The pictures get jumbled; you tend to miss a lot. And then afterward, when you go to tell about it, there is always that surreal seemingness, which makes the story seem untrue,

but which in fact represents the hard and exact truth as it *seemed.*

O'Brien is hardly thrashing about facts here; he is sifting emotions—anger, ardor, love, grief, despondency, sentiment, shame, sorrow. At the end of "How to Tell a True War Story," from which I've been quoting, O'Brien (the character? the real person?) complains about people—particularly women—who complain about his war stories, his "true" stories:

> All you can do is tell it one more time, patiently, adding and subtracting, making up a few things to get at the real truth. No Mitchell Sanders, you tell her. No Lemon. No Rat Kiley. No trail junction. No baby buffalo. No vines or moss or white blossoms. Beginning to end, you tell her, it's all made up. Every goddamn detail—the mountains and the river and especially that poor dumb baby buffalo. None of it happened. *None* of it. And even if it did happen, it didn't happen in the mountains, it happened in this little village on the Batangan Peninsula, and it was raining like crazy, and one night a guy named Stink Harris woke up screaming with a leech on his tongue. You can tell a true war story if you just keep on telling it.

"Absolute occurrence is irrelevant," O'Brien states earlier. Absolute occurrence does not constitute the truth a true war story depends on. "A thing may happen and be a total lie; another thing may not happen and be truer than the truth."

. . .

It's a commonplace—isn't it?—that most fiction is, on some level, *true*, though perhaps not striving for this condition as assiduously as nonfiction. But both forms are after—aren't they?—what we call willingly a *larger truth*? It's mushy, though, because truth with a capital T is hardly universal or given to convincing verification. Facts can be checked and confirmed of course, but absolute truth remains in debate—which is why in courtrooms we lower our aim for a "reasonable" truth. Acknowledging such may also be why we have witnessed the rise of *creative nonfiction*, a term as bewildering, perhaps, as it is accurate. Fiction and non-fiction writers share more than they don't, and face (as they ransack memory and imagination) the same holy mess in their constructions. Why wouldn't they reach for the same problem-solving contraptions: dialogue, description, plot, detail, characterization, point of view, image, metaphor?

. . .

Metaphor—that old instrument of perception—is the very heart of whatever gifts a writer has to offer and whatever gifts a reader is prepared to receive, and yet is in fact a small lie. No metaphor is factually true, but we accept, if not believe them. Graham Greene: "Innocence is like a dumb leper who has lost his bell, wandering the world, meaning no harm." Or David Keplinger: "The smell of a man's hat—an old man's hat—is like the nostril of a horse." Jean Cocteau, on coming upon stacks of Marcel Proust's notebooks after Proust's death, characterized them as "watches ticking on the wrists of dead soldiers." Metaphor, in all its variations—similes, and the like—become the little lies we live by. Ennobled lies that persist.

. . .

In Harriet Doerr's semi-autobiographical novel *Stones for Ibarra*, there is a chapter in which the American Sara Everton takes Spanish lessons from an older Mexican nun. The novel takes place in Mexico. Sara is blessed with a busy imagination, from which place she constantly invents the nun's former life. Simultaneously, she works to imagine a future for her husband, who has contracted terminal cancer.

"Where were you born?" asked Sara.

"For your next lesson please write a paragraph on an event of the coming week," said the nun.

As simply as this, without method or rules, the line of skirmish was drawn between the two women, one resolved to close off the past, the other to reject the future.

Because the nun has shut the door to her past, Sara feels compelled to invent it. What else is she to do? In controlling the past, Sara appears to feel more secure in imagining a future that contains a cure for her husband. Richard senses what Sara is doing and calls her on it. Sara parries the way a writer might. After one particularly extravagant slice of the nun's former life, Richard examines his wife's face:

"Are you sure this is what Madre Petra told you?"

Sara thought of the convent *sala*, its sparse furnishings, the nun's seamed face, her crippled hand.

"It's what I heard her say."

And then later:

"Is that what the madre told you? In those words?"

"Almost," she said.

. . .

Tobias Wolff concludes his first story collection with a story entitled "The Liar." The character of interest in this story is a sixteen-year-old who confabulates. The stories he tells are fake tragedies, such as his mother suffering from appalling disease. James is an accomplished liar. He is good at what he does. In one of the most deft set pieces in contemporary fiction, James conscripts a neighbor kid to help him move his father's body into an upstairs bedroom. James's father has died on the couch after a prolonged illness. James is proud that his father has "died well"—that is, as Wolff puts it, without complaining or overly inconveniencing those who are to be left behind.

> He died downstairs in a shaft of late afternoon sunlight on New Year's Day, while I was reading to him. I was alone in the house and didn't know what to do. His body did not frighten me but immediately and sharply I missed my father. It seemed wrong to leave him sitting up and I tried to carry him upstairs to the bedroom but it was too hard, alone. So I called up my friend Ralphy across the street. When he came over and saw what I wanted him for he started crying but I made him help me anyway. A couple of hours later Mother got home and when I told her that Father was dead she ran upstairs, calling his name. A few minutes later she came back down. "Thank God," she said, "at least he died in bed." This seemed important to her and I didn't tell her otherwise. But that night Ralphy's parents

called. They were, they said, shocked at what I had done and so was Mother when she heard the story, shocked and furious. Why? Because I had not told her the truth? Or because she had learned the truth, and could not go on believing that Father had died in bed? I really don't know.

Wolff finishes "The Liar" with James on a bus, traveling to spend time with his elder brother. The bus breaks down, and James, given a chance to confabulate, takes it. He can't seem to help himself, but put yourself on the stalled bus and see if you don't welcome this weakness. The bus is stuck, and a friendly fat woman is passing around cold fried chicken.

The wind was blowing hard around the bus, driving sheets of rain against the windows on both sides. The bus swayed gently. Outside the light was brown and thick. The woman next to me pumped all the people for their itineraries and said whether or not she had ever been where they were from or where they were going. "How about you?" She slapped my knee. "Parents own a chicken ranch? I hope so!" She laughed. I told her I was from San Francisco. "San Francisco, that's where my husband was stationed." She asked me what I did there and I told her I worked with refugees from Tibet.

"Is that right? What do you do with a bunch of Tibetans?"

"Seems like there's plenty of other places they could've gone," said a man in front of us. "Coming across the border like that. We don't go there."

"What do you do with a bunch of Tibetans?" the woman repeated.

"Try to find them jobs, locate housing, listen to their problems."

"You understand that kind of talk?"

"Yes."

"Speak it?"

"Pretty well. I was born and raised in Tibet. My parents were missionaries over there."

Everyone waited.

"They were killed when the Communists took over."

The big woman patted my arm.

"It's all right," I said.

"Why don't you say some of that Tibetan?"

"What would you like to hear?"

"Say 'The cow jumped over the moon.'" She watched me, smiling, and when I finished she looked at the others and shook her head. "That was pretty. Like music. Say some more."

"What?"

"Anything."

They bent toward me. The windows suddenly went blind with rain. The driver had fallen asleep and was snoring gently to the swaying of the bus. Outside the muddy light flickered to pale yellow, and far off there was thunder. The woman next to me leaned back and closed her eyes and then so did all the others as I sang to them in what was surely an ancient and holy tongue.

. . .

Tobias Wolff is a memoirist as well as a fiction writer, and his prefatory note to *This Boy's Life* is, well, memorable. "I have been corrected on some points," he says, "mostly of chronology."

> Also my mother thinks that a dog I describe as ugly was actually quite handsome. I've allowed some of these points to stand, because this is a book of memory, and memory has its own story to tell. But I have done my best to make it tell a truthful story.

. . .

My earliest mentor would say, "Art and life are different. If they weren't, we wouldn't need art."

. . .

What is art, but a remaking of the world into forms more acceptable to us?

Entr'acte

I turn to reading or making fiction to clarify reality. Though Life is under no obligation to make sense, Art promotes a reach toward meaning beyond what in your life may have been at first apparent. Secondary meanings emerge through the noise of words. Language adjusts experience, doesn't it? Meaning, embedded in concreteness, can become a beautiful, ghostly abstraction to the fleshy counterpart. Do you believe it? Here:

A few years back I was flying to Florida for spring break. I had that day finished classes and was taking a night flight from Colorado to South Florida. My wife was already there. I had a layover in Cincinnati. It was about 7:00 PM. The sun had set and it was rainy and cold. At the end of the terminal I spied a Starbucks. Just what I need, I thought: a seven-dollar cup of coffee. I started that way.

At the counter, ahead of me, was a dwarf. My reaction was as yours might have been. It made me think of words like, *Well*, *now*, or *Oh!* My reaction was compounded by the fact that the little woman was lovely, shockingly gorgeous. I felt confused and affronted. Brainless. What right had I to decide that this dwarf did not look as she should have?—like *I* expected her to? Something felt wrong. What was it? I knew I would have to write about the experience to understand the least of it. The essay was published in the *North American Review*. It was listed under Nonfiction and titled "Stunted."

The woman was so small—the height and size of a three-year-old—that the clerk behind the Starbucks counter in the Cincinnati airport didn't see her. When the clerk asked for my order, I, along with a hand gesture, said, "I believe she was first." Was I trying to pretend it was normal for a grown person to be thirty inches tall? The clerk—bless her heart—then leaned over the counter. To be fair, it was a wide counter, though I don't think higher than standard.

"Oh," the clerk said. "What would you like?"

"A small latté," the dwarf said.

The clerk, taller than I, was a thin black girl with straightened hair. She was kind and probably some years younger than the white dwarf below her.

When the clerk set the latté on the counter to reach for the money, she inadvertently set the cup beyond the dwarf's reach. The clerk handed over the change, then asked for my order. I pointed at the cup.

What was I feeling? Shame? Fear? Pride? Generosity? What I knew for sure was that whatever the feeling was, it was anchored in an awkward self-centeredness. What did this woman's growth have to do with me?

The clerk saw she had to push the latté closer, and she did. I ordered a small latté. I didn't want to give the impression that my body could absorb more liquid than the dwarf's. Besides, how to utter the Starbucks word for small: *tall*?

The woman had to reach as high as she could to remove the plastic lid from her cup to add sugar. She'd moved down the counter, sliding the capped cup toward the stirrers, the honey and sugars. I was worried she'd pull the hot cup over onto her head—her uplifted face—and had to resist helping. Craning, she managed to add raw cane sugar, stir the coffee, and replace the lid. When she headed off in her little beige London Fog, navy slacks, and kid's clogs, I noticed her hands were the size of a woman's, strong and dexterous enough to hold her latté and to maneuver her rolling luggage. If her clothes were doll-size, her pull luggage wasn't.

For her height and size her head was, as seems the case for dwarves, disproportionate. Too large, of course, but in this case—her case—only slightly. And her features were fine, not distorted. Her long hair was tended and high-lighted professionally with streaks of blond.

I boarded my plane. Late that night, I told my wife about the little woman and her latté.

What I've just reported is factual. It is, as best as I recall, what happened in the airport. I did, that night, tell my wife about the dwarf. What Ellen said—and it is *all* she said—was this: "She was probably going to a conference." I needed dialogue, so I wrote some.

[Late that night, I told my wife about the little woman and her latté.]

"She had glorious hair—really—I have to say," I say to Ellen. "A little kid's voice but a grown-up's hair. Luxurious. And she was neat and urbane in her kid's clothes, her little purse."

"You don't have to feel bad for her," my wife says. "Why do you feel bad? You feel bad, don't you? You do."

"Well, God," I say, "I think of Marnie racing her bike in that mountain thing in Moab." Marnie is one of our daughters. As the local joke goes, you can tell she's from Boulder, Colorado: She owns a $500 car, but pedals a $3,000 bicycle made from space-age metals.

"When I saw the little woman walking away," I say, "pulling that suitcase her size, I thought about Marnie talking about her bike's composite frame, the composite shifters, titanium gears, step-in pedals."

I say: "Her feet lock into her pedals like ski boots. That little woman will never ride a mountain bike. They don't make good bikes that small. She'd have to buy a tricycle for chrissake—a Goddamn Big Wheel or something. You know?"

"Why is this personal?" Ellen asks. "Is this personal?"

"I don't know."

"Dwarves attend conferences. I've read about this," Ellen says. "They have dwarf stores for clothes and furniture. Car stuff. A lot of dwarves drive cars." Then: "Dwarfism is treated as a disability. There are lobbies for this.

'Little People' lobbies. And: *conferences.* She was probably on her way to a conference. They meet at these places, fall in love, marry, have babies."

"What kind of babies? Regular or small?"

"Regular," she says.

"Why would they be regular? A bald guy's son is usually bald. Big noses run in families. A son of an alcoholic is an alcoholic risk. A fat woman's mother is generally large, right? You think I didn't check out your mother?"

I should tell you that my wife heard me read this essay at a conference in Key West. After my reading, she said, "I didn't say those things." I know," I said, "but you should have." And there you have the hazard—on both sides—of having a writer in the house. In my defense, there were people in the audience who know both Ellen and me, and who said, "Sounds just like you, Ellen." I should report too, I suppose, that Ellen was not amused.

["A fat woman's mother is generally large, right? You think I didn't check out your mother?"]

My wife is a slender woman who smokes cigarettes. She walks four miles a day. Power walks. To stay fit, is what she says, and to keep on smoking. My wife buys cheap filtered menthols she stubs out when half puffed. It stunts your growth, she says. I call her E sometimes instead of Ellen.

"You should quit, E," I say.

"You *like* tiny women," she says, lighting up. She raises a kitchen window and sticks her head close. She is a polite smoker insofar as she keeps smoke out of people's faces and houses, even her own.

"Why wouldn't dwarves bear dwarves?" I ask. And when Ellen doesn't answer: "What would a dwarf do with a four-year-old who could knock her over?"

Ellen blows smoke out the window, then swivels her head. "What makes you think all dwarves are actors or circus freaks?"

"I think that?"

"Do you?"

I say that every few years you read in the paper about dwarf tossing or such. "You don't remember Cuomo signing legislation banning dwarf tossing and dwarf bowling in New York bars?" We'd lived in New York for a few years.

"Dwarf bowling?" E says.

"Yes."

"Bowling?"

"They strap them on skateboards and fire them down the lane." Then: "As I understand it, they do wear helmets and the pins are plastic."

I clamp shut because I suddenly remember seeing on TV some little folks wrapped in Velcro clothes. They were hung like pictures on Velcro walls. I don't recall whether they were tossed at the walls, but, in any event, I don't bring it up.

"Bars and bowling alleys," E says. "I take it they throw dwarves in bars."

"Liquor's involved," I say. "It would have to be, right?"

"You tell me," E says.

"Some dwarves have sued for the right to be tossed and bowled." I nod my head to enforce the point.

"Claiming what—the right to make a living?"

"So, maybe there should be a right? I mean, who stops three-hundred-pound blubber boys from squashing skinnier backs and wide-outs? Why isn't that illegal? Pitchers fire balls at batters' heads. We're not talking hockey or Tyson eating Holyfield's ear. Consenting dwarves," I say, "wear sturdy little helmets and padding, and when they're tossed, they land on mattresses—no, usually a pile of them."

"Consenting? Did you say *consenting*?"

"I did." Then: "I say if a man wants to juggle hatchets, let him do it."

"Where would you draw the line," E asks, "chainsaws, grenades, white phosphorus? White phosphorus," she says, "reacts rapidly with oxygen, catching fire at ten to fifteen degrees above room temperature. Dangerous enough, Ace?"

My wife takes a drag on her cigarette. She blows smoke into the room, then shoots me a look. It's the look I imagined on the writer Annie Dillard's face a few years back.

I've never met Ms. Dillard but have taken pleasure in her work and had just finished her book *For the Time Being*. It's hardly a book in an obvious sense of unity and purpose. It is a loose yet rich federation about human abnormalities, sand, clouds, numbers, China, Israel, God, evil, archaeology, and life-size Chinese clay soldiers and their horses—thousands of them sculpted for, then buried with the Emperor Qin to honor and protect him for the past two thousand years. The clay soldiers and their mounts were a whole new idea. It had been the practice to bury an emperor's living army with him when he passed.

In the book, Dillard not only covers a variety of human abnormalities—noting, in particular, mentally deficient bird-headed dwarves—but a variety of human cruelties as well, such stunted acts as the flaying of the eighty-five-year-old Rabbi Akiva for teaching Torah. The Romans, more than a hundred years before Christ, stripped the rabbi's living flesh to its bones with horse currycombs, all the while the rabbi singing Shema, *Hear O Israel, the Lord our God, the Lord is One.*

When I talk about the look on the writer's face, I'm thinking of a look that must have accompanied a one-sentence paragraph three-quarters of the way into the book. Dillard, a smoker, notes: *Do you think I don't know cigarettes are fatal?*

In her book, for every heartening note such as seventeenth-century Jews who so respected books that when books wore out, they were buried like a person, there *is* a person like Joseph Stalin who took the long view: "One death is a tragedy; a million deaths are a statistic." Or Mao, who told Nehru that the atomic bomb was nothing to be afraid of. Or a Ted Bundy who, with an invested sense of chilled proportion, is able to explain his serial killings: "I mean, there are so many people."

When I finally get into bed, Ellen is asleep. I lie on my back, eyes wide. What I see is my dwarf careening down a boulder trail in Utah. It's a full-size bike. There are metal extenders strapped to her feet and locked into her pedals. At times, as she flies down the trail, she's airborne. In this picture I'm painting, my dwarf is unhelmeted, her streaked locks like some nation's flag. But my eyes adjust to the bedroom's dark, my picture dissolves. I'm past sixty, and I lie on my back thinking about college some forty years before and the fraternity I joined. It was a group known for drinking and reliable and current exam files. The president of the fraternity didn't live in the house on Greek Row. He bought one of his own, a three-story deal where he lived with eight roommates who covered his mortgage each month. I was one of the renters. "Grog" Greer was, during his junior and senior year, the Bareback Bronc Riding champion in collegiate rodeo. He was better known, though, for the annual Frat Bash, which featured competitive dwarf tossing.

. . .

I did live with a cowboy at Utah State University who was a champion rider and who owned enough funds and foresight to buy a house he lived in for free, and from which upon graduation, he garnered a profit. I leave it to you to decide whether or not this smart cowboy sponsored dwarf tossing. Do you think it matters? Do you think the essay is about short people?

. . .

Perhaps like you I've felt comfortable with, become accustomed to, the thought of word as concept made flesh, but why not the William Gass perception: "It's not the word made flesh that we want in writing…but the flesh made word."? Gass puts it this way too:

> Every loving act of definition reverses the retreat of attention to the word and returns it to the world. The landscape which emerges from the language which has made it is quite as lovely, vast and curious, as rich and prepossessing, as that of the deity who broke the silence of the void with speech so perfect the word "tree" grew leaves and the syllables of "sealion" swallowed fish.

. . .

Or Diane Ackerman: "We inhabit a deeply imagined world that exists alongside the real physical world. Even the crudest utterance, or the simplest, contains the fundamental poetry by which we live."

. . .

Writing is not apart from living.

. . .

Aristotle's notion that History accumulates but only Poetry unifies is a notion we can subscribe to. Art grants access to a larger world, allows us to live other lives, allows us to examine the quality and meaning of our own lives.

. . .

Whose very earliest recollections do not include the request, *Tell Me a Story*?

. . .

Before we made fire, before we made tools, before we made weapons, we made images.

—Wright Morris

. . .

Art, at its deepest level, is about preserving the world.

. . .

Perhaps my factories will put an end to war even sooner than your congresses. On the day when two army corps may mutually annihilate each other in a second, probably all civilized nations will recoil with horror and disband their troops.

—Alfred Nobel, 1892, the fourth World's Peace Conference, Bern, Switzerland; qtd. in Nicholson Baker, *Human Smoke*

. . .

What is the difference between throwing 500 babies into a fire and throwing fire from aeroplanes on 500 babies?

—Captain Philip S. Mumford, British officer who joined the Peace Pledge Union, 1937; qtd. in Nicholson Baker, *Human Smoke*

. . .

My grandfather taught me to tie my shoes. He kept a pair of boxing gloves beside his bed. Hung. On a nail. The six teeth in a cup.

. . .

Napoleon Bonaparte died at fifty-one. Alexander the Great at thirty-three. You know about Jesus. I had a baby brother who, as I understood, lived a few days. When my mother came home from the hospital, she was alone. The baby was never talked about, though I know his name was David. And his middle name was Ross. If my mother were alive, I'd ask about the child, in the hope to find some way to comfort her. The last few years of her life she was without real memory. When I phoned her one Mother's Day, she said, "I've no idea who you are, but thank you for the kind wishes."

. . .

I did not attend my mother's funeral. I had no interest in seeing her dead.

. . .

I attended my father's funeral, but that was for my mother, not me.

. . .

Aujourd'hui, maman est morte.

. . .

The Mother's Day card that reads, *You've been like a mother to me.*

. . .

Mother had died
that morning.

In the closet
a chalice of her last night's urine,
now numinous relic.

And yet, without fanfare,
what is to be done
but empty it into the weeds.
        —Jonathan Greene, from "Vestige"

. . .

What are obituaries but performance reports?

. . .

The same year that the Mormon Church fully admitted blacks—1978—is the same year that the National Oceanic and Atmospheric Administration announced that hurricanes would no longer be given only female names.

. . .

Nations and groups of nations act through their armed forces, which can only act with the maximum of imprecision, killing, maiming, starving and ruining millions of human beings, the overwhelming majority of whom have committed no crime of any sort.

—Aldous Huxley

. . .

Bombing was, to Churchill, a form of pedagogy—a way of enlightening city dwellers as to the hellishness of remote battlefields by killing them.

—Nicholson Baker, from *Human Smoke:*
The Beginnings of World War II, the End of Civilization

. . .

As of June 1941, nearly twice as many British civilians had died in bombing raids—35,756—as British troops had died in combat.

. . .

In six months of fire bombing, starting with the Tokyo raid, civilian casualties in Japan doubled those suffered by the Japanese military worldwide in forty-five months of war.

. . .

The great tragedy unfolding in Hue seemed not to register with those in charge. Neither Saigon nor the MACV—nor the press, for that matter—expressed concern for the masses of people trapped by the fighting. The only concern expressed about collateral damage concerned Hue's historical treasures.... None of the stories written about the fierce fighting in the city mentioned mounting civilian casualties.... Avenues of escape were few in the fortress, so the crisis there was particularly dire.... When civilians did make it into stories filed from the battlefield, it was only to describe the mounting logistical challenge of dealing with them.

There's no doubt that an authoritarian state can more easily absorb battlefield deaths than a democracy, where every one is a blow to public support. It is to democracy's credit, and benefit, that casualties dampen enthusiasm for all but the most vitally important conflicts. Hanoi, on the other hand, had millions of men at its disposal, and could justify its suffering and sacrifice by asserting the noble cause of independence—more inspiring than some abstract theory about the balance of power.

—Mark Bowden, from *Hue 1968*

. . .

re: Overheard, various locations
If I owned a diner, I'd call it "Mildred's."

What was he doing wearing an earring?

Coaches coach; players play.

Forgotten, but not gone…

More ways to be unfaithful than just sleeping with someone.

Now you know how I feel.

If you blanch kale, it tastes better?

Do you know anyone named Thor?

When pigs fly.

Why are you crying?

Is there a doctor in the house?

Despite anyone's certainty, most of what we think we know is provisional.

Raccoons like dog food.

Do bats bite during the day?

You know Regina. She looks everything up on the internet. She read where a four-year-old's brain has not developed enough so they are unlikely to lie. But Rocco, she says, lies all the time. Everything that comes out of his mouth, she says, is a lie. I ask him anything, she says, and he tells me a lie.

Cards are dealt. You play 'em.

Hey—this *is* everybody's first rodeo.

They are less likely to go up from where they are than to go down from where they are.

Ignorance is one thing, sincerity about it is another.

True dat.

. . .

The *Playboy* cartoon in which a Pilgrim woman, full-bosomed, is featured with a very coy look. Pilgrim men staring. She wears an embroidered letter on her low-necked dress: **A+**.

. . .

The North Vietnamese soldier lived with the land. He farmed its fields, cut his bed and his fighting place into it, walked paths, drank its water, used its leaves to hide his movements, and tunneled into its depths. The Americans bulldozed the land, dynamited it, burned it with napalm, and dosed it with chemicals and pesticides.

Ships full of hand grenades, corn on the cob, napalm, wristwatches, artillery shells, pigs, plastic explosives, lawnmower engines, rifle ammunition, tank parts, and c-rations were unloading *one million tons a month* by late 1967.... The United States had been spending about a half billion dollars a year when Westmoreland arrived to replace General Harkins; Westmoreland's tab for 1968 would run closer to thirty billion dollars.

The tidal wave of American dollars swamped the Vietnamese economy. Whores earned more than cabinet ministers, and shoemakers more than veteran ARVN sergeants.

—Robert Pisor, from *The Siege of Khe Sanh*

. . .

Shouldn't we remember that at the time of the Fall of Saigon, our presence in Southeast Asia constituted America's longest war? The same war for Vietnam—in its longer history—was its shortest.

. . .

In the end, America's well-armed and well-provisioned troops proved an inferior match. Defending what other generals labeled an unnecessary outpost, Westmoreland called Khe Sanh's resupply effort "the premier logistical feat of the war." Marine and Army artillery had distinguished themselves by firing 158,891 shells during the siege—answering every enemy shell with more than ten. The Air Force made 9,691 fighter bomber attacks at Khe Sanh, the Marines 7,078, and the Navy 5,337—delivering 39,178 tons of bombs, rockets, and napalm, contributing their share to what Westmoreland called, with satisfaction, "one of the heaviest and most concentrated displays of firepower in the history of warfare." B-52s added an additional 75,000 tons in 2,602 sorties.

Five months after the siege of Khe Sanh began and six days after Westmoreland left Vietnam, "the Marines began slashing sandbags, blowing up bunkers with plastic explosives, filling in trenchlines with bulldozers, and peeling up the pierced steel plates of the airstrip. All supplies, equipment, ammunition, vehicles, building beams, and airfield matting were to be trucked out, the order read "[and] everything else buried by bulldozer, burned, or blown up."

—see Robert Pisor, *The Siege of Khe Sanh*

. . .

During the early schoolboy exchanges between Donald Trump and Kim Jong Un, the specter of devastation on the Korean Peninsula rose. Trump was informed that a million people could die. He is reported to have responded, "But it would be over there, right?"

. . .

So far, the United States has been in Afghanistan longer than America's Civil War and involvement in World War I combined.

. . .

In America, while we were simultaneously engaged in Iraq and Afghanistan (with side bombing in Libya) everyone's Netflix still arrived on time…

. . .

Trump is what he is, a floundering, inarticulate jumble of gnawing insecurities and not-at-all compensating vanities, which is pathetic.

Donald Trump, with his feral cunning, knew. The oleaginous Mike Pence, with his talent for toadyism and appetite for obsequiousness, could, Trump knew, become America's most repulsive public figure…his is the authentic voice of today's lickspittle Republican Party, he clarifies this year's elections: Vote Republican to ratify groveling as governing.

—George F. Will

. . .

The rise of *alternative facts…*

. . .

Hugh was late picking up his fiancée Trish for the election party. She arrived at her door dressed as Donald Trump, and later in bed Hugh Johnson was unable to maintain an erection.

— Phillip Gardner, from "Election Return"

. . .

re: On Meeting Churchill, 1941
His real tyrant is the glittering phrase—so attractive to his mind that awkward facts may have to give way.

—Robert Menzies, prime minister of Australia

. . .

*…the first time
in the history of America*

*a white billionaire has
moved into public housing
vacated by a black family.*

—Donal Mahoney, from "Analyzing the Election"

. . .

Who said women need a reason, men a place? Was she right?

. . .

What my Father said:
You can be right or you can be happy.

What he also said:
If you ever have to fight a Negro, hit him in the nose. It takes the starch right out of them.

. . .

What is this Royal Wedding crap? I am supposed to care?

. . .

How do you get vitamin D from the sun? Human photosynthesis? Who figures out this stuff?

. . .

Is death as the consequence of a space shuttle accident more significant than death as the consequence of a school bus accident? Really?

. . .

Colonel Enrique Zanetti, a chemistry professor at Columbia University, reported for active duty at the Chemical Warfare Service of the U.S. Army. It was July 1941.

Zanetti was America's expert in fire warfare. His interest in incendiary weapons, which began during World War I, had quickened with the Italian invasion of Ethiopia—a reporter for the New York *Herald Tribune* had sent him a partly burned Italian firebomb, which he inspected and handed over to the Chemical Warfare Service. In 1936, Zanetti wrote that fire was the "forgotten enemy"—more dangerous to a large city than poison gas. "Gas *dissipates* while fire *propagates*," he wrote. Each diminutive firebomb holds within itself "the devastating possibilities of Mrs. O'Leary's cow."

Enrique Zanetti's Incendiaries Branch, Chemical Warfare Service, U.S. Army, got its first assignment. It was supposed to find a way to make twenty-five million four-pound fire-bombs: one hundred million pounds of fire. It was August 28, 1941.

Zanetti knew he would need a lot of powdered magnesium. And fortunately for him, a new, federally financed, sixty-three-million-dollar magnesium plant, powered by Boulder Dam, was going up near Las Vegas. Las Vegas was destined to grow in the desert, fed in part by money from the men and women who made the raw materials for firebombs.

—Nicholson Baker, from *Human Smoke*

. . .

I can conceive that in 1943, when Britain has achieved a tremendous air superiority, the ruthless bombing of the war-weary population of Germany on far more gigantic scale than has been experienced by any British city may well be the most effective way to bring about a German revolution. By butchering the German population indiscriminately it might be possible to goad them into a desperate rising in which every member of the Nazi party would have his throat cut.

—David Garnett, from *The War in the Air*

. . .

Firebombing is efficient, as most of the weight of a firebomb is fuel.

. . .

PART II

The only true aristocracy is that of consciousness.

—D. H. LAWRENCE

Never laugh at live dragons.

—J. R. R. Tolkien

. . .

I know not with what weapons World War III will be fought, but World War IV will be fought with sticks and stones.

—Albert Einstein

. . .

Who said *People who burn books will eventually burn people*?

. . .

Scientists are not perfect but the discipline has checks and balances. Peer reviews and attempts to replicate findings ensure that errors are eventually discovered and discredited. Whereas wishful thinking, hunches, political dogma, passionate feelings, and conspiracy theories are untested. Also, scientists are competitive. A consensus among competitors provides a measure of certainty. Lawmakers and the public should pay attention to scientific consensus even when it makes us uncomfortable.

—Krista Kafer

. . .

Global Warming is a Chinese hoax.

—Donald J. Trump

. . .

Sit down before fact as a little child, be prepared to give up every preconceived notion, follow humbly wherever and to whatever abyss Nature leads, or you shall learn nothing.

—Thomas Henry Huxley

. . .

Henry Shrapnel survived his creation to a ripe and fine age: eighty-one. Unhonored during his military career for his invention, he was promoted near life's end to the rank of lieutenant general. Years hence, his weapon proved in particular effective in the full trenches of World War I. Time has refined the original hollow shell packed with musket balls and powder, but the idea was first Henry's. He survives. You might know him. I know him. Generations of close-packed bodies of men on their hunkers know him. Like any artist, he exists in his work.

. . .

The world today doesn't make sense, so why should I paint pictures that do?

—Pablo Picasso

. . .

It is all practice: when we emerge from experience we are not wise but skillful. But at what?

—Albert Camus

. . .

It occurred to me that if I could invent a machine—a gun—which could by its rapidity of fire, enable one man to do as much battle duty as a hundred, that it would, to a large extent supersede the necessity of large armies, and consequently, exposure to battle and disease be greatly diminished.

—Richard Jordan Gatling

. . .

Gatling was, by education, a physician. He never practiced.

. . .

Verdun, the longest battle during World War I, lasted ten months, claiming the lives of over three hundred thousand French and German soldiers, not to count the wounding of hundreds of thousands of others. Between February and March of 1916, sixty million shells were fired, rendering acres and acres of land uninhabitable and not fit for farming. One hundred years past, unexploded ordnance remains an issue.

. . .

Frederick Douglass, former slave, and then accomplished journalist, author, orator, statesman, and abolitionist (he taught himself to read and write) was the most widely photographed American of the nineteenth century. He was denied U.S. citizenship for most of his life.

During the first year of his term in office, Donald Trump spoke of Frederick Douglass as if Douglass were contemporary and actively contributing to, say, Black Lives

Matter—despite the generally known fact that Douglass died in 1895, after a life of extraordinary achievements impossible to account for, given the man's beginnings and opportunities.

Compare and Contrast:
I am very proud now that we have a museum on the National Mall where people can learn about Reverend King, so many other things, Frederick Douglass is an example of somebody who's done an amazing job and is getting recognized more and more, I notice. Harriet Tubman, Rosa Parks, and millions more black Americans who made America what it is today. Big impact.

—Donald J. Trump

Yes, African Americans have felt the cold weight of shackles and the stinging lash of the field whip. But we've also dared to run north and sing songs from Harriet Tubman's hymnal. We've buttoned up our Union Blues to join the fight for our freedom. We've railed against injustice for decade upon decade, a lifetime of struggle and progress and enlightenment that we see etched in Frederick Douglass's mighty, leonine gaze.

—Barack Obama

. . .

The distinction between revenge and justice is always a question of authority.

—Greg Laski

. . .

Kierkegaard believed that knowledge preceded all acts. If so, how are we off the hook for anything?

. . .

I rubbed the sleep out of my eyes and stood up. Gerry was pointing toward the east. "What?" I asked.

"That red streak," he said. It was gone, but I could see the lights of an airplane circling in the sky far out over the dunes, maybe six or seven miles, out near the ocean. I was awake now.

"Keep watching," I said. The lights continued to circle over the same spot. The aircraft was too far to hear the engines. Suddenly a brilliant red streak silently began to descend toward the earth until it connected the flashing lights to the ground below with a solid bar of color. Many seconds later, as the flashing lights and red bar continued to move like a spotlight sweeping the sky from a flexed point on the ground, a sound like the dull buzz of a dentist's slow-speed drill came floating lazily through the humid night air. Sound and visual image appeared to be synchronized for a while. Then the red streak slowly fell away from the circling lights and disappeared into the earth, leaving the thick sound humming alone in a black vacuum. Finally, long after the lights had stopped circling and begun to move off in a straight line toward the south, the sound abruptly stopped.

"That's Puff the Magic Dragon," I said. "The gunship."

"What's that?"

"Air Force C-47 with Vulcan cannons." I explained that the old transporter plane, a military version of the DC-3, had been converted into a flying battleship by mounting three Vulcan cannons along one side of the fuselage. The

Vulcan worked like a Gatling gun; it had six barrels that rotated as the gun was fired, so that each barrel fired only once every six shots. Each of the three cannons could fire 6,000 bullets per minute. Since the guns were in fixed mounts they could only be aimed by tilting the entire aircraft toward the ground and circling around and around over the target.

"That's 18,000 rounds a minute, my man," I said, "300 bullets per second. Chops up anything and everything like mincemeat: fields, forests, mangroves, water buffalo, hooches, people. Everything. Take a patch of redwood forest and turn it into matchsticks before you can hitch up the horses. I've seen places where Puff's left his calling card. Unbelievable. Looks like a freshly plowed field ready for planting. I saw a body once, got chopped up by Puff. You wouldn't have known it had ever been a human being. Just a pile of pulp stuck to little pieces of cement and straw that used to be the guy's hooch—or her hooch, absolutely no way to tell the difference. It was so gross, it wasn't even sickening. It was just there, like litter or something."

—W. D. Ehrhart, from *Vietnam-Perkasie*

.   .   .

Guilt tells you about yourself.

—William Trevor

.   .   .

Whether we can fully describe anxiety matters not. It is central to everything.

—see Kierkegaard, Nietzsche, Camus, and Sartre

.   .   .

—look west at the hill of water: it is half the planet:
this dome, this half-globe, this bulging
Eyeball of water, arched over to Asia,
Australia and white Antarctica: those are the eyelids that
  never close;
this is the staring unsleeping
Eye of the earth; and what it watches is not our wars.

—Robinson Jeffers, from "The Eye"

. . .

Soldiers are witnesses and there is a false belief that they should recover from what they have seen and done, and had done to them. Combat is so separate, so distant from normalcy that to expect soldiers to return easily from battle during or after war is a dreamy prospect. All to say that much of what propels a soldier's worldview and living must stem from war-learned behavior—reliance on instinct and the ugly effectiveness of violence—controlled and uncontrolled, scheduled and unplanned.

. . .

Those who actually fought on the line in the war, especially if they were wounded, constitute an in-group forever separate from those who did not. Praise or blame does not attach; rather there is the accidental possession of a special empirical knowledge, a feeling of a mysterious shared ironic awareness manifesting itself in an instinctive skepticism about pretension, publicly enunciated truths, the vanities of learning, and the pomp of authority. Those who fought know a secret about themselves, and it's not very nice.

—Paul Fussell, from "My War"

. . .

War is a lot of things, and it's useless to pretend that exciting isn't one of them. It's insanely exciting. The machinery of war and the sound it makes and the urgency of its use and the consequences of almost everything about it are the most exciting things anyone engaged in war will ever know. Soldiers discuss that fact with each other and eventually with their chaplains and their shrinks and maybe even their spouses, but the public will never hear about it. It's just not something that many people want acknowledged. War is supposed to feel bad because undeniably bad things happen in it, but for a nineteen-year-old at the working end of a .50 cal during a firefight that everyone comes out of okay, war is life multiplied by some number that no one has ever heard of.

Combat is not where you might die—though that does happen—it's where you find out whether you get to keep on living. Don't underestimate the power of that revelation. Don't underestimate the things young men will wager in order to play that game one more time.

Combat was a game that the United States had asked Second Platoon to become very good at, and once they had, the United States had put them on a hilltop without women, hot food, running water, communication with the outside world, or any kind of entertainment for over a year. Not that the men were complaining, but that sort of thing has consequences. Society can give its young men almost any job and they'll figure out how to do it. They'll suffer for it and die for it and watch their friends die for it, but in the end it will get done. That only means that society should be careful about what it asks for.

—Sebastian Junger, from *War*

. . .

We hear of, say, My Lai or Abu Ghraib, and want to believe—don't we?—that our choices would have been different from those who will find their place in history as moral dwarfs. Except: as the Milgram and the Stanford Prison experiments uncomfortably disclose—humans are only too willing to obey authority, even when that authority conflicts with their conscience. As we should by now know, it is in this way that ordinary folk, by merely "doing their jobs," become agents in persecution, "cleansing," and genocide. Now and again during the Milgram experiments, someone would refuse to "obey," either to start or to continue to administer what they had every reason to believe was debilitating, if not fatal, electrical shock to unseen but screaming recipients. But such forswearing individuals were always in the minority.

. . .

If you can't imagine yourself an SS officer hustling the Jewish women and children to the gas chamber, you need to be more closely in touch with your buried self.

—Paul Fussell, from *Thank God for the Atom Bomb*

. . .

"We could take those guns out with a little napalm." Hynes, a former marine pilot, thought, *You have never seen napalm dropped, you don't know how it flows and spreads like a wave of fire and burns* everything.

—Samuel Hynes, from *The Soldiers' Tale*

. . .

And this:

**From World War I—a soldier marches
through a ruined village:**
Just past the last house on the left was a small pond, whence
protruded the grey-clad knee of a dead German. The water
around him was green and on his knee was perched a large
rat making a meal.

**From World War II—a German infantryman
is retreating on the Russian front:**
We had just passed a bunker in which we noticed a body
lying at the bottom. Two emaciated cats were eating one
of its hands.

From the Vietnam War—a young officer remembers:
A man saw the heights and depths of human behavior in
Vietnam, all manner of violence and horrors so grotesque
that they evoked more fascination than disgust. Once I
had seen pigs eating napalm-charred corpses—a memorable sight, pigs eating roast people.

—Samuel Hynes, from *The Soldiers' Tale*

. . .

re: Overheard, various locations
Forsooth?

Zip it.

When you are seventy, do you still want people saying,
"What a fine young man…"?

His idea of a perfect round of golf is going home with more balls than he showed up with.

Love is compulsion welded to delusion.

There are carpeted towers in all the picture windows. How do I know they accommodate cats?

I know I was fucking somebody else, but it still bothers me that she was too.

You live in a million-dollar house and have one set of sheets?

So drop off some starving polar bears at the White House.

Beat me like a red-headed stepchild. For fighting.

It's like understanding that for a stack of $1000 bills to be a million dollars, the stack would be four inches high, but for a trillion, the stack would be like sixty-plus miles high or something. Four inches and sixty miles…Is that math correct?

Sometimes we just outfox Nature.

Nothing to see here.

Really?

Put a coat on now and then. Who wants to live where it's always summer afternoon?

My wife's idea of camping is a hotel with thicker towels than we have at home.

Ignorance camouflaged as piety.

'Sup?

. . .

No one spits, no one calls him a baby-killer. On the contrary, people could not be more supportive or kindlier disposed, yet Billy finds these encounters weird and frightening all the same. There's something harsh in his fellow Americans, avid, ecstatic, a burning that comes of the deepest need. That's his sense of it, they all need something from him, this pack of half-rich lawyers, dentists, soccer moms, and corporate VPs, they're all gnashing for a piece of a barely grown grunt making $14,800 a year. For these adult, affluent people he is mere petty cash in their personal accounting, yet they lose it when they enter his personal space. They tremble. They breathe in fitful, stinky huffs. Their eyes skitz and quiver with the force of the moment, because here, finally, up close and personal, is the war made flesh, an actual point of contact after all the months and years of reading about the war, watching the war on TV, hearing the war flogged and flacked on talk radio. It's been hard times in America—how did we get this way? So scared all the time, and so shamed at being scared through the long nights of worry and dread, days of rumor and doubt, years of drift and slowly ossifying angst. You listened and read and watched and it was *just, so, obvious*, what had to be done, a mental tic of a mantra that became second nature as the war dragged on. *Why don't they just...*

Send in more troops. Make the troops fight harder. Pile on the armor and go in blazing, full-frontal smackdown and no prisoners. And by the way, shouldn't the Iraqis be thanking us? Somebody needs to tell them that, would you tell them that, please? Or maybe *they'd* like their dictator back. Failing that, drop bombs. More and bigger bombs. Show these persons the wrath of God and pound them into compliance, and if that doesn't work then bring out the nukes and take it all the way down, wipe it clean, reload with fresh hearts and minds, a nuclear slum clearance of the country's soul.

—Ben Fountain, from *Billy Lynn's Long Halftime Walk*

. . .

Don't talk about shit you don't know, Billy thinks, and therein lies the dynamic of all such encounters, the Bravos speak from the high ground of experience. They are the authentic. They are the Real. They have dealt much death and received much death and smelled it and held it and slopped through it in their boots, had it spattered on their clothes and tasted it in their mouths. That is their advantage, and given the masculine standard America has set for itself it is interesting how few actually qualify. *Why we fight*, yo, who is this *we*? Here in the chickenhawk nation of blowhards and bluffers, Bravo always has the ace of bloods up its sleeve.

—Ben Fountain, from *Billy Lynn's Long Halftime Walk*

. . .

Birdwatching?

. . .

Thomas Andrews, who built the *Titanic*, actually went down with it. Fair enough?

. . .

re: Of His Reputation for Throwing at Batters
I wasn't really throwing at them, but I didn't care whether I hit them or not.

—Bob Gibson, St. Louis Cardinals

And this:
I'm not throwing at him. If I threw at him, I would hit him.

. . .

They have a huge shoulder-fired rocket called a Javelin, for example, that can be steered into the window of a speeding car half a mile away. Each Javelin round costs $80,000, and the idea that it's fired by a guy who doesn't make that in a year at a guy who doesn't make that in a lifetime is somehow so outrageous it almost makes the war seem winnable.

—Sebastian Junger, from *War*

Entr'acte
Some possible risks of laser varicose vein surgery include: infection, pain, bleeding, bruising, nerve damage, inflammation, clots…. These warnings were included in the release I signed, a form I skimmed. I signed a number of documents. It was like buying a house, or horse. But whatever I properly signed, I properly threw a clot following the surgery—a clot to the lung, which, as it turns out, is unpleasant.

Whether the clot was a consequence of the surgery remains unknown, or, at least, unadmitted. When I informed the vascular surgeon about the post-surgery PE, he appeared bewildered. I'd first gone to the Vein Institute with a saphenous, or *surface* vein, clot. I'd undergone the surgery precisely to avoid deep vein thrombosis—DVT in the trade—which are the sort of clots that can kill, as they pass to the lung by way of the heart.

Dr. Talbot. We met at his Vein Institute, a posh complex on the north side of Colorado Springs, Colorado. Across the interstate, you can see the U.S. Air Force Academy, nestled in the foothills of the Rockies, Pikes Peak just off to the south. I arrived early at the institute and set up shop in the waiting room, which was well appointed—leather and mahogany—and peopled with women sporting pricey jewels. In addition to saving lives, the institute performed cosmetic repair of spider veins and other procedures involving Botox. The room's two wall TVs were tuned to HGTV.

I had seen my family physician, who identified the foot-long clot extending up my left calf. "You probably noticed that," he said. You think of a clot as a ball-ish thing, a sink stopper, say, but it's not. Clots are more like ropes, and the pain like embedded heated rebar. My doc recommended 680 mg of aspirin, an elevated leg, and moist heating pad, but undiminished pain drove me to the vein institute, where I was informed that my saphenous veins needed immediate attention. It was then that the doctor administered Lovenox and wrote a prescription for two weeks' worth of injections twice a day. I then asked if after the Lovenox I would need to undergo varicose vein treatments. (I'd read on the institute's website about the

Cool Touch endovenous saphenous vein ablation laser protocols.) "If you last that long," Talbot said.

What Talbot said felt more like blunt fact than scare tactic, so that's how I took it. Talbot then excused himself and an assistant took over. Before I left I was fully informed that part of the clot needed dissolving so as not to break away to scoot to the upper nether parts of my body: my heart and lungs.

At first, I injected myself with the Lovenox, but it was so daunting that my wife took over. Ellen immediately became proficient and accomplished the injections without the pain and bruising I'd been inflicting on myself. I'd been able to accomplish the self-injections only by backing up against a wall. If I hadn't known before, hara-kiri is out of the question for me. That aside, the Lovenox began and did its duty of working to dissolve the rope of coagulated blood. This first clot I knew about: could run my fingers along its length. The later lung clot caught me altogether unawares. What I knew was that pain had bloomed, then spread, extending from hip to shoulder. After two days, I popped a leftover Vicodin (from an old root canal) before attempting to go to bed. About 9:00 PM, my wife said: "Get dressed."

At the ER, I was asked if I'd ever experienced kidney stones. In fact, I had—had passed my first and only stone *in* an ER. That passing had taken morphine, time, and a catheter. I attended to this line of thought but sensed what was at present occurring was different. I said so. My oxygen intake was so diminished and painful that the nurse inquired whether I'd ever been on oxygen.

"*On* oxygen?"

"You know," she said, "breathing with a tank."

I visualized old folk in grocery stores, plastic tubing hooked over the ears and up the nose, green tanks nesting in shopping carts where toddlers can sit.

"No," I said. My breathing was labored. The nurse conferred with the ER doc, and I was scheduled for a CAT scan. It was now 2:00 AM and I hadn't seen an actual doctor yet—a good nurse, but no doctor.

To lie on my back for the scan was crippling, as if I'd been clobbered with a bat in a street fight. It was almost impossible to lie still. The technician warned that the fluid pumped into the IV port for CAT scan picture contrast would make me feel as if I'd wet myself. She was correct, and I looked at myself to check.

Back in my room, the ER doc appeared.

"The good news is I know what's causing the pain. The bad news is it's a PE." Then: "You know, a clot. In the lung—. We're admitting you. Get you started on some thinners. Some oxygen too."

"I'm for that," I said. "And the pain…"

"Sure." She nodded at the nurse.

The nurse returned to inject something into the IV port. "Morphine," she said. I asked for and received two more injections during the night. About 5:00 AM, just before discharge, I received an injection of Lovenox to start the thinning. Why had they waited so long? I had tubing in my nose for breathing.

At home, I moved from morphine to OxyContin. But after two days the OxyContin made me nauseous, and rather than vomit, I switched to Tylenol and thence to nothing. Why is it, I wondered, that I'm tolerant of morphine but intolerant of OxyContin? Codeine can also make me sick, as will Percocet. Morphine had helped with the earlier kidney stone, though not completely. At the time I joked that a kidney stone can be compared to *Crucifixion*. The overstatement holds because passing a stone is *Resurrection*. When I passed the stone, my body temperature dropped four degrees.

Twenty years before, my intestine, riddled with diverticula, burst and more than an arm's length of that organ had to be removed. The colon was reconnected six months after. Meantime, I was reduced to attaching a plastic bag to my gut for shitting. It shouldn't surprise that this predicament affects beach time and, ever after, any feelings of superiority.

One of the cheers of the hospital, though, during the week-long recovery, was my then new pal, morphine. In this case, I was hooked up to my own private drug dealer, an apparatus allowing me to administer the juice sans nurse intervention. Computerized, these machines won't let you overdose. But you are in charge: don't have to beg or wait for dosings. For what it's worth, I have been since informed that research reports that patients in charge of their own narcotics use less. For my new time in the hospital, I liked that morphine was making a return appearance.

Back when my intestine burst, I should have died, and would have save for an experienced surgeon, who had spent an early part of his medical career in Nepal where he had cut from dawn till dusk without paperwork or fear of malpractice. He had seen and done it all. It was the sort of doctor I wanted now. And I found him in Talbot, a board-certified cardiologist turned vascular surgeon.

The medical-speak for what had happened to me was, as the doctor had put it, PE—that is, pulmonary embolism—from the Greek *embolus*, meaning *plug*. The precise number of people affected by DVT/PE is uncertain, although it is estimated that as many as 900,000 people could be affected (one to two per 1,000) each year in the United States. Sudden death is the first symptom in about one-quarter of people who contract a PE. More sobering for me was to realize that to get to my lung the clot had had to pass first through my heart, its little doors and exits. I also learned that an untreated clot can kill the lung in the area where it arrests the flow of blood, permanently damaging that organ and possibly others, as the PE can reduce the overall amount of oxygen in the blood. As the Lovenox worked, the pain from the lung clot receded until I felt like a pulp Western novel's hero: *The gambler's sputum was flecked with blood....* I coughed such phlegm for a week.

When your legs' surface, or *saphenous*, veins, fail—like frozen canal locks—blood flows backwards, pooling in the veins and clotting. As the veins clot and harden, pain presents. Moreover, to repeat myself, should any portion of such a clot break off to travel to your legs' deeper veins, they are contenders to complete the journey to the oxy-genating organs above your groin, where they mean to do harm.

More than three hundred million people travel on long-distance flights (generally more than four hours) each year. Blood clots are a risk. Most information about clots and long-distance travel comes from information that has been gathered about air travel. That said, anyone traveling more than four hours—by air, car, bus, or train, long sitting at a desk—can be at risk. The longer you are immobile, the greater the risk. Problem: I'm a writer. I sit a lot. (I've tried the standing desk, but my legs can't hack it, so I sit. I'm sitting right *now*.) Additional problem: About half of people with DVT have no symptoms.

Calling endovenous saphenous vein ablation lasers "Cool Touch" is misleading. The procedure harvests heat from the laser's light to reduce varicose veins. The thin beam of radiation in the form of light closes and shrinks the vein, causing scar tissue within the vessel that seals off the vein. Blood then reroutes through healthier veins nearby. The laser's concentrated energy razes the inside lining of the affected veins and they collapse. In time, the cooked protein structure will be absorbed by the body. Your body creates new veins. But, if you are prone to varicosity, all repeats itself. This was explained to me in the aftermath of conscious sedation as two nurses were swabbing clean and wrapping my legs prior to discharge from Dr. Talbot's institute. Established in a wheelchair where I was handed orange juice and an energy bar, I was, in time, wheeled to my waiting ride by Talbot himself. I asked him just how hot the Cool Laser was.

"In some experiments," he said, "the laser's tip's been measured at 1800°F."

"Wow," I said. "Like welding."

"In practice," he said, "it's less than that."

There have been two surgeries since (the second one possibly causing the offending lung clot). I'm careful to don compression stockings for long plane rides. I swallow blood thinners twice a day. So, when I began to feel shortness of breath when walking or climbing stairs, it jammed my brain with dark thoughts of clots and heart plugs. The shorter of breath I felt, the slower I walked, the fewer stairs I climbed. Finally, I made an appointment with a cardiologist, who scheduled a treadmill stress test and ultrasound. I passed and the doctor recommended *more* exercise, not *less*—faster walking, more stairs, core work, etc. He pointed out that the shortness of breath was the consequence of aging, diminished exercise, and muscle loss. These were facts I hadn't dreamed of. I bought a Fitbit. From the treadmill test, what I remember is this: As I watched on the screen my heart's surgings—without thought or orders from me—I dwelt on my wet red motor's involuntary rhythmic and consistent effort. I admired then, as I admire now, its work ethic.

. . .

I took a deep breath and listened to the old brag of my heart. I am, I am, I am.

—Sylvia Plath, from *The Bell Jar*

. . .

I just regret everything and using my turn signal is too much trouble. Fuck you. Why should you get to know where I'm going, I don't.

—Mary Robison, from *Why Did I Ever*

. . .

When I landed a few feet up the trail from the booby-trapped howitzer round that I had detonated, I felt as if I had been airborne forever.... I thought initially that the loss of my glasses in the explosion accounted for my blurred vision, and I had no idea that the pink mist that engulfed me had been caused by the vaporization of most of my right and left legs. As shock began to numb my body, I could see through a haze of pain that my right thumb and little finger were missing, as was most of my left hand, and I could smell the charred flesh which extended from my right wrist upward to the elbow. I knew that I had finished serving my time in the hell of Vietnam.

—Lewis Puller Jr., from *Fortunate Son*

. . .

Lewis Puller Jr., son of Chesty Puller (the Marine Corps's most decorated general) lived with his wreckage for twenty years. He killed himself in 1994.

. . .

John Wolfe, who himself lost a leg in Vietnam, was medevaced and nearly died three times (surviving two open-heart massages and the infusion of thirty-nine pints of blood) before being delivered to a hospital ship where, sometime after, he underwent the following:

Semiconscious and strapped into a wheelchair, I was wheeled down to a physical therapy room with various exercise bars, tables, and gym equipment around. Weights about the size of baby rattles were placed in my hands. Just a few feet away, a physical therapist was busy balancing something on a table that at first looked like a sack of potatoes. When I focused, I saw that it was a young Asian man, probably Korean, who had lost both arms and both legs close to the torso. No sooner would the therapist balance the torso on its buttocks than it would topple over on its face with a painful-looking impact, and then the process would be repeated. The Korean's eyes met mine, and for a long moment the presence of everything and everybody else in the room blurred, faded out, dematerialized, leaving only his mind and mine on that spatial plane in an uninterrupted convergence, and then we both started to laugh hysterically.

—John Wolfe, from "A Different Species of Time"

. . .

I'm amazed at how polite people are in warzones. Chalk this up to the fact that nearly everyone is armed. Or, maybe it's a sense that we're all locked down in this compound together. Despite technology, there's a tangible isolation within each base's walled perimeter. Events in other parts of this country, such as the assassination of three doctors or the British helicopter crash that killed five, might as well have occurred on the other side of the globe. Regardless, people make an extra effort to open doors and offer help. Drivers stop traffic to wave pedestrians across. Everyone smiles and says, please, thank you, sir, and ma'am.

—Nick Willard, from "How I'll End the War:
My First Week Back in Afghanistan"

. . .

John Coltrane was handed a transcript of one of the solos he had played and said, "I can't play that!"

. . .

Writing about music is like dancing about architecture. Nobody knows for sure who said that first, but why not pin it on Thelonious Monk?

. . .

Men's memories are uncertain and the past that was differs little from the past that was not.

     —Cormac McCarthy, from *Blood Meridian*

. . .

What makes life livable if not penicillin, hot water heaters, and birth control?

. . .

When black people protest in whatever place or about whatever issue, they are wrong. When white people protest they are exercising their God-given rights. Ever notice that?

. . .

The Bombay I drink is based on a recipe dated 1761. Sometimes things get done right the first time.

. . .

Since when is kneeling a sign of disrespect? Isn't it more of a plea, a supplication?

. . .

Frederick Downs writes about counting bodies, or parts of them, to sustain the American policy of attrition. Some

Vietcong, accidently or not, had detonated their own land-mine:

> There were three penises, two complete faces, which looked like masks they were so complete, five soles of feet, their hands, and a few other parts. The largest body part was a section of a rib cage with parts of four rib bones connected to a small section of the shoulder.

After counting, Downs's men situated one of the hands into the soft ground and stuck a cigarette between two fingers. "It looked great," Downs said.

> It looked like someone lying underground had paused in the motion of moving his cigarette from his mouth to his side. Everyone took pictures of this bizarre construction. We never thought it was ghoulish.

—see Samuel Hynes, *The Soldiers' Tale*

. . .

Years after, veterans still find memories of combat victory and killing exhilarating. Soldiers as yet "uncooked" by combat often scrutinize the face and body of the killed enemy in wonder at their ability to create something as profound and enduring as death. Soldiers tie themselves to the dead by photographing dead enemy soldiers or by taking the possessions of the dead as trophies to preserve the moment.

—Theodore Nadelson, from *Trained to Kill: Soldiers at War*

. . .

The resistance to the close-range killing of one's own species is so great that it is often sufficient to overcome the cumulative influences of the instinct for self-protection, the coercive forces of leadership, the expectance of peers, and the obligation to preserve the lives of comrades. The soldier in combat is trapped within this tragic Catch-22. If he overcomes his resistance to killing and kills an enemy soldier in close combat, he will be forever burdened with blood guilt, and if he elects not to kill, then the blood guilt of his fallen comrades and the shame of his profession, nation, and cause lie upon him. He is damned if he does, and damned if he doesn't.

—Dave Grossman, from *On Killing*

. . .

Memory is an internal rumor.

—George Santayana

. . .

Winston Churchill submitted a war-cabinet paper recommending that all men over eighteen and a half and under fifty-one should perform compulsory military service. It was November 6, 1941. "The campaign for directing women into the munitions industries should be pressed forward," Churchill also recommended. A month later, Parliament passed a National Service Act, which included conscription for unmarried women between twenty and thirty. Women had a choice of joining the armed services or working in a government factory, such as the Royal Ordinance Factory at Bridgend, which employed thirty thousand people.

At the Bridgend factory, where workers made incendiary and high-explosive bombs, TNT powder dyed a person's skin, hair, and teeth yellow—as a result, the women who filled bombs with it were sometimes called "canaries." "Accidents were frequent and were mainly in the detonator assembly shops," according to a history of Bridgend. "The main casualties were the young women workers with the unfortunate ones losing fingers or suffering more serious injuries." Once, on an icy morning, a woman was carrying a tray of detonators from one building to another. She slipped and shook the tray, "causing the detonators to explode and blow her breasts off."

—Nicholson Baker, from *Human Smoke*

. . .

During World War II, Japanese planes dropped wheat, rice, paper, and fluffs of cotton tainted with the bubonic plague on cities in China.

. . .

Before Hiroshima and Nagasaki, the powers that were applied what they designated the "Saipan ratio" to the inevitable land invasion of Japan. This ratio, based on the Battle of Saipan, was 9.5:1 in favor of the United States. Percentage advantage aside, U.S. commanders ordered a half million Purple Hearts, that, as we now gratefully know, went unused. For years, I thought of these figures as "military preparation." This jaded outlook held sway until I heard Donald Rumsfeld defending unarmored Humvees by announcing, "You go to war with the army you have." Though such an utterance is a chilling truth, it qualifies as insensitive as the answer to the soldier who was asking why his unit had to rummage through trash heaps for scrap metal to weld onto old Humvees. Rumsfeld would go on to "clarify" at a later press conference that *There are things we know that we know. There are known unknowns. That is to say there are things that we now know we don't know. But there are also unknown unknowns. There are things we do not know we don't know.*

· · ·

re: How to Begin

My first memory is of a time ten years before I was born, and the memory takes place where I have never been and involves my daddy whom I never knew. It was in the middle of the night in the Everglades swamp in 1925, when my daddy woke his best friend Cecil out of a deep sleep in the bunkhouse just south of the floating dredge that was slowly chewing its way across the Florida Peninsula from Miami on the Atlantic to Naples on the Gulf of Mexico, opening a route and piling dirt for the highway that would come to be known as the Tamiami Trail. The night was dark as only a swamp can be dark and they could not see each other there in the bunkhouse. The rhythmic stroke of the dredge's engine came counterpoint to my daddy's shaky voice as he told Cecil what was wrong.

When Cecil finally did speak, he said: "I hope it was good, boy. I sho do."

"What was good?"

"That Indian. You got the clap."

But daddy had already known. He had thought of little else since it had become almost impossible for him to give water because of the fire that started in his stomach and felt like it burned through raw flesh every time he had to water off. He had thought from sunup to dark of the chickee where he had lain under the palm roof being eaten alive by swarming mosquitoes as he rode the flat-faced Seminole girl, whose name he never knew and who grunted like a sow and smelled like something shot in the woods.

—Harry Crews, from *A Childhood: The Biography of a Place*

. . .

re: Other Beginnings
"It was love at first sight."

"If I am out of my mind, it's all right with me, thought Moses Herzog."

"Lolita, light of my life, fire of my loins."

"Like all men, I tell a hundred lies a day."

—Heller, Bellow, Nabokov, Bourjaily

. . .

My story begins, like everything else, on the beach. Beaches are the same the world over, you peel down, then you peel off; they serve you up raw meat, dark meat, or flesh nicely basted in olive oil. A strip of sun and sand where the sex is alert, the mind is numb. The beach in question, one of the best, is near where Sunset Boulevard meets the sea. I don't mean to be ironic. California is that way naturally. It's hard to do malice to California, but this particular strip might have been in Acapulco, or down in Rio, or along the Riviera. If it's world brotherhood you want, go to the beach. If you like parallels, the beach is where we came in, and where we'll go out. Having crawled from the sea, we're now crawling back into it. That solution of salt in the blood is calling us home. And in a mammary age, what better place to compensate for an unsuckled childhood?

—Wright Morris, from *Love Among the Cannibals*

. . .

In our family, as far as we are concerned, we were born and what happened before that is myth. Go back two generations and the names and lives of our forebears vanish into the common grass. All we could get out of Mother was that her grandfather had once taken a horse to Dublin; and sometimes in my father's expansive histories, his grandfather had owned trawlers in Hull, but when an abashed regard for fact, uncommon in my father, touched him in his eighties, he told us that this ancestor, a decayed seaman, was last seen gutting herrings at a bench in the fish market of that city.

—V. S. Pritchett, from *A Cab at the Door*

. . .

If you really want to hear about it, the first thing you'll probably want to know is where I was born, and what my lousy childhood was like, and how my parents were occupied and all before they had me, and all that David Copperfield kind of crap, but I don't feel like going into it, if you want to know the truth.

—J. D. Salinger, from *Catcher in the Rye*

. . .

Entr'acte
I was seventeen years old. The copy of *Catcher* I bought, I still have. It cost $1.25. Try to imagine my reading about eastern prep schools in Butte, Montana. I mean, I went to

high school with Evel Knievel—well, I knew his brother who, as it turns out, was to fall to his death in a mineshaft in that mining city. I was lucky enough to enroll in college like Gary. Gary Turner, a year ahead of me at Butte High, was on Christmas break from Snow College, a Mormon college in southern Utah. He arrived for break with a copy of *Catcher*.

The summer before college, I worked on the 5200 level of the Mountain Con Mine, a full mile below the surface of the earth—a long distance to fall. Gary never worked a day in the mines. He was crippled.

"The Richest Hill on Earth," as Butte was dubbed, was, by the 1880s, the world's biggest copper producer.

Some related facts: Butte's Miners Union formed in 1878, sending the largest delegation to the International Workers of the World's founding convention in Chicago in 1906. 1917: Butte's population at a peak of 100,000, 168 men were killed in a mine fire—a fire that remains the worst mining disaster in American history. Three heavyweight champions: John L. Sullivan himself as well as Jim Jeffries and Bob Fitzsimmons all fought bouts in Butte. All to say there were no prep schools in my city. Most of Butte's inhabitants were not barons or millionaires—they were miners and boxers and gamblers and whores and bartenders and preachers and drunks.

We owned a cow in the city. Butte was a mining town, but *still.* Our house and field were not in the country. We lived two blocks from my grade school, a half mile from our church. Lenz's Pharmacy and the Cobban Market (where my father and other miners had grocery tabs they could pay once a month) were practically neighbors. I dreamed of the sheriff coming to our house to tell my father it was illegal to keep cows. I didn't hold out much hope because at school we studied Montana history, and I knew there were more cows in my state than people, and my teacher had informed us that Montana statutes dictated death by hanging for cattle rustling but not for human murder. There were no prep schools in Butte.

Gary Turner said it was inevitable I'd meet someone like Holden. "You're going to leave Butte, right?" he said. "Right?" Gary hobbled with a limp that made him seem, at the time to the most of us, a touch prissy. It was polio. Why he caught polio while the rest of us didn't, who dared say? We'd all swum in the same public pool: a huge concrete thing in Clark Park built by the Anaconda Company along with a ball field, a skating rink, teeter-totters, slides, swings, and sunken-pit trampolines that were filled in when Robby Grunnell broke his neck and was paralyzed from his jawbone down.

At some point I was told that Gary had married a dancer, had studied dance history, and was teaching choreography somewhere in Utah or Arizona. His wife was of the exotic sort: Apache or Basque.

Gary Turner once asked me to his house after school. To tell the truth, I was better friends with his brother Teddy, but I went. It was the year Gary was a senior and I was a junior in high school: 1963—the year before Gary left for

Snow. It was late spring (you know what was waiting for us that fall). Gary had asked me to his house to play a record. The record he played was *Sketches of Spain*, which, I now know, had been recorded by Miles Davis the year before. The first black man I saw was on TV. There were no blacks in the mines in Butte. There were Irish, Czechs, Finns, Italians, Jews, Hispanics, Chinese, Filipinos, Crow Indians, but no blacks. Gary danced a little to Davis's good music with his leg in that brace.

· · ·

"It's a poor sort of memory," Lewis Carroll's Queen says, "that only works backwards."

· · ·

re: Usable Toast
To the lucky and the unlucky, to the swindlers and the swindled, the living and the dead.

· · ·

I see Jeter firing into a corpse with his M16. The corpse is dancing. Jeter is red-faced, like a thwarted child. His eyes are all pupil. This is the kid who most often makes me laugh, who makes me feel most protective, the eighteen-year-old whose parents had to sign for him when he joined up at seventeen. He empties one magazine and slaps in another. He fires again into the corpse. The corpse dances, arms and legs flail, the flat face peeling off the shattered skull, the pink-blue brains scattering, the ground black with blood. Jeter stops suddenly, looks dazed.

—Doug Anderson, from *Keep Your Head Down*

· · ·

You could do anything you wanted—shit, I was eighteen—
kill anyone or anything in Vietnam and get away with it. It
was like being drunk and walking around with a hard-on.
—Theodore Nadelson, from *Trained to Kill*

. . .

re: What Hank Williams's best friend said
the last time he saw him just before he died…
He looked like Death eating a cracker.

. . .

November 6
The King Who Was Not
King Charles II was born in Madrid in 1661.

During his forty years he never managed to stand up
or speak without drooling or keep the crown from falling
off his head, a head that never hosted a single idea.

Charles was his aunt's grandson, his mother was his
father's niece and his great-grandfather was his great-
grandmother's uncle: the Hapsburgs liked to keep things
close to home.

So much devotion to family put an end to them.

When Charles died, the dynasty in Spain died with
him.

—Eduardo Galeano, from *Children of the Days*

. . .

Lightning struck the house today and fried the garage door
opener. Here on the mesa, across the street though, this
same lightning struck a neighbor. His name is Fred Mix.
The police accident report reported unspecified neurolog-
ical damage. It is a form report his wife showed me. In the

section where it asks if weather was a factor, the police officer checked *Yes*.

. . .

Why are there no Russian golfers? And why do golfers flourish in smaller countries like Ireland, Sweden, South Africa?

. . .

What doesn't kill you doesn't make you stronger, it just doesn't kill you.

. . .

After a rain, my father would pick mushrooms in the cow field. He knew which ones to pick. Do you?

. . .

Sartre said even the grimmest literature is optimistic since it proves those things can be thought about.

. . .

1964: Panama
Twenty-Three Boys Are Pumped Full of Lead
when they try to hoist the flag of Panama on Panamanian soil.

"*We only used bird-shot*," the commander of the North American occupation forces says defensively.

Another flag flies over the strip that slits Panama from sea to sea. Another law prevails, another police keep watch, another language is spoken. Panamanians may not enter the Canal Zone without permission, even to pick up fallen fruit from a mango tree, and they work here at second-class pay, like blacks and women.

The Canal Zone, North American colony, is both a business and a military base. The School of the Americas' courses are financed with the tolls that ships pay. In the Canal Zone barracks, Pentagon officers teach anticommunist surgery to Latin American military men who will soon, in their own countries, occupy presidencies, ministries, commands, and embassies.

"They are the leaders of the future," explains Robert McNamara, secretary of defense of the United States.

Wary of the cancer that lies in wait for them, these military men will cut off the hands of anyone who dares to commit agrarian reform or nationalization, and tear out the tongues of the impudent or the inquisitive.

—Eduardo Galeano, from *Century of the Wind*

. . .

Nobody on U.S. bases in Baghdad celebrated Bin Laden's death as thousands did in the United States. The public celebration proved embarrassing to try to explain to our Iraqi counterparts. The only reaction to his death I heard came in a conversation with an Army captain on his third deployment after two tours in Afghanistan: "Fuck that mother fucker, he cost me my first wife!"

—Brandon Lingle, from "I Thought You Were in Afghanistan"

. . .

We'll die and it's going to take a lot for our children and theirs to remember us accurately—and they won't—because we are all made up of details many of which—most of which—nobody knows about.

. . .

I knew him in the Air Force—a guy who posted a half dozen DUIs until forced into detox and rehab. When he emerged I asked how it had gone. He had lost weight and was pale. "I do not believe I can face my life without the prospect of drink," he said. I've no idea where things went from there.

. . .

The cat who knew me is buried under the bush.
>   —Naomi Shihab Nye, from
>   "Trying to Name What Doesn't Change"

. . .

re: Too Much Money
For $100,000, a buyer from Southeast Asia recently purchased a 125-year-old pair of Levi Strauss & Co. blue jeans…

re: Too Much Time
The world record for the tallest stack of waffles was just broken in some guy's backyard in Denver. (After hours of mixing, waffle-ironing, and hardening in the oven, the twenty-three-year-old produced a column of waffles standing sixty-seven centimeters, surpassing the previous record of fifty-one centimeters.)

. . .

In Poland alone, 860,000 Jews were resettled, with 75,000 Germans taking over the acquired lands. One million three hundred thousand Poles were shipped to Germany as slave labor, while another 330,000 were simply shot. The invading Germans and the remaining Poles and Jews now stood in breadlines or, rather, three separate lines. Germans received 2,613 calories, Poles 669, Jews 184.

—see Diane Ackerman, *The Zookeeper's Wife*

. . .

Peace seems to allow so little space for belief in destiny, fate, God, or ghosts.

—Anthony Loyd, from *My War Gone By, I Miss It So*

. . .

William Smith was a young supervisor of construction on the Somerset Coal Canal. On the evening of 5 January 1796, he was sitting in a coaching inn in Somerset when he jotted down the notion that would eventually make his reputation. To interpret rocks, there needs to be some means of correlation, a basis on which you can tell that those carboniferous rocks from Devon are younger than these Cambrian rocks from Wales. Smith's insight was to realize that the answer lay with fossils. At every change in rock strata, you could work out the relative ages of rocks wherever they appeared. Drawing on his knowledge as a surveyor, Smith began at once to make a map of Britain's rock strata, which would be published after many trials in 1815 and would become a cornerstone of modern geology.

Smith's revelation regarding strata heightened the moral awkwardness concerning extinctions. To begin with, it confirmed that God had wiped out creatures not occasionally but repeatedly. This made Him seem not so much careless as peculiarly hostile. It also made it inconveniently necessary to explain how some species were wiped out while others continued unimpeded into succeeding eons. Clearly there was more to extinctions than could be accounted for by a single Noachian deluge, as the biblical flood was known. Cuvier [the paleontologist] resolved the matter to his own satisfaction by suggesting that Genesis applied only to the most recent inundation. God, it appeared, hadn't wished to distract or alarm Moses with news of earlier, irrelevant extinctions.

—Bill Bryson, from *A Short History of Nearly Everything*

. . .

Why wasn't I born in Syria? Why wasn't I born black? Blind? Why weren't you?

. . .

Now this is halfway round the world,
the other side with all its smell and it's almost like
you don't have to care
or there is no need
until somebody eats it,

buys the farm *and then*
all Asia bears down;
you never been so put upon

your whole life and it is your life
so you are moaning it don't mean nothin'
and it doesn't

and that's why you keep track of
it's all you care about and that's too much
one more day, one more dark

one more dying:
so you lie awake and repeat
hometown, girl friend
say '59 Ford coupe
    —D. F. Brown, from "Keeping Days and Numbers Together"

. . .

In the moment after the explosion, an old man
staggers in the cloud of dust and debris, hands
pressed hard against bleeding ears
as if to block out the noise of the world
at 11:40 A.M., *the broken sounds of the wounded*
rising around him, roughened by pain.

Buildings catch fire. Cafes.
Stationary shops. The Renaissance Bookstore.
A huge column of smoke, a black anvil head
pluming upward, fueled by the Kitah al-Aghani.
al-Isfahani's Book of Songs, *the elegies of Khansa,*
the exile poetry of Youssef and al-Azzawi,
religious tracts, manifestos, translations
of Homer, Shakespeare, Whitman, and Neruda—
these book-leaves curl in the fire's
blue-tipped heat, and the long centuries
handed down from one person to another, verse
by verse, rise over Baghdad.
    —Brian Turner, from "The Mutanabbi Street Bombing"

. . .

re: What You Learn at the Twentieth High School Reunion

You were right to go for the first-chair oboe player and not the cheerleader who ended up with triplets and hauling around that extra hundred pounds.

. . .

A *miracle*, someone said, *is a violation of experience.*

. . .

Antique restoration. What is that?

. . .

Does whiteness always find someone to violate?

. . .

From the user's point of view, artillery is an ideal weapon. It does enormous destruction without exposing the user to much risk. Better still, the users rarely suffer the dismay of seeing their mangled victims. However, artillery is a rich man's weapon. A less wealthy army can be just as destructive, but at greater human cost to itself. Throwing shells instead of infantry at the enemy is preferable, if you can afford it.

—James F. Dunnigan, from *How to Make War*

. . .

During World War II, artillery caused nearly 60 percent of all casualties. World War II still holds the record for the most artillery fire thrown at the most troops.

—see James F. Dunnigan, from *How to Make War*

. . .

It has been said that consciousness is the ability to know and understand that we will die. Probably not, because children don't know that they are going to die until we explain it to them. We wouldn't say, would we, that children lack consciousness?

. . .

In the twentieth century, civilized people killed 150 million other civilized people.

. . .

Descartes, the so-called father of modern philosophy, had no care or concern for animals—in fact, practiced dissection on live subjects.

. . .

While I'm looking for handrails, I watch my students dance down the granite stairwells, texting.

. . .

Male lions live an average of fourteen years.

. . .

Wall Street was named for an actual wall built by seventeenth-century Dutchmen as protection from the British.

. . .

What is Wall Street but Las Vegas without hotels and pools?

. . .

In a better world, poetry would need no justification beyond the sheer splendor of its existence. As Wallace

Stevens once observed, "The purpose of poetry is to contribute to man's happiness." Children know this essential truth when they ask to hear their favorite nursery rhymes again and again. Aesthetic pleasure needs no justification, because a life without such pleasure is one not worth living.

—Dana Gioia, from *Can Poetry Matter?*

. . .

The poet's central mission is "to purify the words of the tribe."

—Stéphane Mallarmé, qtd. in Dana Gioia, *Can Poetry Matter?*

. . .

We love poetry in part because it is useless. In an age when everything seems to have its price and schedule, poetry is without deadlines or market value; it is undenominated by party or church or special-interest lobby. Its playfulness both serves and is subversive to causes we solemnly admire. Poetry's power is very real, though indirect. A great poem can affect the lives of all, whether they read it or not. As poetry is based on the gold standard of experience, so experience is keyed to the bedrock of the best expression. My understanding of tradition is that our language and age are writing us, in ways we can't always see. An individual may have nothing better to contribute than a radical, humble attention that both startles and reassures.

—Robert Morgan, from *Good Measure*

. . .

To pay attention is the great act of love, whether to a person or to the world.

. . .

I like the way poetry finds brightness in the ordinary and imperfect, the way memory turns out to be prediction. Poetry connects the instant with all times, and irrigates a present that seems otherwise diminished, a prison, a weak imitation of the past.

—Robert Morgan, from *Good Measure*

. . .

A. R. Ammons, in a poem about the plague in Strasbourg in 1349, has a line, "Dogs ate their masters' empty hands."

. . .

It is objectivity and precision that can be translated and that translates, the love of the humble detail, a sensitivity to the eros in all things, focused recognition.

—Robert Morgan, from *Good Measure*

. . .

…Two cabs almost
collide; someone yells fuck in Farsi.
I'm sorry, she says. The comforts
of loneliness fall in like a bad platoon.
The sky blurs—there's a storm coming
up or down. A lank cat slinks liquidly
around a corner. How familiar
it feels to feel strange, hollower
than a bassoon. A rill of chill air
in the leaves. A car alarm. Hail.

—William Matthews, from "Morningside Height, July"

. . .

It is time to experiment, time to leave the well-ordered but stuffy classroom, time to restore a vulgar vitality to poetry and unleash the energy now trapped in the subculture. There is nothing to lose. Society has already told us that poetry is dead. Let's build a funeral pyre out of the desiccated conventions piled around us and watch the ancient, spangle-feathered, unkillable phoenix rise from the ashes.

—Dana Gioia, from *Can Poetry Matter?*

. . .

The broom hill shines like a fox running.
. . . .
In the moon-polished sky stars crawl out
and press like spiders

deep inside a horse's eye.

—Robert Morgan, from "Close"

. . .

I have for many years now relished the textures of Robert Morgan's words and objects. He has more touchable things per line than one would think the world offers; but that is exactly how he gets us to stop ignoring our world.

—Sandra McPherson

. . .

Art moves you before you understand why.

. . .

re: Sometimes words mesh so well
it is almost language beyond language
casually triumphant
provoking defeat
festively disputatious
violent retreat
miraculously mundane
dedicated hypochondria
captive whale
benignly aggressive
varnished truth
discomfiting epiphany
commendable wounds
kidney stones
blemished virgin
striving pain
vice cop
criminally admired
malignantly intelligent
fish mongering to fear mongering to war mongering...
portentous vitality
blinkered moralism
luscious predictability
monstrous euphemism
tyrannical benevolence
darkness visible
unpardonable beauty
unforecastably large
ship-wrecking water

. . .

re: Overheard, various locations
What's going to happen to Christians when they are informed that Jesus is not white and not from Iowa?

Can you help this man find his friend?

Life without a Porsche in the garage?

La-Di-Da…

An ice shelf the size of Florida is about to break off in Antarctica. How far above sea level is actual Florida?

Good thing the Russians didn't beat us into space. They did?

If you were working to have a baby, would you have pythons for pets?

You're not going to like what happens.

No, try this.

How is it that firemen are all young, strong, and handsome? Makes you *want* to get stuck in an elevator.

Dahlias are the prettiest.

Yes, there was a joust, but cancer has been unhorsed.

Wherever you go, there you are.

Yikes!

Boyo!

Cruises are like being in prison with the chance of drowning.

Cripes!

It should be all right to steal food and books.

.   .   .

Are memory and longing fraternal or identical twins?

.   .   .

In *Girls*, Frederick Busch describes the scent of a woman yielding to cancer: "She smelled like wood that's been in pond water too long." And he begins "Widow Water": "What to know about pain is how little we do to deserve it, how simple it is to give, how hard to lose. I'm a plumber. I dig for what's wrong. I should know." Don DeLillo on the first page of his first novel, *Americana*: "The santas of Fifth Avenue rang their little bells with an odd sad delicacy, as if sprinkling salt on some brutally spoiled piece of meat." Ann Beattie, in "Snow," presents a marriage: "It was as hopeless as giving a child a matched cup and saucer."

.   .   .

re: Language
...a city to the building of which every human being has brought a stone.

—Ralph Waldo Emerson

.   .   .

It is not the work of art to make order, but to complicate order in just such a way that it begins to resemble living.

. . .

We should read as we probably ought to live—*alertly, receptively, expectantly.*

. . .

Friends Don't Let Friends Read Junk.

. . .

The leaves are a gift to the wind,
which otherwise, on its own, couldn't be seen.

—Albert Goldbarth, from "Untitled"

. . .

Power can always unleash mayhem in the name of superior virtue.

. . .

re: Nazis

It is worth considering the fact that all of them, master and pupils, gradually took leave of reality at the same pace as their morals became detached from the morals common to every time and every civilization.

—Primo Levi, from *The Complete Works*

. . .

The primary cause of hunger is hunger.

. . .

The sun had struggled all day behind monsoon clouds before finally being extinguished by the turning earth and the dark wet ridges of the Annamese Cordillera. It was February 1969, in Quang Tri province, Vietnam. Zoomer lay above my hole in monsoon-night blackness on the slick clay of Mutter's Ridge, the dark jungle-covered ridge paralleling Vietnam's demilitarized zone where the Third Marine Division and the North Vietnamese Army had struggled together for two years. A bullet had gone through Zoomer's chest, tearing a large hole out of his back. We kept him on his side, curled against the cold drizzle, so the one good lung wouldn't fill up with blood. We were surrounded and there was no hope of evacuation, even in the daylight. The choppers couldn't find us in the fog-shrouded mountains.

I heard Zoomer all night, panting as if he were running the 400, one lung doing for two and a body in shock. In and out. In, the fog, the sighing sound of monsoon wind through the jungle. Out, the painful breath. Zoomer had to go all night. If he slept, he'd die. So no morphine. Pain was the key to life.

To help him stay awake, and to calm my own fear, I'd crawl over to him to whisper stories.

—Karl Marlantes, from *What It Is Like to Go to War*

. . .

The first voice is the voice of the poet talking to himself— or to nobody.

—T. S. Eliot, from "The Three Voices of Poetry"

. . .

All events and experiences are
local, somewhere.

—William Stafford, from *Sound of the Ax*

· · ·

The next time you're with a group of around forty people, perhaps at a meeting, maybe on a city bus, imagine them all with the lean hard bodies of eighteen- to twenty-year-old men. Arm them all with automatic rifles, rockets, and grenades. Add three machine guns and a supply of bullets backed by the industrial might of America. Understand that these armed young men will do, without question, absolutely anything you ask. Now add in the power to call in jet aircraft that shake the earth with engine noise alone and can spew jellied fire over entire football fields, make craters big enough to block freeways, and fire lead so thick and fast that it would pulp the body of a cow in an eye-blink. Add to this artillery with shells as thick as your waist and naval gunfire with shells the weight of Volkswagens. And you're twenty-one or twenty-two and immortal. And no one will ever ask a single question.

—Karl Marlantes, from *What It Is Like to Go to War*

· · ·

Writing starts from the world—doesn't it?—something you see or hear, or hear about. Newspapers. TV. Restaurants. Coffee Shops. Family Reunions. Bus Stops…a "trigger" (it's been put), and it arrives from anywhere, anytime, like meteors, fish bites, hail, or dawn. Sometimes it can be as simple as a word. Take *sabotage*, coming to us from *sabot*, the French word for wooden shoe. The first instances of "sabotage" were likely peasant revolts against oppressive landowners, peasants tossing sabots into machines with the intent to destroy the machines: a word turning into event, or story.

. . .

The Zuni believed that wearing turquoise made a horse sure-footed.

. . .

In Breughel's Icarus, for instance: how everything turns
    away
Quite leisurely from the disaster; the ploughman may
Have heard the splash, the forsaken cry,
But for him it was not an important failure; the sun shone
As it had to on the white legs disappearing into the green
Water, and the expensive delicate ship that must have seen
Something amazing, a boy falling out of the sky,
Had somewhere to get to and sailed calmly on.
                —W. H. Auden, from "Musée des Beaux Arts"

. . .

In other words, he was blessed with that rare self-confidence which does not need admiration and the good opinion of others, and can even withstand self-criticism and self-examination without falling into the trap of self-doubt.
                —Hannah Arendt on W. H. Auden

. . .

It is known that Auden wrote, in a poem, that "poetry makes nothing happen," and he may have said that "no poem ever saved a single Jew from the gas chambers."

. . .

Wallace Stevens criticized Robert Frost for his poems being about *things*. Robert Frost criticized Wallace Stevens for his poems being about *bric-a-brac*.

. . .

Paul West accused literary critics of *garroting earthworms*.

. . .

re: Literary Critics
Park rangers shouting down rock climbers to check permits.
—Sean Purio

...drudges working with computers against Shakespeare.
—Barry Hannah

. . .

The right words matter. When I praise, it's normally on the level of language; when I don't, it's normally because the words are broken. I've striven always to do writers the tremendous dignity of considering their minds—since the culture wants to do them the tremendous indignity of considering only their emotions—and language is our most accurate embodiment of mind.
—William Giraldi, from *American Audacity: In Defense of Literary Daring*

. . .

As kids, we all believed our heights should be recorded on the doorframe and left for posterity. Who wouldn't have wanted to know of our growth?

. . .

re: What Fascists Do
Work to co-opt the justice system; work to diminish the free press; work to scapegoat large groups of humans.

. . .

In college calculus I discovered I needed glasses. Sitting in the rear of the classroom (as usual), I was miscopying math problems from the blackboard and receiving failing grades when I was certain I understood the processes. The bonus to my rising math scores was that the heavens featured stars and the trees revealed leaves.

. . .

For nearly all Americans war is an idea, not an experience.

. . .

re: In the Event of Nuclear War
Don't try to hide, run toward it with your mouth open. That's what I'm doing.

. . .

re: Creepy Enough?
If she wasn't my daughter, I'd probably be dating her.
                                              —Donald J. Trump

re: Dense Enough?
If the Jews had had guns, there wouldn't have been a Holocaust.
                                              —Ben Carson

. . .

At age six, Mozart began composing, writing his first symphonies by the age of eight. He died at thirty-five. His funeral drew few, and he was buried in a common grave.

. . .

It was pointless to tell the truth to anyone who crossed the threshold of the crematorium. You couldn't save anyone there. It was impossible to save people. One day in 1943 when I was already in Crematorium 5, a train from Bialystok arrived. A prisoner on the "special detail" saw a woman in the "undressing room" who was the wife of a friend of his. He came right out and told her: "You are going to be exterminated. In three hours you'll be ashes." The woman believed him because she knew him. She ran all over and warned the other women. "We're going to be killed. We're going to be gassed." Mothers carrying their children on their shoulders didn't want to hear that. They decided the woman was crazy. They chased her away. So she went to the men. To no avail. Not that they didn't believe her: they'd heard rumors in the Bialystok ghetto, or in Grodno, and elsewhere. But who wanted to hear that! When she saw that no one would listen, she scratched her whole face. Out of despair. In shock. And she started to scream.

So what happened? Everyone was gassed. The woman was held back. We had to line up in front of the ovens. First, they tortured her horribly because she wouldn't betray him. In the end she pointed to him. He was taken out of the line and thrown alive into the oven.

—Filip Müller, from Claude Lanzmann, *Shoah*

. . .

The "dead season," as it was called, began in February 1943, after the big trainloads came in from Grodno and Bialystok. Absolute quiet. It quieted in late January, February and into March. Nothing. Not one trainload. The whole camp was empty, and suddenly, everywhere, there was hunger. It kept increasing. And one day when the famine was at its peak, SS-Oberharführer Kurt Franz appeared before us and told us: "The trains will begin coming in again starting tomorrow." We didn't say anything. We just looked at each other, and each of us thought: "Tomorrow the hunger will end." In that period we were actively planning the rebellion. We all wanted to survive until the rebellion.

The trainloads came from an assembly camp in Salonika. They'd brought in Jews from Bulgaria, Macedonia. These were rich people; the passenger cars bulged with possessions. Then an awful feeling gripped us, all of us, my companions as well as myself, a feeling of helplessness, of shame. For we threw ourselves onto their food. A detail brought a crate full of crackers, another full of jam. They deliberately dropped the crates, falling over each other, filling their mouths with crackers and jam. The trainloads from the Balkans brought us to a terrible realization: we were the workers in the Treblinka factory, and our lives depended on the whole manufacturing process, that is, the slaughtering process at Treblinka.

—Richard Glazar, from Lanzmann, *Shoah*

. . .

Shoah is a Hebrew word meaning *catastrophe*. It is often used as a replacement word for *Holocaust*.

. . .

re: Who Said That

during slavery there was no black unemployment?

. . .

My neighbor cannot be Jewish. He is not circumcised and besides…so blond a skin, a face and a body so huge, are characteristics of non-Jewish Poles. He is a whole head taller than me but he has quite cordial features, as have those who do not suffer from hunger.

I tried to ask him if he knew when they would let us enter. He turned to the nurse who resembled him like a twin and was smoking in the corner; they talked and laughed together without replying, as if I was not there. Then one of them took my arm and looked at my number and then both laughed still more strongly. Everyone knows that the 17400s are the Italian Jews, the well-known Italian Jews who arrived two months ago, all lawyers, all with degrees, who were more than hundred and are now only forty; the ones who do not know how to work, and let their bread be stolen, and are slapped from the morning to the evening. The Germans call them "*zwei linke Hände*" (two left hands), and even the Polish Jews despise them as they do not speak Yiddish.

The nurse points to my ribs to show the other, as if I was a corpse in an anatomy class: he alludes to my eyelids and my swollen cheeks and my thin neck, he stoops to press on my tibia with his thumb, and shows the other the deep impression that his finger leaves in the pale flesh, as if it was wax.

I wish I had never spoken to the Pole: I feel as if I had never in all my life undergone an affront worse than this. The nurse, meanwhile, seems to have finished his demonstration in this language which I do not understand

and which sounds terrible. He turns to me, and in near-German, charitably, tells me the conclusion: *"Du Jude, kaput. Du schnell Krematorium fertig."* (You Jew, finished. You soon ready for crematorium.)

—Primo Levi, from *Survival in Auschwitz*

. . .

When I asked my father about his childhood, he said, "I was always hungry and I wore crappy clothes. I wouldn't be a kid again for nothing."

. . .

Stanislas Lefranc, a devout Catholic and monarchist, was a Belgian prosecutor who had come to the Congo to work as a magistrate. Early one Sunday morning in Leopoldville, he heard the sound of many children screaming desperately.

On tracing the howls to the source, Lefranc found "some thirty urchins, of whom several were seven or eight years old, lined up and waiting their turn, watching, terrified, their companions being flogged. Most of the urchins, in a paroxysm of grief...kicked so frightfully that the soldiers ordered to hold them by the hands and feet had to lift them off the ground.... 25 times the whip slashed down on each of the children." The evening before, Lefranc learned, several children had laughed in the presence of a white man, who then ordered that all servant boys in town be given fifty lashes. The second installment of twenty-five lashes was due at six o'clock the next morning. Lefranc managed to get these stopped, but was told not to make any more protests that interfered with discipline.

Lefranc was seeing in use a central tool of Leopold's Congo, which in the minds of the territory's people, soon became as closely identified with white rule as the steamboat or rifle. It was the *chicotte*—a whip of raw, sun-dried hippopotamus hide, cut into a long sharp-edged cork-screw strip. Usually the *chicotte* was applied to the victim's bare buttocks. Its blows would leave permanent scars; more than twenty-five strokes could mean unconsciousness; and a hundred or more—not an uncommon punishment—were often fatal.

Except for Lefranc, few Europeans working for the regime left records of their shock at the sight of officially sanctioned terror. The white men who passed through the territory as military officers, steamboat captains, or state or concession company officials generally accepted the use of the *chicotte* as unthinkingly as hundreds of thousands of other men in uniform would accept their assignments, a half-century later, to staff the Nazi and Soviet concentration camps. "Monsters exist," wrote Primo Levi of experience at Auschwitz. "But they are too few in number to be truly dangerous. More dangerous are…the functionaries ready to believe and to act without asking questions."

What made it possible for the functionaries in the Congo to so blithely watch the *chicotte* in action and…to deal out pain and death in other ways as well? To begin with, of course, was race. To Europeans, Africans were inferior beings: lazy, uncivilized, little better than animals. In fact, the most common way they were put to work was, like animals, as beasts of burden. In any system of terror, the functionaries must first of all see the victims as less than human, and Victorian ideas about race provided such a foundation.

—Adam Hochschild, from *King Leopold's Ghost*

PART III

Life consists in what a man is thinking of all day.

—Ralph Waldo Emerson

re: Trump
Like hiring a clown and getting a circus.

Aux barricades, citoyens!

. . .

Historians will tell you my uncle
wouldn't have called it World War II
or the Great War plus One *or* Tombstone
over My Head. *All this language*
came later. He and his buddies
knew it as get my ass outta here
or fucking trench foot *and of course*
sex please now. *Petunias are an apology*
for ignorance, my confidence
that saying high-density bombing
or chunks of brain in cold coffee
even suggest the athleticism
of his flinch or how casually
he picked the pieces out.

—Bob Hicok, from "The semantics of flowers
on Memorial Day"

. . .

Zebras live in constant fear, but their stomachs don't create ulcers. Scientists don't know why.

. . .

re: Comanches
The greatest threat of all to their identity, and to the very idea of a nomadic hunter in North America, appeared on the plains in the late 1860s. These were the buffalo men. Between 1868 and 1881 they would kill thirty-one million buffalo, stripping the plains almost entirely of the huge, lumbering creatures and destroying any last small hope that any horse tribe could ever be restored to its traditional life. There was no such thing as a horse Indian without a buffalo herd. Such an Indian had no identity at all.

—S. C. Gwynne, from *Empire of the Summer Moon*

. . .

The killing of over thirty million buffalo, in human terms, would have meant the death of every American then living, wiping out America entirely.

. . .

Surprisingly, only a few voices cried out against the slaughter of the buffalo, which had no precedent in human history. Mostly people didn't trouble themselves about the consequences. It was simply capitalism working itself out, the exploitation of another natural resource. There was another better explanation for the lack of protest, articulated best by General Phil Sherman, then commander of the Military Division of the Missouri. "These men [hunters] have done in the last two years...more to settle the vexed Indian question than the entire regular army has done in the last thirty years," he said. "They are destroying the Indian's commissary.... For the sake of a lasting peace, let them kill, skin, and sell until the buffalo are exterminated. Then your prairies can be covered with speckled cattle and the festive cowboy." Killing the Indian's food was not just an accident of commerce; it was a deliberate political act.

—S. C. Gwynne, from *Empire of the Summer Moon*

. . .

She is frightened of her children, because now that they've arrived in the world she has to stay here for as long as she can but not longer than they do.

—Lauren Groff, from "Flower Hunters"

. . .

...a man "so mild-mannered that he thought it was impossible to pick up a telephone in mid-ring."

—Anne Tyler, from *Clock Dance*

. . .

Italian scientists have determined that pasta won't make you fat. Are you good with that?

. . .

Exhibit A: Alban Michael. Out of the 7,700,000,000 people on earth, he was [the] only one left who could speak Nuchatlaht. He lived near Nootka Island, he spoke to his parents in dreams, as there was no one left to speak to him. And then one year ago, he was gone, himself a dream, his language buried with him.

Exhibit B: After millennia of surviving in the Caucasus Mountains on one vowel and 84 consonants, Ubykh died in the grave of Tevfik Esenç. He said, *I see you well* instead of *I love you* and *You cut my heart* instead of *You please me*, the sounds of his words described in a fable as the noise of a bag of pebbles poured on a sultan's marble floor.

Exhibit C: It took 600,000 men working 43 years to build the Tower of Babel. It is said in the Torah that those in charge behaved heartlessly toward the weak and sick who could not assist in its construction. They would not even allow a woman in travail to leave the work. When God smashed the tower to smithereens, many of its builders were changed into apes, evil spirits, demons, and ghosts. The rest wandered the earth, deaf to each other, confounded, babbling a thousand tongues, interpreters racing in the rain to explain the dreams of God. Babel is hence referred to in some texts as the *mother of confusion*. And barbarous, then, or barbarian, is Greek for "one who babbles" while "jabber" pertains to seafowl, fools, Jews, monkeys, and the Flemish.

Exhibit D: Two old women sit stiffly on a small upholstered sofa somewhere in Alaska. *I worked real hard on fish today*, one says improbably to the other. *You rest*, the other responds. I eat today, one says into the camera. *Seaweed, salmon, berries, bread. Hooligan grease, potatoes, tea. Tastes really good.* The other smiles, speaks to the videographer in English. These are some of the only words they still know in the moribund language of Haida. Soon they will be dead but they will leave behind a partial dictionary and a YouTube video of their conversation.

At the edge of the Timor Sea in Australia, **Exhibit E**, the last speakers of Mati Ke, a brother and sister, live in separate villages, and because they are siblings, they may not converse. *I miss you*, one says to the wind. *I have been dreaming of our mother, have you seen the plums this year, the wildfire is fierce, the waterbirds are growing thinner, do you still pray, do you sleep with the language we swam in during the womb?* The wind garbles the messages so when they arrive they are scratchy and unintelligible, like the recordings made by linguists who set up camp in the outback.

—Heather Altfeld, from "Obituary for Dead Languages"

. . .

There must be some so dead we don't
know they existed, but what we mean
by dead is: nobody speaks them anymore.
The bees that made the wax that sank
while scribes scratched late into the night,
the beekeeper, the inkmaker, whoever pared
the quilltips, and the birds who extruded
those quills and the calves who became
vellum, all these fell dead and nameless,
but the languages remain alive.

—William Matthews, from "Dead Languages"

. . .

re: The French Revolution
Men will never be free until the last king is strangled with the entrails of the last priest.

—Denis Diderot

. . .

These fragments I have shored against my ruins…

. . .

My father was happy to have a bathroom *in* the house, a happiness unavailable to us kids. We thought we should have more than one bathroom, and maybe a shower.

. . .

It may be I don't know enough to tell the story.

It may be I don't remember.

I might have to rebuild portions. Refurbish
memory. What I do get back can seed the rest.
                    —D. F. Brown, from "The Other Half of Everything"

. . .

At a party in a Spanish kind of tiled house
I met a woman who had won an award
for writing whose second prize
had gone to me. For years
I'd felt a kinship with her in the sharing
Of this honor;
and I told her how glad I was to talk with her,
my compatriot of letters,
mentioning of course this award.
But it was nothing
to her, and in fact she didn't remember it.
I didn't know what else to talk about.
I looked around us at a room full of hands

moving drinks in tiny rapid circles—
you know how people do
with their drinks.

—Denis Johnson, from "The Honor"

. . .

At a party once someone told another person that I was a writer who had published. That person sought me out. "You know" he said, "I've always thought that if I was in an accident and became like, you know, a quadriplegic or something, that what I'd start to do is to write science fiction novels. What do think of that idea?" I looked at him. I said, "Sounds good."

. . .

…where drunk drivers ought to wear necklaces
made from the spines of children they've run over.

—Jeffrey McDaniel, from "Disasterology"

. . .

Cry "Havoc!" and let slip the dogs of war…

—William Shakespeare, *Julius Caesar*

. . .

I'd start with an obscenity
a fat man in boils
pointing to the battle on a map
the queen secreting away her only son
disguised as a beggar
a labyrinth of sewers

spilling into the sea
an old man's rowboat
and a week's rations
a storm of men panting
behind the tree line
fletchers tearing asunder birds for arrows
pulling taut the gut strain of winches
locking down the catapults
the bones of philosophers tossed in dungeons
as deep as the earth's core

—M. K. Sukach, from "Raising the Dogs of War"

. . .

When we first were dating, I took my second wife into DC to catch a concert: Frank Sinatra and Buddy Rich. Fabulous. In an attempt to beat the traffic back to the Virginia suburbs, I took a turn up the alley behind the theater. There on the loading dock, in dim light, was Sinatra, alone, smoking a cigarette. Ellen begged me to stop. I didn't. I said the man had given his all in a terrific show and deserved a little downtime. "I wanted to talk to him," she said. I continued driving. Thirty years now, she's still upset.

. . .

She can't remember the experience of the concert and that, during that same year, I also took her to see the Coen brothers' first film, *Blood Simple*, as well as to encounter the young and dazzling Gérard Depardieu in *The Return of Martin Guerre*?

. . .

On my parents' honeymoon, my mother stood not
ten feet away from the one and only Frank Sinatra,
who was swaying at the blackjack table, dead drunk
and pissed at being ten thousand down, pissed
at this little shit who's been betting against him
all night, making snide remarks behind his back.
So when he says something really sick about Frank's wife,
he turns and lays the guy out on the plush casino carpet.
Blood everywhere and all the people slapping Frank
on the back. All this happening, when my mother
has one of those epiphanies that hit you right
in the stomach, and she knows she will never love
my father who's back in the room sleeping off three
whiskey sours and a porterhouse steak. She thinks
I shine and that will be enough, some fly boy will come
and take me, part my fine white flesh, flake me off
in tender forkfuls. Thought she was the sole of Dover,
my mother did, as Frank brushed by her, letting his
hand rest for just a second on her hip.

                        —William Loren Smith, from "Sole of Dover"

· · ·

Francis Albert Sinatra (1915–98)

· · ·

How old do you have to be until everyone seems younger,
even the dead as you remember them?

· · ·

"It was a watershed," says one State Department official,
who asked not to be named because his insight runs so
counter to our current foreign policy agenda. "The idea
used to be that terrible countries were terrible because

good, decent, innocent people were being oppressed by
evil, thuggish leaders. Somalia changed that. Here you
have a country where just about everybody is caught up in
hatred and fighting.... People in those countries—Bosnia
is a more recent example—don't want peace. They want
victory. They want power. Men, women, old and young.
Somalia was the experience that taught us that people in
these places bear much of the responsibility for things
being the way they are."

—Mark Bowden, from *Black Hawk Down*

. . .

Human ability to make tools was an early path to mas-
tering the environment. Simple hand blades and hand
axes made from hard rock were most certainly used to kill
and dismember animals but could also have been used
to subdue people. The distinction between hunting and
military use of such tools had to have been quickly blurred.
Handles for length and leverage and throwing had to have
soon followed. The subsequent organization of groups of
humans and tools against other groups of humans and
tools has brought us to now.

. . .

Every battle is a drama played out apart from broader
issues. Soldiers cannot concern themselves with the forces
that bring them to a fight, or its aftermath. They trust their
leaders not to risk their lives for too little. Once the battle
is joined, they fight to survive as much as to win, to kill
before they are killed. The story of combat is timeless. It is
about the same things whether in Troy or Gettysburg, Normandy or the Ia Drang. It is about soldiers, most of them
young, trapped in a fight to the death. The extreme and

terrible nature of war touches something essential about being human, and soldiers do not always like what they learn. For those who survive, the victors and the defeated, the battle lives on in their memories and nightmares and in the dull ache of old wounds.

> —Mark Bowden, from *Black Hawk Down*

. . .

If a novel is a revelation of consciousness, then may I suggest that that is what you are encountering here?

. . .

Drones strike me as cowardly, and yet I know we have been killing people from a distance for a very long time— the longbow replacing the sword, catapults, guns, artillery, ICBMs, manned aircraft. Why does drone warfare strike me as so chickenshit? How do you feel about it?

. . .

The idea of contingency is huge, the notion that lives— whole lives—are shaped by small decisions that go unnoticed or seem inconsequential at the time.

. . .

In a world preoccupied with the problems of war, the morning news brings a word of peace: peace in outer space. This unparalleled agreement prohibits all states from placing nuclear arms, or other weapons of destruction, in an environment empty of, and deadly to, human beings. So there is hope. If you can get into outer space you're safe.

> —Wright Morris, from *A Bill of Rites,*
> *a Bill of Wrongs, a Bill of Goods*

. . .

The world-class mountaineer who falls down her stairs in Telluride, Colorado, and dies.

. . .

The cowboy in my chemistry class at the Montana School of Mines who never removed his cowboy hat and who said, "You can do anything to me you want except break my Merle Haggard records."

. . .

In either the Netherlands or Denmark there was such an embrace of earth-friendly electric cars that the government had to construct additional fossil-fueled power plants in order to charge all the vehicles.

. . .

Jack winks at the boy waiting to get his cut. Jack was a winker long before he got his eye put out in a fight over a card game.

"Just a friendly game," Jack had said to the others when they caught him cheating. "That's the trouble with some people," Jack says to the barber and the boy, "they don't know the difference between a game and real life—between theory and the hard facts."

The hard fact was the toe of a steel-toed boot. Each time Jack winks, the boy disappears.

—Michael Chitwood, from "Practicum"

. . .

Young cat used to teach here,
Chinese guy: philosopher with a freak-flag pony tail.
Kids were ape shit about him.
Thought he was Lao Tze with a side of fries.

This was the nineties
when the whole tattoo thing was starting:
suburban white kids going to Bucktown, getting drunk
    and inked.
Come back feeling all badass.
                    —Benjamin Goluboff, from "Orientalism"

. . .

The moral concern is not that the people in our society have different amounts of money but that too many people don't have enough.

. . .

re: Overheard, various locations
If you are careful enough, nothing good or bad will ever happen to you.

People with that kind of money don't get their hair cut, they get it maintained.

Block chain?

It's why young wives start to look at the tennis pro.

The hundred-mile-long Suez Canal saves ships more than five thousand miles of sea travel around Africa's Cape of Good Hope.

A bit on the side?

Gun control is holding your weapon with both hands.

Why did Lady Godiva remove her clothes?

UTFART in Swedish means EXIT.

Marry somebody with the same age equipment.

Who put the Miller in my cooler?

Wouldn't it be loverly?

Eat your Wheaties.

…the mudslide of life.

What happened to her lips?

It kills weeds.

Take a walk. Leave the fucking phone at home!

. . .

Is it true that in all cultures there is evidence of bread and baskets?

. . .

Panhuman: Dancing and Singing.

. . .

"Anyone wanna get laid tonight?" asked Wally, grinning.

"Where?" asked Seagrave. "Here? In Hue?"

"Yeh," said Wally. "We found a whore over at the University. She'll take us all on and it won't cost us a single piaster. All she wants is food."

"A fuck for a box of C-rations," added Mogerty.

"A case?"

"No. One box. One meal per fuck."

"Count me in," said Hoffy.

"Why not?" said Seagrave.

"All right!" Wally whooped. "Get some!"

"Where's all this gonna happen?" asked Seagrave.

"I got a buddy in the 60-mike-mike platoon by the river," said Mogerty. "It's all set up. He'll let us use his gun pit if we cut him in on it."

"Someone's got to stay here on radio watch," said Seagrave.

I thought about volunteering. I wasn't sure I wanted in on a gang-bang. But I wasn't sure I wanted out either. The idea repelled me, but it aroused my curiosity, too, and I didn't want the others to think I wasn't game.

"I'll keep an eye on the radio," said Morgan. "You guys go on."

The rest of us slipped into the darkness, moving cautiously in single file as though we were on any ordinary patrol. It was raining. Mogerty led us to the river, found his friend, and the two of them muscled the little 60-millimeter mortar out of the gun pit. "I hope to hell we don't get a fire mission," said the friend. Wally arrived a short time later with a Vietnamese woman wearing dark silk trousers and a light silk blouse. It was too dark to see how old she was or what she looked like. Wally and Mogerty counted heads—six—and paid for all of us: one-half a case. We sat in the rain, smoking and listening to the gunfire coming from the other side of the river, while each of us took his turn. No one said much.

When my turn came, I jumped down into the pit. The woman was sitting up on some cardboard, protecting her body from the mud. She was naked from the waist down. I didn't know what to say or where to begin. "Chow Co," I said. "Hello." She just grunted softly and fumbled for my belt buckle. Her hands were cold. I undid the buckle myself and dropped my trousers. Cold air and rain bit at my buttocks and tightened my thighs. I hadn't had much experience at this sort of thing but even I knew that the woman's awkwardness and stiff body suggested either inexperience or deep hatred. "Probably both," I thought. My stomach felt sick. I finished quickly, pulled up my trousers, and climbed out of the pit.

"I don't think she was a whore," I said to Hoffy as we sneaked back through the rain toward the MACV compound. Hoffy said something that I couldn't hear. "What?" I asked.

Hoffy leaned into my ear. "So what?" he said.

—W. D. Ehrhart, from Vietnam-Perkasie

. . .

Plato is credited with the statement, "The unexamined life is not worth living." It comes to us from Plato's *Apology*, which is a recollection of the speech Socrates gave at his trial. Socrates presumably uttered these words after choosing death rather than exile from Athens or a commitment to silence.

. . .

Kurt Vonnegut asks, "But what if the examined life turns out to be a clunker as well?"

—from Wampeters, Foma, and Granfalloons

. . .

Around mid-morning, we came onto a small cluster of houses—or rather, what was left of them. The hooches had been blown to splinters, probably the night before. There was no one around but a middle-aged woman sitting amid the rubble in a dark pool of coagulated blood. She was holding a small child who had only one leg and half a head, and she had a tremendous gaping chest wound that ripped open both of her breasts. Flies swarmed loudly around mother and child. The woman was in a kind of trance, keening softly and gently rocking her baby....

"Holy Christ, what hit this place?" said Pelinski.

"Artillery," I said, trying to hold my voice steady, "or naval gunfire. The VC got nothing big enough to do this kind of damage." One of the corpsmen came over and looked at the woman, then gave her a shot of morphine.

—W. D. Ehrhart, from *Vietnam-Perkasie*

. . .

In the war against the Soviets, Omar was a brave fighter, never more so than on the day he was gravely wounded. The Soviets had laid siege to Singesar, Hassan said, firing a missile into the town's mosque. Shrapnel flew into Omar's right eye.

"Omar just got hold of his eye, took it out, and threw it away," Hassan said. He'd not seen the battle himself, of course; he was too young, but the tale of Omar's eye had the power of a founding myth.

—Dexter Filkins, from *The Forever War*

. . .

I collected Classic Comics. A favorite had to do with Odysseus and the Cyclops. I was informing my father about this race of one-eyed giants who raised giant sheep and ate people. I went on to explain how the clever Odysseus set afire a sharpened timber with which he and his surviving mates then managed to impale the drunken Cyclops's single eye. My father's response was to the point: *a problem with your only eye? not much of a backup there.* It was something to think about. I fell asleep that night, grateful for my double options: dual hands, dual feet, dual ears, dual eyes, nuts, knees, ankles, wrists, elbows, shoulders...

. . .

My father had a damaged left eye. At a young age, he'd caught a flying wood chip in his father's wood yard. It was this impaired vision that kept him out of World War II. Without that handicap, he would have joined the Navy with his best friend Sidney. Like other friends and brothers, they had connived to be assigned to and board the same ship. When Sidney died at Pearl Harbor, it was more than four years before my birth.

. . .

Do you promise to tell the truth, the whole truth, and nothing but the truth? What?

. . .

Attention equals life or is its only evidence.

—Frank O'Hara

. . .

Memory translates experience, writing translates memory.

. . .

re: Excellent Idea Department
An ax-throwing business in, of all places, Salt Lake City, has been granted a beer license. The license had been earlier denied until the business, Social Axe, added billiard tables to satisfy a new law's definition of a "recreational amenity."

. . .

Doesn't wine retain the flavor of the weather the grapes were grown in, the particularities of the soil, storms that came or didn't? Memoir is like that. It picks up the essence of the moment you wrote it, where you were sitting, the quality of the sun, amount of car exhaust or freshness in the air, the quality of your heart, it being open or not, how close its most recent breakage, how you are regarding your family of origin, it is a *they did the best they could* week or a *your best was not fucking good enough* week. All of this will color your story. What you have eaten or haven't, how hungover or not you may be, your various levels— emotional, physical, perhaps you have a toothache, perhaps you took a lovely walk, or else your shoulder is pained from hunching over a deeply non-ergonomic flea market desk. You just read something inspiring or have the theme to a children's song calliopeing through your head. You fear your best friend hates you. You just made up with your partner and are swelled with love and gratitude for them. You will never be in this precise state ever again. Its marks lie all over the version of your story you are telling today.
                    —Michelle Tea, from *Against Memoir:*
                    Complaints, Confessions, and Criticisms

. . .

In a museum, once, I took in a series of a woman's face: six photos. Beneath each view of the face, in this sequence, in the artist's pencil cursive: *Mother, Father, Sex, God, Death, Self.* And to introduce the photos: *The camera trained on Bethany was controlled by her. I provided the six words in sealed envelopes. At the moment Bethany possessed the image or memory by which she most embraced each word, she triggered the shutter.*

EXERCISE: Consider the effect of such an experiment for you.
EXTRA CREDIT: Snap the photos. Cope.
HELPFUL HINT: Memory is imagination
PROBLEM: Memory is imagination.

. . .

The line between fact and fiction is fuzzier than most people find it convenient to admit. There is the common-sensical assertion that while the novelist is engaged on a work of the creative imagination, the duty of the journalist is to tell what really happened, as it happened. That distinction is easy to voice but hard to sustain in logic. For imagination and memory are Siamese twins, and you cannot cut them so cleanly apart. There's a good case for arguing that any narrative account is a form of fiction. The moment you start to arrange the world in words, you alter its nature.

—David Shields, from *Reality Hunger*

. . .

Certain producers of plain prose have conned the reading public into believing that only in prose plain, humdrum or flat can you articulate the mind of inarticulate ordinary Joe. Even to begin to do that you need to be more articulate than Joe, or you might as well tape-record him and leave it at that. This minimalist vogue depends on the premise that only an almost invisible style can be sincere, honest, moving, sensitive and so forth, whereas prose that draws attention to itself by being revved up, ample, intense, incandescent or flamboyant turns its back on something almost holy—the human bond with ordinariness. I doubt if much unmitigated ordinariness can exist. As Harold Nicolson, the critic and biographer, once observed, only one man in a thousand is boring, and he's interesting because he's a man in a thousand. Surely the passion for the plain, the homespun, the banal, is itself a form of betrayal, a refusal to look honestly at a complex universe, a get-poor-quick attitude that wraps up everything in simplistic formulas never to be inspected for veracity or substance. Got up as a cry from the heart, it is really an excuse for dull and mindless writing, larded over with the democratic myth that says this is how most folks are. Well, most folks are lazy, especially when confronted with a book, and some writers are lazy too, writing in the same anonymous style as everyone else.

—Paul West, from "In Defense of Purple Prose"

. . .

Sampling, the technique of taking a section of existing, recorded sound and placing it within an "original" composition, is a new way of doing something that's been done for a long time: creating with found objects. The rotation gets thick. The constraints get thin. The mix breaks free of the old associations. New contexts form from old. The script gets flipped.

—David Shields, from *Reality Hunger*

. . .

We never see Indians having sex on TV, which is odd, considering there are a billion of us on the planet and we did
invent the Kama Sutra.

—Neel Patel talks to Mira Jacob

. . .

Art is illusion, and what's needed is an art that temporarily
blots out the real.... It's when the words blot out the real,
and displace it, that prose comes into its own, conjuring,
fooling, aping, yet never quite achieving the impression
that, in dealing with an elephant, it is actually working in
elephant hide. There lingers always, just out of view, on the
conjectural fringe of vision, the fact that what's going on is
verbal. The prose will not turn to the sun, like a plant, or
wither without actually falling off its stem, or spawn tapeworms in its interior. Yet it has mass, texture and shape.
It calls into play all the senses, and it can interact at the
speed of ionization with the reader's mind. HOW extraordinary: our minds loll in two states, ably transposing
words into things, things into words. What goes on in this
hybrid mental shuttling to and fro is something passive
but active, a compromise in affairs of scale, dimension
and abstraction. The phrase "teddy bear" is smaller than
the toy animal, which in turn is smaller (usually) than the
big bear from the wilds; is almost entirely flat (a printed
phrase stands up a little from the surface it is printed on);
and lacks physical attributes conspicuous in any bear. The
words represent, but they also re-present, and when the
wordsmith turns to purple various things happen. The
presence of the supervising wordsmith becomes more
blatant, but the objects being presented in words have a

more unruly presence. They bristle, they buzz, they come out at you.

—Paul West, from "In Defense of Purple Prose"

. . .

In 2008, more votes were cast for *American Idol* than were cast for Barack Obama for president.

. . .

If I had the slightest grasp upon my own faculties, I would not make essays. I would make decisions.

—Michel de Montaigne

. . .

This morning I watched a flock of magpies run a coyote off a dead rabbit. *Air superiority.* Coyote gone, the magpies went to work on the opened rabbit.

. . .

People who, over time, resemble their musical instruments, their cars, their dogs...

. . .

Before a recent surgery, I attempted to make friends with the anesthesiologist. I asked what had prompted him to go to medical school. He said he had been unable to get into a veterinary program.

. . .

The very pregnant cashier's name tag, "Hi, My Name is Chasity," that you could never write convincingly but could film—the camera silently panning. See what I mean?

. . .

In art, meaning must try to surface like a held-underwater beach ball. "So much depends on a red wheelbarrow" is superior to a dreary disquisition on the concept of contingency, in which you employ the word *contingency.*

. . .

L'absence est à l'amour ce qu'est au feu le vent;
Il éteint le petit, Il allume le grand.
> —Roger Rabutin, Comte de Bussy (1618–93),
> from his *Maximes d'Amour*

. . .

Why is there sand in deserts? Because windblown sand collects in every low place, and deserts are low, like beaches. However far you live from the sea, however high your altitude, you will find sand in ditches, in roadside drains, and in cracks between rocks and sidewalks.

Sand collects in flat places too, like high-altitude deserts. During interglacials, such as the one in which we live now, soils dry. Clay particles clump and lie low; sand grains part and blow about. Winds drop sand by weight, as one drops anything when it gets too heavy for one's strength. Winds carry light stone dust—loess—far afield. Wherever they drop it, it stays put only in a few places: in the rich prairies in central North America, and in the precious flat basins in China and Russia.

> —Annie Dillard, from *For the Time Being*

. . .

The wind bloweth where it listeth, and thou hearest the sound thereof, but canst not tell whence it cometh, and whither it goeth.

—John 3:8

. . .

The Winds of War...

. . .

The more nearly spherical is a grain of sand, the older it is. "The average river requires a million years to move a grain of sand one hundred miles," James Trefil tells us. As a sand grain tumbles along the riverbed—as it saltates, then lies still, then saltates for those millions of years—it smooths some of its rough edges. Then, sooner or later, it blows into a desert. In the desert, no water buoys its weight. When it leaps, it lands hard. In the desert, it knaps itself round. Most of the round sand grains in the world, wherever you find them, have spent some part of their histories blowing around a desert. Wind bangs sand grains into one another on dunes and beaches, and into rocks. Rocks and other sands blast the surfaces, so windblown sands don't sparkle like young river sands.

—Annie Dillard, from *For the Time Being*

. . .

On September 8, 1900, an unexpected hurricane with sustained winds of 140 miles per hour slammed into Galveston, Texas, killing eight thousand people. With no radar, tracking, or predictions, no preparations were made for the storm. A fifteen-foot storm surge flooded the city, which was then situated at less than nine feet above sea level. In terms of loss of life, this hurricane remains the worst weather-related disaster in U.S. history.

. . .

Hurricane Andrew struck in 1992 and devastated the Homestead and southern Miami-Dade areas with sustained winds of over 156 miles per hour. The estimated cost of the damage was $26.5 billion. In Dade County alone, the forces of Andrew resulted in fifteen deaths and up to one-quarter million people left temporarily homeless. An additional twenty-five lives were lost in Dade County from the indirect effects of Andrew.

. . .

The total cost of damage from Katrina is estimated at $81.2 billion, more than double the cost of the previously most expensive storm, Hurricane Andrew. Some eighteen hundred people died as a consequence of Katrina.

. . .

Over the Labor Day weekend in 1935, a hurricane struck the Florida Keys, with record-setting low barometric pressure of 892 mb. Some four hundred of the then Keys population of one thousand died. Roads, buildings, viaducts, bridges, and the railroad were completely wiped out. The Great Labor Day Hurricane's sustained winds are estimated to have reached two hundred miles per hour. The highest elevation of the Florida Keys is eighteen feet above sea level.

. . .

People still intentionally live in Galveston, New Orleans, and the Florida Keys.

. . .

windscreen, wind shear, windshield, windburn, windborne, windblown, windbreak, windbag, windpipe, windrow, windlass, wind harp, windmill, windsock, windfall, windjammer, windage, windswept, windward, winded, windy...

. . .

mid-argument
> *wind chimes*
we gave each other.

—Peter Newton

. . .

On May 9, 1934, a flock of whirlwinds started up in the northern prairie, in the Dakotas and eastern Montana, where people had fled the homesteads two decades earlier. The sun at midmorning turned orange and looked swollen. The sky seemed as if it were matted by a window screen. The next day, a mass of dust-filled clouds marched east, picking up strength as they found the jet stream winds, moving toward the population centers. By the time this black front hit Illinois and Ohio, the formations had merged into what looked to pilots like a solid block of airborne dirt. Planes had to fly fifteen thousand feet to get above it, and when they finally topped out at their ceiling, the pilots described the storm in apocalyptic terms. Carrying three tons of dust for every American alive, the formation moved over the Midwest. It covered Chicago at night, dumping an estimated six thousand tons, the dust slinking down walls as if every home and every office had sprung a leak. By morning, the dust fell like snow over Boston and Scranton, and then New York slipped under partial darkness. Now the storm was measured at 1,800 miles wide, a great rectangle of dust from the Great Plains to the Atlantic, weighing 350 million tons. In Manhattan, the streetlights came on at midday and cars used their headlights to drive. A sunny day, which had dawned cloudless, fell under a haze like that of a partial eclipse. From the observatory at the top of the Empire State Building, people looked into a soup unlike anything ever seen in midtown. They could not see the city below or Central Park just to the north. An off-white film covered the ledge. People coughed, rushed into hospitals and doctors' offices asking for emergency help to clear their eyes. The harbor turned gray, the dust floating on the surface. The grass of the parks and the tulips rising to break the Depression fog were coated in fine sand. From Governors Island, visibility was so bad a person could not see the boats just beyond the shore. Baseball players said they had trouble tracking fly balls.

—Timothy Egan, from *The Worst Hard Time*

. . .

Unimpeded by vegetation, desert winds can desiccate seedlings in minutes and carry enough sand and dust to cut visibility to zero, make bare skin bleed, bury human settlements, and drop dust thousands of miles from its source. These winds, which typically come at regular times of the year, have such strong personalities that they have names:

khamsin, sharav, simoom, shamal, Santa Anna, cherguli, ghibli, haboob, harmattan, bad kessif, brickfielder, sirocco.

—SueEllen Campbell, from *The Face of the Earth*

· · ·

"Remember Knobloch?"

   "IED, right?"

"Yeah, Mosul."

"Motherfucker sure could play Texas Hold 'Em."

"Damn straight."

We were standing around after the memorial service. Seven of us, the ones who'd made it this far.

The afternoon wind kicked up and we bent our heads, tucking up under our Kevlars. Two of us realized the dust covers on our 16s were open and clicked them shut. To someone passing by, it might have looked like we were praying, huddled in a tight circle of faith and brotherhood.

Bullshit. It was just the motherfucking wind.

—David Abrams, from "Roll Call"

· · ·

In Iraq, dirt was the environment. The soil was capable of rising above ground-level, billowing into atmospheric clouds, moving, the landscape shedding its skin. In June, when my mother was watching seedlings emerge from moist earth, I wrote home about the desertic soil:

It is now hot enough to sweat spinal fluid. Truly miserable and not yet even July. Dust storms have poured out of the dry spaces to the west. The air turns opaque with an orange tan of migrating particles. They move with the freedom of the air that moves them and cannot be kept out of anything. Eyes, nose, weapons. Dust seems to seek the places that it becomes most noticeable. When the wind finally thins, the entire city is left covered with a fragile layer of fine powder. The resident dust beneath is revealed to be a different, older hue of dirt by the first footsteps of the next day. More gray than colored, as if it has aged by settling. Our trudging begins the blending of sediments. Of dunes and riverbeds. Of bones and buildings. Mountains and of what lies beneath. There is something to be said about being dust. It is where we are all heading.

Northern Africa had the highest fecal content blowing in its winds, Kuwait had grit, Los Angeles had petroleum soot, central New York had my dander, and Iraq would have death in its dust. The Pentagon was still denying Gulf War syndrome as veterans hollowed out and died from it in VA hospitals. T. S. Eliot wrote, "I will show you fear in a handful of dust." There was something else in the air with all of that dust and ash.

—Benjamin Busch, from Dust to Dust

. . .

For health reasons, an anti-smoking campaign in the middle of a war zone?

. . .

The army wanting credit for using lead-free paint on artillery shells?

. . .

What is life but a long series of digressions? Where did I read that?

. . .

The answer my friend is blowin' in the wind...

. . .

No weapon frightens me as much as the shell. Bullets have a certain logic. Put a sizeable enough piece of concrete between yourself and the firer and you will be untouched. Run between cover, for it is difficult even for an experienced shot to hit a man who sprints fast. Even when people around you are hit the wounds seldom seem so bad, unless the bullet has tumbled in flight or hit them in the head. But shells? They can do things to the human body you never believed possible; turn it inside out like a steaming rose; bend it backwards and through itself; chop it up; shred it; pulp it: mutilations so base and vile they never stopped revolting me. And there is no real cover from shellfire. Shells can drop out of the sky to your feet, or smash their way through any piece of architecture to find you. Some of the ordnance the Russians were using was slicing through ten-storey buildings before exploding in the basement. Shells could arrive silently and unannounced, or whistle and howl their way in, a sound that somehow seems to tear at your nerves more than warn you of anything. It's only the detonation which always seems the same—a feeling as much as a sound, a hideous suck-roar-thump that in itself, should you be close enough, can collapse your palate and liquefy your brain.

—Anthony Loyd, from *My War Gone By, I Miss It So*

. . .

Seeing is metamorphosis, not mechanism. Seeing changes both you and what you're looking at.

—James Elkins, from
The Object Stares Back: On the Nature of Seeing

. . .

There is a philosophical element to it all too: a bullet may or may not have your number on it, but I am sure all shells are merely engraved with "to whom it may concern."

In Sarajevo there were times when we thought it was a bad day if a few hundred shells fell on the city. During the second half of the battle for Grozny the Russians sometimes fired over 30,000 shells a day into the southern sector. It was an area less than a third the size of Sarajevo.

And so Grozny had the life torn out of it by the second most powerful military machine on the planet and the lethal dynamics were breathtaking in every sense. A concrete killing zone, it was as if a hurricane of shrapnel had swept through every street, leaving each perspective bearing the torn, pitted scars, the irregular bites of high-explosive ordnance. The remaining trees were shredded and blasted horizontal, while the snow on the pavements became covered in a crunching carpet of shattered glass.

Artillery, tanks, mortars, rocket systems, jet aircraft, helicopter gunships—the permutations of incoming fire were endless. It left the dead plentiful: dead people blown out of their flats; dead pigeons blown out of their roosts; dead dogs blown off the street. Death became too frequent and too abundant to deal with, so that often the bodies were left where they had fallen to become landmarks in their own right: "Turn left past the dead guy with the yellow shopping bag and his wife, then right to Minutka..."

—Anthony Loyd, from *My War Gone By, I Miss It So*

. . .

A poet friend, when he heard I'd begun attending Mass with my wife, said he was an agnostic Catholic. When I asked what he meant, he said he didn't believe in Jesus but that Mary was His mother.

. . .

At the state fair this year, you could purchase a Twinkie deep-fried and wrapped in bacon. Who thinks up this stuff?

. . .

Desire is the inconvenience of its object. Lourdes isn't Lourdes if you live in Lourdes.

—Don Paterson, from *The Book of Shadows*

. . .

How powerful men deal with accusations of sexual harassment and assault: *Deny, Degrade, and Dig In.*

. . .

Where *do* these guys get the idea that young women have been waiting all along just to catch a glimpse of their hairy bellies and ancient dicks?

. . .

Bernardine:
Thou hast committed…

Barabas:
Fornication?
But that was in another country:
And besides, the wench is dead.

—Christopher Marlowe, from The Jew of Malta

. . .

re: In 2002
The woman in Pakistan who was raped—and under Muslim law convicted of adultery and sentenced to be stoned to death.

—David Markson, from Vanishing Point

. . .

What farmers know: *weather and weeds win.*

. . .

The poor have always lived in a world without much shield from pain.

. . .

August 6
God's Bomb
In 1945, while this day was dawning, Hiroshima lost its life. The atomic bomb's first appearance incinerated this city and people in an instant.

The few survivors, mutilated sleepwalkers, wandered among the smoking ruins. The burns on their naked bodies carried the stamp of the clothing they were wearing when the explosion hit. On what remained of the walls, the atom bomb's flash left silhouettes of what had been: a woman with her arms raised, a man, a tethered horse.

Three days later, President Harry Truman spoke about the bomb over the radio.

He said: "We thank God that it has come to us, instead of to our enemies; and we pray that He may guide us to use it in His ways and for His purposes."

—Eduardo Galeano, from *Children of the Days*

. . .

We look at the world once, in childhood.
The rest is memory.

—Louise Glück, from "Nostos"

. . .

re: How to Finish

Moments of kindness and reconciliation are worth having, even if the parting has to come sooner or later. I wonder if those moments aren't more valued, and deliberately gone after, in the setups some people like myself have now, than they were in those old marriages, where love and grudges could be growing underground, so confused and stubborn, it must have seemed they had forever.

—Alice Munro, from "The Progress of Love"

. . .

She hasn't even put a hand on the door, she hasn't made a move to leave. Doesn't he know what's happening? Maybe you need the experience of a lot of married fights to know it. To know what you think—and for a while, hope—is the absolute end for you can turn out to be only the start of a new stage, a continuation. That's what's happening, that's what has happened. He has lost some of his sheen for her; he may not get it back. Probably the same goes for her, with him. She feels his heaviness and anger and surprise. She feels that also in herself. She thinks that up till now was easy.

—Alice Munro, from "Five Points"

. . .

So we went on, with the two in the back seat trusting us, because of no choice, and we ourselves trusting to be forgiven, in time, for everything that had first to be seen and condemned by those children: whatever was flippant, arbitrary, careless, callous—all our natural, and particular, mistakes.

—Alice Munro, from "Miles City, Montana"

Entr'acte

Deaf or *Blind?* I speak for myself: *Deaf.* I eat the world with my eyes. I don't want to read with my fingers. My son dreaded his high school wrestling matches with the School of the Deaf and Blind. The kids attending that school and choosing to wrestle were tough. My son was better if he drew a deaf wrestler but beside himself if his opponent were blind. How to pin a blind kid to win and how not to pin a blind kid to lose?

Central retinal vein occlusion (CRVO) is a blockage of the main vein in the retina. The blockage causes the walls of the vein to leak blood and excess fluid into the retina. When this fluid collects in the macula (the area of the retina responsible for central vision), vision blurs.

I was in Key West with my wife when a vein near my retina clogged. The pain was decisive. It was also temporary. The effect on my vision, however, was not. If I shut the right eye, the world distorted. I couldn't read with the right eye shut, the letters on the page narrowing like squiggled heads on thin necks: a Modigliani painting.

Ellen and I headed north to Fort Lauderdale and the Rand Eye Institute to which we'd been granted an emergency appointment. As we were completing preliminary paperwork and a questionnaire, in walked a man with a balled-up shirt pressed to his eye (also the left). There was blood. The man was squat and solid—Guatemalan, I guessed—black thick hair coated in drywall dust. The little man was trying to explain himself in a moaning Spanish. His translator, we guessed, was the construction site's white foreman. We were near enough the reception desk to gather that the Hispanic worker had somehow been shot in the eye with a pneumatic nail gun.

"Nail in the eye?"

"It is," said the foreman.

"Still?" asked the nurse.

"I don't know how deep." Then: "He won't uncover."

"Length?"

The foreman gauged the nail's length with his thumb and forefinger. He showed an inch or so, give or take.

When the nurse asked could the man remove the shirt from the eye, this request was translated until the man said "No." He said he would reveal the damaged eye when he could see a doctor with his undamaged one. He pointed out that he wanted a *man* doctor, an *hombre*, *El Doctor.* The nurse then asked the foreman to escort the worker and to follow her. Ellen and I exchanged looks. We almost stood and left.

My eye examination felt trivial and I honestly admitted to no pain. The right eye had already begun its work of compensation. Dr. Rand, himself, explained that an occluded retina will sometimes resolve itself and that with luck this could be my case. Rand then excused himself to check on his colleague and the foreign man with the nailed eye.

Eight years pass as I wait for my eye's conceivable resolution.

The retina—the layer of light-sensitive cells at the back of the eye—is nourished by blood flow, which provides nutrients and oxygen that nerve cells need. When there is blockage in the veins (age, cholesterol, hypertension, diabetes) into the retina, retinal vein occlusion will generally occur.

Finally, I arrange for an appointment with a retina man in my own town in Colorado:

"We've had some success with a protocol of injections."

"Injection?"

"Injection."

"Needle in the eye?"

"Yes. Needle."

"Any clue about the fruitfulness of my imagination?"

"Maybe."

"Fucking fruitful."

"We could do this now," the doctor says, ignoring, consulting computer-generated photos. In an attempt to involve me in his process, he keeps pointing to areas on the screen. "We can do this now," he repeats.

I raise my hands to prevent violation of my re-valued personal space. "I need to circle my brain around this."

"This?"

"This. Eyes. Needles. That *this.*"

The doctor shrugs, consults the record. "Eight years," he says. "What's a couple of weeks?" Before I leave, Dr. Williamson wants me to know he has performed the procedure on children as young as five years old, and that the week previous he'd treated a patient whose age was 107. I cast him a look and almost quote from *Catch-22* when Yossarian complains to Clevinger that "*They're* trying to kill me." "*No one* is trying to kill you," Clevinger informs. "Then why are they shooting at me?" Yossarian asks. "They're shooting at *everyone,*" Clevinger answers. "They're trying to kill *everyone.*" "And what difference does that make?" Yossarian asks. It was what I was thinking, but I spare the retina man my reference.

You know the story... Desiring to thwart the prophecy that his child would grow up to murder him and marry his wife, King Laius pins Oedipus's feet together and leaves him to perish on a mountainside. Found by kind-hearted shepherds and raised by another king and queen in a different city, Oedipus learns of the prophecy, and believes he is fated to murder King Polybus and marry Queen Merope, and so leaves Corinth. On his way to Thebes, Oedipus encounters Laius and slays him, Laius being nothing to Oedipus but a quarrelsome stranger at a crossroads. Solving the Sphinx's riddle (who, inexplicably but fortunately, kills herself), Oedipus frees Thebes, wins the throne of the murdered king and the hand in marriage of the king's widow, Oedipus's own mother, Jocasta. In time all is revealed, and Jocasta hangs herself. Oedipus, discovering her body, unclasps a brooch from his mother's gown, to stab himself in not one but both eyes.

I steer clear of Retina Consultants of Southern Colorado until Dr. Williamson's assistant calls: "Dr. Williamson is asking for you to come in."

"For what?"

"He told me to tell you 'for a consult.'"

I concede.

Prior to "consulting" with Dr. Williamson both my eyes are dilated twice and I'm ıved with a dye that the nurse hopes doesn't make me feel too itchy.

"My eyes, you mean?"

"No, your body," she says, "your throat. Your breathing." She then situates me in front of a machine that tracks the passage of dye through the veins of both retinas. When another nurse arrives to accompany me to Williamson's exam room, the first nurse says, "So don't be surprised when you urinate."

"What does that mean?"

"It means your stream will appear more colorful than you are used to."

"Colorful?"

"Yes."

Before Williamson shows, the nurse re-dilates both eyes and tells me to keep them shut.

I don't open my eyes when I hear the doctor enter. I do, though, when he reclines the chair so that my feet rise above my head. He then empties what he tells me later is a small bottle of Lidocaine—the anesthesia that dentists use. But this is not a dentist's needle; it is a bottle, and he pours it into my eye before he attaches a cold metal contraption he says will prop the eye open without effort on my part.

"Why is that?" I ask.

"Because we're doing this now," he says, sliding the needle in.

I'll say this: It was over before I knew it. Williamson then smeared Vaseline-like gel into the eye. Now it was viewing Modigliani's world as seen through a frozen cube of sediment and water. As for the surprise attack, I had apparently signed a release on the first visit as I sat waiting for the doctor, eyes wide.

"Check with the receptionist on the way out. We generally have to repeat the procedure, you know?"

I said, *No. I didn't know.*

I had little business driving home, what with the blinded eye and the other so dilated that even squinting through polarized sunglasses hurt. As advised, I did take Tylenol when I got home and lay on my back with my eyes closed. When the greasy smear dissipated, I could see the black hole the needle had made, a needle as thin as an antiseptic hair. It wasn't until the next morning that the eye stopped aching. It was, after all, microscopic as it was, an invasion. I was unable to not think of the Guatemalan dealing with the carpenter's nail, a question, no doubt, of morphine, regimes of antibiotics, medically induced comas, etc. I decided that I'd survive.

Six weeks or so passed before my next appointment. It was the same business, dilation, dye, reclined chair, Lidocaine, the Spanish Inquisition apparatus propping wide the eye. This time, though, I knew the needle was coming and turned my head when the doctor struck. There was more pain at that instant than I had felt the first time when I was surprised and still. There was more pain later, too, the black hole enlarged. With the third visit scheduled in six weeks, I resolved to do my best to be still for the next injection, which came and went.

Although Sigmund Freud chose the term Oedipus complex to describe a son's feeling of love toward his mother and jealousy toward his father, these were not emotions that motivated Oedipus's actions or determined his character in any ancient version of his story. What led to Oedipus's self-inflicted blinding, in my interpretations, was bad luck, timing, and a misunderstanding of himself, an un-seeing. Not so, my Greek scholar friend informs. Oedipus had no choice in the matter. He was destined by Fate, all ordered before his birth. When the Gods dictate your future, your only effect on the outcome is to accept it reluctantly or enthusiastically, which in the end is no choice at all. All to say: When a nail gun is pointed your way, whether it fires intentionally or accidently makes no difference. What you have is a nail in the eye.

It is time to report that over the course of the three injections, my vision improved. My worldview had moved from Modigliani to more of a Greco. I knew instinctively that I was never going to get to Mondrian, and that short of perfect would have to do, a notion the doctor confirmed while saying we might need a fourth or a fifth injection. By the time the fourth scheduled visit arrived, the Retina Consultants group had moved to new digs: a place palatial and jammed with old people who couldn't see. I became suddenly too aware of too many eye patches and dark glasses. A lot of bad posture, too—people staring at the floor as if looking for what? blind mice? near-sighted squirrels? matched socks? I prepared my speech for Williamson. "Look," I practiced. "I didn't expect perfection. I didn't even before you confirmed it wouldn't occur. I'm ready to fold and to collect my winnings. Not in the mood, Doc. I'm through." My speech prepared, I was shuffled through the new set of rooms and equipment. It was the usual, but in a larger and better-appointed setting. Dilation, dye, filming, et al.

I meant to inform you earlier about my reaction to the dye and the nurse's warning. She'd told me the urine would be yellow.

"*Yellow?*"

"You'll see."

My urine appeared radioactive. The brightest yellow you'll never see, not even on the best-painted Japanese car.

By the time I was seated in the big chair in Williamson's exam room, I was more than ready: *My eye, Doc. Finis.*

The doctor entered the room with copies of my eye's photos in hand. "These look good," he said. "Ready to call it quits?"

"What? You sure?"

. . .

When one of my daughters was three or four, she split the tender flesh between her big toe and the next on broken bottle glass on the front lawn. The gash was a mouth speaking blood. I bound her foot in a bath towel and sped to the hospital. It was on an Air Force base in Omaha, Nebraska, where I was stationed. The ER doc told me he thought he could close the wound with one stitch and that a numbing shot would hurt just as much, so he thought he'd just take the stitch and be done with it. I okayed this approach, cradling my child in my arms. It took three stitches with a cruel curved needle that could have hooked carp.

. . .

I later lied to her about her cocker spaniel Brandy. The dog had bitten a neighbor's two-year-old in the face, barely missing the child's eye, and I had to put the dog down. When my daughter asked where her dog was, I said that Brandy had been unexpectedly selected to be a star drug dog for the Air Force and had been assigned to Hawaii. I told my daughter that she should be proud. My daughter, now nearing fifty, has never asked whether the story is true.

. . .

re: Additional Endings

Now he did what his father had done—unlaced his shoes, tore at the buttons of his shirt, and knowing that a mossy stone or the force of the water could be the end of him he stepped naked into the torrent, bellowing like his father. He could stand the cold only for a minute but when he stepped away from the water he seemed at last to be himself. He went on down to the main road, where he was picked up by some mounted police, since Maria had sounded the alarm and the whole province was looking for the maestro. His return to Monte Carbone was triumphant and in the morning he began a long poem on the inalienable dignity of light and air that, while it would not get him the Nobel Prize, would grace the last months of his life.

—John Cheever, from "The World of Apples"

. . .

Oh, what can you do with a man like that? What can you do? How can you dissuade his eye in a crowd from seeking out the cheek with acne, the infirm hand; how can you teach him to respond to the inestimable greatness of the race, the harsh surface beauty of life; how can you put his finger for him on the obdurate truths before which fear and horror are powerless? The sea that morning was iridescent and dark. My wife and sister were swimming—Diana and Helen—and I saw their uncovered heads, black and gold in the dark water. I saw them come out and I saw that they were naked, unshy, beautiful, and full of grace, and I watched the naked women walk out of the sea.

—John Cheever, from "Goodbye, My Brother"

. . .

As before, the it in me was crying: a tear on one cheek, a second on the other. Its mouth dropped open and its face, I suppose, was like Purvis L. Watkin's own, wonder-filled and baffled, the victim of ten or ten thousand ideas at once. As before, it, the me I was, desired answers. To questions about the forward movement of living life. About what to do with weakness. About why it is we have the hearts we do, and how it is they work.

—Lee K. Abbott, from "How Love Is Lived in Paradise."

. . .

He was thinking about Mindy Griffith, that sophomore from Philadelphia, that one whose major in communications science had taught her, doubtlessly, the subtle but potent differences between talk and speech; yes, that fetching, unsafe creature who'd nearly fled her desk that noontime when he'd read from the *Biographia* of shag and rack and the dim, wicked hunter. Oh, he knew now what he would do, all right. And he knew, too, that while one might say that Mozer was a pretty slimy motherfucker, at thirty-five, to hustle the innocent, another might say that he was one hell of a fine person, confident as a gambler, with the courage of Columbus, to share, to shepherd someone into that new world of love, that enchanted province of paradise and dread.

—Lee K. Abbott, from "The Eldest of Things"

. . .

In August, Mr. Dillon Ripley sold his house and moved his family twenty miles further south in the desert, to Hatchita, where, as we understand it, there is no sport at all save hunting and where the winds, infernal and constant, blow as if from a land whose lord is dark and always angry.

—Lee K. Abbott, from "The Valley of Sin"

. . .

re: Overheard, various locations
The free dive record? Did you say four minutes?

No phonebooks?

Mexicans: stucco and landscaping; Chinese: restaurants and laundries; Koreans: liquor stores and massage parlors; Vietnamese: nails and toes. Listen to me on this. And by the way, if you're looking for the best Chinese food, look for the place frequented by Chinese *and* Jews—that's the one.

Get it?

I want to play golf where there are cloth towels in the locker room and garlic butter in the restaurant.

Extinction will kick our ass.

If you're in love, is monogamy irrelevant?

Prescription ads tell you not to use their product if you are allergic to it, but how do you know if you don't use it?

In 1492, there were five million Native Americans. By 1890, there were a quarter million. Do the math.

Booze is over there in the corner doing pushups. Pay attention.

Could you be a dog groomer?

Put a sock in it.

Could it be otherwise?

My dog won't eat leftover pancakes unless you add syrup.

Do you still think of crutches?

That's a Boston terrier? I want one.

It's like saying I struck out Roger Maris.

Being married twice I get. Three times?

…often in error but never in doubt.

Her last name is Frisbee?

Winter's coming.

. . .

Sir Isaac Newton once intentionally inserted a bodkin—a long needle of the sort used for sewing leather—into his eye socket and "rubbed it around 'betwixt my eye and the bone as near to [the] backside of my eye as I could' just to see what would happen…. On another occasion, he stared at the Sun for as long as he could bear, to determine what effect it would have on his vision…. An analysis of a strand of Newton's hair in the 1970s found it contained mercury at a concentration some forty times the natural level." For all of his brilliance, half of Newton's working life was given over to alchemy.

—see Bill Bryson, *A Short History of Nearly Everything*

. . .

City grass doesn't want much of anything,
it's not out there trembling with desire,
minds its own business, leeching slowly upward from
    busted pipe.

—Marsha de la O, from "Nobody Knows"

. . .

Scientists say Hurricane Sandy is likely linked to record Arctic Sea ice loss...but fuck them, they're just scientists. What does the Bible say?

—Bill Maher

. . .

Yes. History has you in it.

. . .

No great dependence is to be placed on the eagerness of young soldiers for action, for the prospect of fighting is agreeable to those who are strangers to it.

—Vegetius, Roman military writer, fourth century AD

. . .

re: the fuller quote
In such condition there is...no account of time; no arts; no letters; no society; and which is worst of all, continual fear and danger of violent death; and the life of man, solitary, poor, nasty, brutish, and short.

—Thomas Hobbes, from *Leviathan*

. . .

Everything rotted and corroded quickly over there: bodies, boot leather, canvas, metal, morals. Scorched by the sun, wracked by the wind and rain of the monsoon, fighting in alien swamps and jungles, our humanity rubbed off of us as the protective bluing rubbed off the barrels of our rifles. We were fighting in the cruelest kind of conflict, a people's war. It was no orderly campaign, as in Europe, but a war of survival waged in a wilderness without rules or laws; a war in which each soldier fought for his own life and the lives of the men beside him, not caring who he killed in that personal cause or how many in what manner and feeling only contempt for those who sought to impose on his savage struggle the mincing distinctions of civilized warfare— that code of battlefield ethics that attempted to humanize an essentially inhuman war. According to those "rules of engagement," it was morally right to shoot an unarmed Vietnamese who was running, but wrong to shoot one who was standing or walking; it was wrong to shoot an enemy prisoner at close range, but right for a sniper at long range to kill an enemy soldier who was no more able than a prisoner to defend himself; it was wrong for an infantrymen to destroy a village with white-phosphorus grenades, but right for a fighter pilot to drop napalm on it. Ethics seemed to be a matter of distance and technology.

—Philip Caputo, from *A Rumor of War*

. . .

All marriages have their own set of needs, flaws, laws, fantasies, and protocols.

. . .

With the leaves all gone, you can see the branches real good.

. . .

At the age of twenty-four, I was more prepared for death than I was for life. My first experience of the world outside the classroom had been war. I went straight from school into the Marine Corps, from Shakespeare to the *Manual of Small-Unit Tactics*, from the campus to the drill field and finally Vietnam. I learned the murderous trade at Quantico, Virginia, practiced it in the rice paddies and jungles around Danang, and then taught it to others at Camp Geiger, a training base in North Carolina.

When my three-year enlistment expired in 1967, I was almost completely ignorant about the stuff of ordinary life, about marriage, mortgages, and building a career. I had a degree, but no skills. I had never run an office, taught a class, built a bridge, welded, programmed a computer, laid bricks, sold anything, or operated a lathe.

But I had acquired some expertise in the art of killing. I knew how to face death and how to cause it, with everything on the evolutionary scale of weapons from the knife to the 3.5-inch rocket launcher. The simplest repairs on an automobile engine were beyond me, but I was able to field-strip and assemble an M-14 rifle blindfolded. I could call in artillery, set up an ambush, rig a booby trap, lead a night raid.

—Philip Caputo, from *A Rumor of War*

. . .

There were a bunch of guys like me at Walter Reed—severe burn cases, the faceless. You would think we would have hung out together, but we avoided it as much as possible. We all looked the same; being around one another was like looking in a mirror. None of us wanted that. We wanted to forget.

Sleed was not faceless. He was okay—a few scars—but mostly intact. Back at Camp War Eagle, he had been standing beside me in the awards ceremony, both of us receiving commendation medals from the Division Commander, when the suicide bomber ran up and exploded himself.

Sleed lost his cock and balls and one of his legs above the knee. My privates survived the blast—my right leg shielded them—but I was never going to need them again, not with how I looked. I don't know how it was Sleed took most of the shrapnel while I got the brunt of the fireball. There's no explaining these things.

   —Brian Van Reet, from "Big Two-Hearted Hunting Creek"

. . .

Let us not burden our remembrances with
A heaviness that's gone.

   —William Shakespeare

. . .

The wicked are always ungrateful.

   —Miguel de Cervantes

. . .

You live the first half of your life
Afraid that something will happen.
Then something happens

   —Cary Tennis, from "That's What Experience Is All About"

. . .

Who said that death is not a curable disease?

. . .

The mercy of the world is that you don't know what's going to happen.

   —Wendell Berry, from *Jayber Crow*

. . .

Certainty is certainly the province of youth and the faithful, but my youth is passed and faith, for me, is out of reach.

. . .

Time only knows the price we have to pay.

—W. H. Auden

. . .

Eyewitness misidentifications are thought to be the leading cause of wrongful criminal convictions in the United States.

. . .

In the face of such overwhelming statistical possibilities, hypochondria has always seemed to me to be the only rational position to take on life.

—John Diamond

. . .

some assembly required…

. . .

re: Overheard in a restaurant

"Colorado? People use rock to landscape, instead of grass. No lawns. It's hard to walk on. I don't like it. They call it zeroscape, I think." The woman saying this had flopped out a breast and was nursing a child. She wasn't looking around to see who was looking. She was put out about rocks in her new state.

"Rocks?" One of the men at the table—an uncle or brother—not from Colorado, said, "That would not be good for Christmas inflatables."

. . .

re: Overheard on the sidewalk
in front of a CVS pharmacy
"Gum? You don't need gum. You never brush your teeth, you sick fuck!" The girl, displaying an array of piercings and tattoos, socked her boyfriend in the shoulder. Her spiked hair looked clean.

. . .

Out to grab the morning newspaper, just after dawn, I felt a presence on the patch of lawn beside my driveway. There, a prairie falcon, the size of a dwarf, perched atop a dying rabbit it had taken. The tall bird swiveled its head to stare at me. If the falcon spoke English, it would have said, "You have a problem with this?"

. . .

The following day, I saw in a field three rabbits grazing. A falcon—perhaps the same one—swooped down to take one. If rabbits could think and philosophize, would the remaining two have tried to comprehend the falcon's decision?

. . .

The summertime traffic on the bridges crossing the Potomac was always stop-and-go or stalled. You'd switch off your car and lower the windows so as to not overheat your engine. The garbage barges on the river brought colonies of flies and gnats. The heat stuck to your teeth. Adding to the overall misery was the jerk driving a black BMW, flying up the emergency lane each day to get to the front of the jam. People waited to lay on their horns when he passed. No one ever followed his example. On the day I'm talking about, I spied the dude in my side mirror, coming up fast.

Four or five vehicles in front, I could also see a farmer's face in *his* large flatbed's side mirror, making up his mind. Just as the Beamer arrived, tooling along unimpeded, the farmer flung open the truck's passenger door. The Beamer tore off the door. To our outside-the-car standing applause, the farmer stepped down to stare at the Beamer's driver, who stayed locked in his car. He picked up the door and threw it up on his flatbed. The traffic began to move past the luxury sedan. The Beamer's radiator spewed fluid and steam, adding to the humidity.

. . .

The transit of Venus was a phenomenon by which scientists were able to finally calculate the distance from the earth to the sun. The careful measurement of the shadow of the planet Venus as it moved across the face of the sun from several locations on our planet allowed for triangulation and the accurate calculation of 149.59 million kilometers.

Transits of Venus come in pairs eight years apart, but then are absent for a century or more. The measurements made in the eighteenth century were the consequence in 1861 of history's first international scientific venture. Scientists set off for locations around the globe. Many observers were waylaid by war, sickness, or shipwreck. Among the unluckiest was Guillaume Le Gentil, who set off a year in advance but was still at sea on the day of the transit, where pitching seas made it impossible to measure anything.

Undaunted, Le Gentil continued on to India to await the next transit in 1769. With eight years to prepare, he erected a first-rate viewing station, tested and retested his instruments and had everything in a state of perfect readiness. On the morning of the second transit, June 4, 1769, he awoke to a fine day, but, just as Venus began its pass, a cloud slid in front of the Sun and remained there for almost exactly the duration of the transit: three hours, fourteen minutes, and seven seconds.

Stoically, Le Gentil packed up his instruments and set off for the nearest port, but en route he contracted dysentery and was laid up for nearly a year. Still weakened, he finally made it onto a ship. It was nearly wrecked in a hurricane off the African coast. When at last he reached home, eleven and a half years after setting off, and having achieved nothing, he discovered that his relatives had had him declared dead in his absence and had enthusiastically plundered his estate.

—Bill Bryson, from *A Short History of Nearly Everything*

. . .

Were it not for unexpected cloud cover, the city of Kokura would have been bombed instead of Nagasaki. What would you have felt—a Kokuran—when you found out after?

. . .

I lived in France during the late sixties, managed on $100 per month, rent and food. You shopped (in your own neighborhood) for every meal and just bought what you needed. No one I knew owned a fridge. Generally you had a gas or coal heater in one of the rooms. Once a week you went to the public bathhouse and paid for thirty minutes in a tub. If you wanted to talk to someone in a different city, you went to the post office and mailed a card to that city with the time and date of the desired conversation. Both callers then showed at the designated post offices at the designated time in each city to converse their few minutes on the phone.

. . .

[The German] guns' cyclic rate had always appalled me: while we stuttered and pattered along with our 30's at 350, they were throwing 550 at us with the sound of a ripping sail, a giant canvas sail tearing itself across in the wind; and even with the decreased accuracy, enough lead must have flown across my back to have sewn an intricate seam.... But as I lay there at last "under the guns," I found on an instant lost and atavistic senses that had been numb since my birth: every minute centimeter of my body, my flesh, was alert, apprehensive, waiting for the impact of its bullet; each pore totally sensitive to and sensing the flight of those bullets towards me, into me. It was only gradually that the mind apprehended that the mounted guns, fixed for their killing zones, undoubtedly could depress no further in their mounts, and that it was to the almost invisible, indistinguishable contours of that land that I owed my momentarily saved life.

—Robert E. Gajdusek, from *Resurrection: A War Journey*

. . .

Run a whorehouse to fund an orphanage. Establish a hospital next to an anti-aircraft battery. Vietnam had both, according to vets I know.

. . .

He realized that his legs could not be saved, one was shattered, but both were long ago frozen and without feeling, probably in unarrestable gangrene, but he well knew that life without his legs was a question of amputations and adjustment. He accepted that—if only he could live. He had also largely lost feeling in his torn and frozen hands, and he wondered if, indeed, it was a sentimentality to believe that he would be willing to live life as a quadruple paraplegic. He considered that question soberly and long and knew that, yes, he could accept that—if only he could live. He knew that life was more impossible than that, that after this long time of freezing he probably had pneumonia and, to judge by his chest pain and his occasional lapsing away towards unconsciousness, he probably was ill and shattered in some way beyond reparation, and he wondered if he was willing to accept his quadriplegic life if he were not surrounded by the love of those he loved. So one by one, he thought of those he loved: of Lee, who was his girl, who was the center of his life—and he knew that he would be willing to live, if he lost her, without her, for could he, after all, wish upon her what he would be if he survived? And, similarly, he thought long and carefully about his brother and mother and father, and slowly, reluctantly, let each fall from his hands, fall from his consciousness, knowing that life, to be had at all, had to be had at that severe a cost, the loss of all and every one of them. It was not as though he were falling into death so much as he was releasing them, one by one, to a great darkness, letting them fall like irreplaceable jeweled stones of solid weight irretrievably through space and away into an impenetrable darkness. They were the sacrifices and the cost. Not he. At last he, seeing himself alone, in an empty room in a ward somewhere, and without a soul about him, near him, caring for or aware of his existence, he asked, BUT WHAT IF you were not only a quadruple amputee but also blind? Could you accept life on those conditions? Yes, yes, said his heart. Yes. But what if you were not only a quadriplegic blind man but also deaf and dumb? You know what I am saying, you hear what I am saying? And he, inside himself, shouted, yes, yes. Even then, Yes! All right, You, You Nameless, you Trunk of Body, you Flesh, you Thing, what if you were only Torso, to be propped by day against the rotting doorway of a shitted mud hut in the wastes of Siberia, and deaf and dumb and blind? Would you truly settle for life on those terms? And he felt the soft wind of evening go across his cheek, and he said yes, yes, if only to feel the warmth of sunlight in the morning move across the side of my face, to be able to feel the coolness coming on of evening; if only to feel the wind touch my hair, touch my cheek, if only that.

—Robert E. Gajdusek, from *Resurrection: A War Journey*

. . .

War stories are always about more than war. They are about memory and love and resentment and loss and disbelief and defiance and humiliation and earnestness and blame and shame and blood and sacrifice and courage and sorrow. War stories, even if set in the past, seem to exist in the urgent and immortal present. They identify us, war stories. They are about us.

. . .

I was born at the start of World War II, and my father was in Italy, distinguishing himself while getting blown up as he served in the ski troops of the 10th Mountain Division. I lived with wars—Korea when my father was home, and of course Vietnam, which harvested so much of my generation. My son is a major in the US Marine Corps, waiting in North Carolina to be sent to the Gulf. I was born in war and conflict between states informs my most interior visions of American life.

—Frederick Busch, from *A Memory of War*

. . .

If you stare too long at anything in the dark, you'll see whatever your imagination invents.

—Army training principle

. . .

If it weren't for the Spaniards, the Pueblo people may never have ended up with doors or horses. That rustic tree-branch ladder you see gracing upscale adobe homes was never meant as mere cosmetics. The Pueblo entered their homes through their roofs, pulling up the ladder after themselves for safety.

. . .

In the language of the Dakota
um pao wasta we
means beautiful daybreak woman.

—Dale Ritterbusch, from "What the Light Would Say"

. . .

The British admiralty
with all its admirable genius
became convinced that the proper stratagem
for combating submarines
and winning the war at sea
was to train seagulls to defecate
on the periscopes of German U-boats.

—Dale Ritterbusch, from "World War I and Beyond"

. . .

Unprotected human ears can spend eight hours a day exposed to the noise of a freeway or crowded restaurant (85 decibels) without incurring hearing loss. Increase that noise to 115 decibels (chainsaw, mosh pit) and your safe exposure is halved. An AT4 anti-tank weapon creates a 187-decibel boom. The problem with ear protection of course is that during heavy combat being able to hear your comrades and leaders may be the difference between life and death. Consider those who serve in Special Operations. Because these soldiers don't want to be prevented from doing what they both love and think of as their duty, they seldom, if ever, report hearing loss, going so far, even, to cheat on hearing tests. When things go kinetic, there's a greater than 50 percent chance that a member of the team will be injured or killed. Hearing loss isn't something Spec Ops troops spend time worrying about. It's a given.

An artilleryman said he wanted hearing loss, because everyone in his unit had hearing loss. If you didn't have a hearing loss it meant you hadn't done anything. One of the reasons the government wants scientific help with ear protection is that the Veterans Administration spends $1 billion a year on hearing loss and tinnitus. That a Special Operations soldier might fire a hundred thousand rounds in ten years of service is part of that end-game expense. The crack of an M16 creates 160 decibels.

—see Mary Roach, *Grunt: The Curious Science
of Humans at War*

· · ·

Good food, good eating, is all about blood and organs, cruelty and decay. It's about sodium-loaded pork fat, stinky triple-cream cheeses, the tender thymus glands and distended livers of young animals. It's about danger—risking the dark, bacterial forces of beef, chicken, cheese, and shellfish. Your first two hundred and seven Wellfleet oysters may transport you to a state of rapture, but your two hundred and eighth may send you to bed with the sweats, chills, and vomits.

Gastronomy is the science of pain. Professional cooks belong to a secret society whose ancient rituals derive from the principles of stoicism in the face of humiliation, injury, fatigue, and the threat of illness. The members of a tight, well-greased kitchen staff are a lot like a submarine crew. Confined for most of their waking hours in hot, airless spaces, and ruled by despotic leaders, they often acquire the characteristics of the poor saps who were press-ganged into the royal navies of Napoleonic times—superstition, a contempt for outsiders, and a loyalty to no flag but their own.

—Anthony Bourdain, from "Don't Eat Before Reading This"

PART IV

Babies do not want to hear about babies;
they like to be told of giants and castles.

—Dr. Johnson

When we allow mythic reality to rule, as it almost always does in war, then there is only one solution—force. In mythic war we fight absolutes. We must vanquish darkness. It is imperative and inevitable for civilization, for the free world, that good triumph, just as Islamic militants see us as infidels whose existence corrupts the pure Islamic society they hope to build.

The potency of myth is that it allows us to make sense of mayhem and violent death. It gives a justification to what is often nothing more than gross human cruelty and stupidity. It allows us to believe we have achieved our place in human society because of a long chain of heroic endeavors, rather than accept the sad reality that we stumble along a dimly lit corridor of disasters. It disguises our powerlessness. It hides from view our own impotence and the ordinariness of our own leaders. By turning history into myth we transform random events into a chain of events by a will greater than our own, one that is determined and preordained. We are elevated above the multitude. We march toward nobility. And no society is immune.

The hijacking of language is fundamental to war.

—Chris Hedges, from *War Is a Force That Gives Us Meaning*

. . .

re: King Louis of France, 1214–1270

He seemed to live for God alone. Not once did I hear him address the devil by name. Countless hours day and night he devoted to prayer, oppressed by the knowledge that our Lord was neither adequately served nor loved, grieved by the existence of infidels, certain that he himself did not honor God deeply enough. Offices he had read in the king's chapel as though it were the chapel of a monastery. There also he had the Hours sung. By his request was the Office for the Dead included. He would hear two masses, at times three. Very little would he study but Scripture and the Fathers. He would ask that a candle as high as his waist be lighted and while it burned he would read the Bible. So long did he remain on his knees in prayer that sight and wit intermingled and he would rise up dazed, murmuring, not certain where he was, unable to find his bed. At midnight he was up to hear matins sung by his chaplain, rising so quietly that equerries failed to note or got up late and chased after him barefoot. Each Friday he made confession after which his confessor must apply the discipline with five iron chains his majesty carried in an ivory box. Similar boxes he ordered, with similar little chains, giving them to his children and to friends, and counseled them to make good use of scourging. Should the confessor strike him gently he would demand harder blows. One such did strike with force enough to lacerate his majesty's sensitive flesh, yet the king held his peace, nor afterward mentioned it save with amusement. Most were less tenacious. Indeed, they reproved him for auster-ities that imperiled his health, persuading him to give up a hair shirt he wore during Advent and Lent and on the vigil of numerous feasts. In its place he adopted a horsehair girdle. Good Friday he walked to church barefoot. Which is to say, he wore shoes for the sake of appearance but had the soles removed. Before approaching the cross he took off his upper garments excepting vest and coat. On his knees he would advance a short distance, stopping to pray, advancing further. Beneath the cross he would prostrate himself as though crucified, arms outflung, weeping. And if during litanies he heard that verse appealing for a fountain of tears he would respond.

O Lord, I dare not ask so much, but a few drops to water my parched and sterile heart.

—Evan S. Connell, from *Deus lo Volt: Chronicle of the Crusades*

. . .

King Louis personally and vigorously participated in the Seventh and Eighth Crusades (when he was in his thirties and later in his fifties). He expanded the Inquisition in France. He punished blasphemy by mutilation of the tongue and lips. He ordered the burning in Paris in 1243 of twelve thousand manuscript copies of the Talmud and other Jewish books. But he was renowned for his charity too. Beggars were fed from his table, he ate their leavings, washed their feet, ministered to the wants of the lepers, and daily fed over one hundred poor. He founded many hospitals and the House of the Filles-Dieu for reformed prostitutes and the Quinze-Vingt for blind men. He is the only French king to be canonized by the Catholic Church and sainted by the Anglicans.

. . .

In all, eight major Crusade expeditions occurred between 1096 and 1291, both sides with many of the same prophets fighting over God for holy places. These ruthless conflicts resulted in nearly two million deaths, with both Muslim and Christian being informed by their religious leaders of eternal sanctification. Despite the blood lust and plundering, Christian knights were promised absolution as the primary consequence of participation. Begun in the Middle East, and still in the Middle East, the Crusades lumber on.

· · ·

Fat women work to walk gracefully, as if light on their feet, or they are vociferously political, arguing, say, for whales or Peru. Fat men just wear their pants lower.

· · ·

The excellent French restaurant run by Guatemalans…

· · ·

Wonderful things were to be viewed. Numbers of Saracens were beheaded. Others were tortured for several days and then burned in flames. In the street were seen piles of heads and hands and feet.

> —priest Raymond of Agiles, on the First Crusade;
> qtd. in David Markson, *This Is Not a Novel*

· · ·

re: Religious Wars
Fighting to decide who has the better imaginary friend…

· · ·

Are Time and Space as buttoned down as we pretend?

· · ·

Chronology is imposed.

. . .

We live and understand our lives by means of association, not linearity. Don't we?

. . .

There's poem about a little girl tonguing out jelly from one of those little packets you find on restaurant tables. The final line runs, I think, "I like strawberry because it tastes like strawberry."

. . .

The man pulling radishes
pointed my way
with a radish.

—Issa (1763–1827)

. . .

Thucydides said that safety and self-interest go comfortably together but that the path to justice and honor is both difficult and dangerous.

. . .

In late 2015, a bus in eastern Kenya was stopped by gunmen from an extremist group named Al-Shabaab that made a practice of massacring Christians as part of a terrorism campaign against the Western-aligned Kenyan government. The gunmen demanded that Muslim and Christian passengers separate themselves into two groups so that the Christians could be killed, but the Muslims—most of whom were women—refused to do it. They told the gunmen that they would all die together if necessary, but that the Christians would not be singled out for execution. The Shabaab eventually let everyone go.

—Sebastian Junger, from *Tribe*

. . .

Say *Ting Ling Lee* quickly.

. . .

When Special Forces soldiers receive a mission, they call it "getting work."

. . .

New health studies have reported that handling toilet seats in restaurants is safer than handling the menus.

. . .

I worked one summer in Preston, Idaho, at a Del Monte canning factory. Twelve-hour shifts. All we ever canned was creamed corn. I have some advice for you: *Do not Eat Creamed Corn*. I mean it.

. . .

As great a sacrifice as soldiers make, American workers arguably make a greater one. Far more Americans lose their lives every year doing dangerous jobs than died *during the entire Afghan War*. In 2014, for example, 4,679 workers lost their lives on the job. More than 90 percent of those deaths were of young men working in industries that have a mortality rate equivalent to most units in the US military. Jobs that are directly observable to the public, like construction, tend to be less respected and less well paid than jobs that happen behind closed doors, like real estate or finance. And yet it is exactly these jobs that provide society's immediate physical needs. Construction workers are more important to everyday life than stockbrokers and yet are far lower down the social and financial ladder.

—Sebastian Junger, from *Tribe*

. . .

Bigotry does not privilege nuance.

. . .

I believe in church basements and all the steps,
not just the 12 famous ones, every slogan,
and I especially believe in that guy in Saint Paul
*   who used to say,*
"Fuck your bad day, work the program."

—Mick Cochrane, from "Stage Four"

. . .

When Stalin attended the Potsdam Conference with Churchill and Roosevelt, he was so paranoid that he brought along eighteen thousand bodyguards.

. . .

re: Saddam rumors
His staff cooked every meal every day at every one of his eighty palaces, just in case.

. . .

Since September 11, 2001, we have witnessed an escalation of rhetoric within the United States that has led us to war twice in two years. We have heard our president, our vice president, our secretary of defense, and our attorney general cultivate fear and command with lies, suggesting our homeland security and safety must reside in their hands, not ours. Force has trumped debate and diplomacy.

Our language has been taken hostage. Words like patriotism, freedom, and democracy have been bound and gagged, forced to perform indecent acts through the abuse of slogans. Freedom will prevail. We are liberating Iraq. God bless America.

—Terry Tempest Williams, from commencement address,
University of Utah, 2003

. . .

I was always embarrassed by the words sacred, glorious, and sacrifice and the expression in vain. We had heard them, sometimes standing in the rain almost out of earshot, so that only the shouted words came through, and had read them, on proclamations that were slapped up by billposters over other proclamations, now for a long time, and I had seen nothing sacred, and the things that were glorious had no glory and the sacrifices were like the stockyards at Chicago if nothing was done with the meat except to bury it.... Abstract words such as glory, honor, courage, or hallow were obscene beside the concrete names of villages, the numbers of roads, the names of rivers, the numbers of regiments and the dates.

—Ernest Hemingway, from *A Farewell to Arms*

. . .

Spontaneity is the consequence of constant revision.

. . .

What constitutes the bulwark of our own liberty and independence? It is not our crowning battlements, our bristling sea coasts, our army and our navy. These are not our reliance against tyranny.... Our reliance is in the spirit which prized liberty as the heritage of all men, in all lands everywhere. Destroy this spirit and you have planted the seeds of despotism at your own doors. Familiarize yourself with the chains of bondage and you prepare your own limbs to wear them. Accustom to trample on the rights of others and you have lost the genius of your own independence and become fit subjects of the first cunning tyrant who rises among you.

—Abraham Lincoln, 1858

. . .

Hope is the thing with feathers
That perches in the soul.

—Emily Dickinson

. . .

Faith, like a jackal, feeds among the tombs, and even from these dead doubts she gathers her most vital hope.

—Herman Melville

. . .

The arctic is balancing on an immense mirror. The water table is visible. Pools of light gather: lakes, ponds, wetlands. The tundra is shimmering. One squints perpetually.

Drinking from the river—I am drinking from the river—this tincture of glaciers, this press of ice warmed by the sun. My arid heart has been waiting for decades, maybe three, for the return of this childhood pleasure of drinking directly from the source.

When my father asks me what it was like to visit the Arctic National Wildlife Refuge, I will simply say, "We drank from the river."

—Terry Tempest Williams, from "Ground Truthing"

. . .

re: Overheard, various locations
Hotter than two rats fucking in a wool sock.

I need a phone charge cord that reaches the bed.

But he's never bitten anyone...

Snap, Crackle, Pop.

A habitual observer of his own moods.

Everything in the fucking brewery broke. Like, seriously.

In old movies, people smoke. In movies now, they jog.

Academics display more fears than medieval peasants.

If you were going to feature your bowling trophies, would you choose the kitchen window?

Like hunting bear with a piano.

Praise the Lord and pass the ammunition.

Dentists and sheepherders have, by profession, the highest rates of suicide. Is that true?

I wore a coonskin cap during the Davy Crockett phase. Did you?

Has no one condemned you…

Being a trial judge is like directing a grammar school picnic.

We're defined, aren't we, by choice, mistake, and circumstance?

Battleworthy. Is that a compliment?

Self-delusion is the same as success, only you don't have to work as hard.

. . .

The Salem witch trials occurred in the Massachusetts colony during the years 1692–93. More than two hundred were accused of practicing witchcraft (acting strangely on Satan's behalf to the detriment of the world). Twenty people (mostly women) and two dogs were executed.

. . .

In 1976, Dr. Linnda Caporael of the Rensselaer Polytechnic Institute found evidence that the brief and intense illnesses suffered by so many of the Salem Village townspeople were not bewitchment but quite possibly ergotism, a disease commonly contracted by rye. Ergotism forms in rye after a severe winter and a damp spring—conditions that Caporael and other historians claim were present in 1691 and therefore affected the rye harvested for consumption in

1692. After the rye plant contracts ergot, the fungus grows and replaces shoots on the grain with sclerotia. Ergot sclerotia are purple-black growths that contain lysergic acid and ergotamine. "Once contracted from rye bread, ergotism (also called St. Anthony's fire) causes severe convulsions, muscle spasms, delusions, the sensation of crawling under the skin, and, in extreme cases, gangrene of the extremities. Severe hallucinations can also be a symptom, as lysergic acid is the substance from which the drug LSD is synthesized. These symptoms were the same as those shown by the accused in Salem: mostly young girls whose immune systems had not fully developed, leaving them susceptible." The village doctor, more religious than scientific, and, unaware of ergotism as a disease, attributed the strange symptoms to a *known* evil: witchcraft.

—Kate Lohnes, from "How Rye Bread
May Have Caused the Salem Witch Trials"

. . .

During the slaughter of plumage birds in the nineteenth century for feathered hats, the killing got so out of hand that the Gulf's population of snowy egrets dipped below the population of the endangered American bison. Five million birds annually fed the hat business, leaving the Gulf with 10 percent of the previous bird population by the beginning of the twentieth century.

. . .

When the cavalry chased Chief Joseph and the Nez Percé, they followed them through Yellowstone Park, which had been established five years earlier. The soldiers enjoyed the park, catching trout in the streams and poaching them in the geysers.

. . .

re: U.S. Naturalization Final Question
Where do you do your shopping? (Answer in English)

. . .

I do know one thing—the paleo diet is horseshit. Why would you listen to a caveman about what to eat? Cavemen ate whatever they could get their hands on.

. . .

My father could frame a window, hang a door, glaze glass, thread pipe, repair a carburetor, dehorn a calf, lay down a blacktop driveway, install a heat coupler in a furnace, fell a tree (hanging over a house), butcher a cow. Where did he learn to do these things?

. . .

There was a period during the run-up to the Iraq War in 2003 when a bumper sticker that read NO BLOOD FOR OIL started appearing on American cars. Implicit in the slogan was the assumption that the Iraq War was over oil, but the central irony of putting such a message on a machine *that runs on oil* seemed lost on most people.... I was deeply opposed to the Iraq War for other reasons. But the antiwar rhetoric around the topic of oil by people who continued to use it to fuel their cars betrayed a larger hypocrisy that extended across the political spectrum. The public is often accused of being disconnected from its military, but frankly, it's disconnected from just about everything. Farming, mineral extraction, gas and oil production, bulk cargo transport, logging, fishing, infrastructure construction—all the industries that keep the nation going are mostly unacknowledged by the people who depend on them most.

—Sebastian Junger, from *Tribe*

. . .

My confining drinking has less to do with my health than with improving the quality of my dreams.

. . .

If you peered into the fridge in my childhood home, you would have detected both butter and margarine. The butter was my father's, the margarine for us, the remaining eight. Whether my father thought butter unhealthy for us, or whether he thought the spread too dear, I haven't a clue. I know he savored cream and red meat and butter, and that, in the end, his slathered heart struck back four times in fourteen hours and he died. All through my thirties and early forties, I was a committed vegetarian until my intestines burst, eaten through by diverticula. I should have died, but fell into the hands of an experienced surgeon in upstate New York where I was attending Cornell University. During this time when I thought I was eating healthily, I was also training for and running at least a marathon a year. When I asked the surgeon who saved my life what changes I could make to live my life more safely, he advised exercise and a high-fiber diet. You don't realize how much you might have wanted to live in a world of direct cause and effect, a sphere wherein virtue is blessed, sin punished. What you find is that virtue is sometimes rewarded, that crime often pays, that love hardly conquers all, and that Nature, though interested, perhaps, in preserving the species, is not particularly attentive to the individual.

. . .

The land masses of all of China, the United States, India and Japan, plus nearly all of Europe, fit within the borders of the African continent. Did you know that?

. . .

For all experiences, it's one thing to be prepared, quite another to be present.

. . .

There are places in Africa where people who have never used an elevator have cellphones.

. . .

Native Americans considered the dragonfly a sign of happiness, speed, and purity. Purity because the dragonfly "eats from the wind itself."

. . .

President Bush's war plans are risky, but Mr. Bush is no gambler. In fact he denies the very existence of chance. "Events aren't moved by blind change and chance" he has said, but by "the hand of a just and faithful God." From the outset he has been convinced that his presidency is part of a divine plan, even telling a friend while he was governor of Texas, "I believe God wants me to run for president."
    —Jackson Lears, from "How a War Became a Crusade"

. . .

There may be no atheists in foxholes, but there are not many believers in Providence in them either. Combat soldiers have always been less confident than politicians that God is on the premises. They have paid homage to an older deity, Fortuna. From the Civil War through the Persian Gulf War, American soldiers have festooned themselves with amulets and lucky charms—everything from St. Christopher medals and smooth stones to their girlfriends' locks of hair. And why not? Ritual efforts to conjure luck speak directly to their own experience.

—Jackson Lears, from "How a War Became a Crusade"

. . .

In explaining any puzzling Washington phenomenon, always choose stupidity over conspiracy, incompetence over cunning. Anything else gives them too much credit.

—Charles Krauthammer

. . .

The politician who promises you the universe, then shows up with one of Jupiter's minor moons, claiming he is the only person who ever lived who could have managed it.

—see Trump

. . .

When asked why he performed so many feats of heroism, Audie Murphy explained, "They were trying to kill my friends." What does such a notion and action have to do with generals or politicians?

. . .

Not everything that counts can be counted.

—Albert Einstein

. . .

We are only two years removed from our withdrawal from Iraq and the al Qaeda flag flies over the city of Fallujah, in which more than 120 American service members died. The ultimate failure of American military might to secure Fallujah does nothing to diminish the honorable nature of their service. But likewise, all their gallantry cannot change the fact that they died for an unfulfilled cause. The honor is theirs alone. The disgrace belongs to America.

It's the disgrace of a country that abandoned its civic duty to execute due diligence in weighing the decisions of whether and how to go to war, and then later to hold accountable those that spent precious blood and vast treasure for meager gains. All the while, we convinced ourselves that we were supporting our fighting forces simply by saying that we were. We even made bumper stickers to prove it, never considering what it said about us to wear our hearts next to our exhaust pipes.

—Jim Gourley, from "Yes Marcus. They Did Die in Vain"

. . .

Throughout history, our nation's greatest leaders have understood on a deeply personal level that however honorably a soldier acquits himself, he can die in vain, and that it is the responsibility of the leaders and citizenry to see to it that they don't. Our country has lost its sense of that responsibility to a horrifying extent. Our generals have lost the capability to succeed and the integrity to admit failure. Our society has lost the courage and energy to hold them accountable. Over the last decade, our top leaders have wasted the lives of our sons, daughters, and comrades with their incompetence and hubris. After each failure, our citizens have failed to hold them accountable, instead underwriting new failed strategies as quickly as their predecessors with our apathy and sense of detachment. And then we use the tired paeans of "never forget" and "honor the fallen" to distract ourselves from our guilt in the affair. When we blithely declare that they did not die in vain, we deface their honor by using it to wipe the blood from our hands.

—Jim Gourley, from "Yes Marcus. They Did Die in Vain"

. . .

Tu Fu wrote that poetry is useless,
in a poem alive these thousand years.

Today our news is much the same.
Near Srebrenica, skulls dot fields
like cabbages, while in Rwanda,
the short tribe hacked up the tall.
"Blood is smeared on bush and grass,"
yet poetry persists through slaughter,
as if the systoles in our raging hearts
held rhythms that could heal, if heard.

—John Balaban, from "Reading the News
and Thinking of the T'ang Poets"

. . .

A poem should not mean
But be.

—Archibald MacLeish, from "Ars Poetica"

. . .

Is it true that Li Po and Tu Fu stood on a bridge together, inscribing poems on leaves, then tossing them into the river?

. . .

A poem is an event, not the record of an event.

—Robert Lowell

. . .

When you confuse art with propaganda, you confuse an act of god with something which can be turned on and off like the hot water faucet.

—E. E. Cummings

. . .

…language is the most fundamental and powerful instrument we have. It is the forerunner of every invention, every technical invention. Before there was space travel there was literature about space travel. Literature is the instrument through which all the gods have been imagined and all the religions built. It gives hue and character to every society, shapes and aggregates individuals; constructs, sustains, and demolishes belief systems.

—George Hutchinson, from
"Why You Should Want Me on the Life Raft"

. . .

Human decency is not derived from religion. It precedes it.

To "choose" dogma and faith over doubt and experience is to throw out the ripening vintage and to reach greedily for the Kool-Aid.

I leave it to the faithful to burn each other's churches and mosques and synagogues, which they can be always relied upon to do.

—Christopher Hitchens, from *God Is Not Great:*
How Religion Poisons Everything

. . .

Clarity of language breeds clarity of thought and vice versa. It wins converts, creates solidarity among strangers, confers leadership, expresses one's inmost feelings and beliefs. Through it we ask the most fundamental questions about how to live together and what we want in life. A thought or feeling hovering on the edge of consciousness, and when we put a word to it we feel satisfied; and then it opens a new vista on experience. The language grows and language grows us.

—George Hutchinson, from
"Why You Should Want Me on the Life Raft"

. . .

You'll never be able to make a living writing poems.... You might make a living as a teacher of poetry writing or as a lecturer about poetry, but writing poems won't go very far toward paying your electric bill. A poem published in one of the very best literary magazines in the country might net you a check for enough money to buy half a sack of groceries. The chances are much better that all you'll receive, besides the pleasure of seeing your poem in print, are a couple of copies of the magazine, one to keep and one to show to your mother. You might get a letter or postcard from a grateful reader, always a delightful surprise. But look at it this way: Any activity that's worth lots of money, like professional basketball, comes with rules pinned all over it. In poetry, the only rules worth thinking about are the standards of perfection you set for yourself.

—Ted Kooser, from *The Poetry Home Repair Manual*

. . .

Memory is memory, and imagination is in part the re-assembly of things we remember.

—Ted Kooser, from *The Poetry Home Repair Manual*

. . .

I like words like *windowsill, curbstone, passport, sundown, wetland.* I also like words like *perspicacious, mellifluous, basbousa, vellum. Coldening.* Is that a word? It should be.

. . .

There are three religious truths: (1) Jews do not recognize Jesus as the Messiah. (2) Protestants do not recognize the pope as the leader of the Christian faith. (3) Baptists do not recognize each other in liquor stores or Hooters.

. . .

A lock of hair from the head of George Armstrong Custer recently sold at auction for $12,000. Who had kept it since before the Battle of the Little Bighorn which occurred in 1876? Do you need Custer's hair?

. . .

My mother heard a man plead for his life once. She remembers the stars, the dark shapes of trees along the road on which they were fleeing the Austrian army in a slow-moving ox-cart. "That man sounded terribly frightened out there in the woods," she says. The cart went on. No one said anything. Soon they could hear the river they were supposed to cross.

—Charles Simic, from "Three Fragments"

. . .

Collage, the art of reassembling fragments of the pre-existing images in such a way as to form a new image, was the most important innovation in the art of the twentieth century...

—Charles Simic reflecting on Joseph Cornell

. . .

Beneath the swarm of high-flying planes we were eating watermelon. While we ate the bombs fell on Belgrade. We watched the smoke rise in the distance. We were hot in the garden and asked to take our shirts off. The watermelon made a ripe, cracking noise as my mother cut it with a big knife. We also heard what we thought was thunder, but when we looked up, the sky was cloudless and blue.

—Charles Simic, from "Three Fragments"

. . .

Dysentery "has been more fatal to soldiers than powder and shot," wrote William "Father of Modern Medicine" Osler in 1892. ("Dysentery" is an umbrella term for infections in which the pathogens invade the lining of the intestine, causing cells and capillaries to ooze their contents and creating dysentery's hallmark symptom, the one that sounds like British profanity: bloody diarrhea.) For every American killed by battle injuries during the Mexican War of 1848, seven died of disease, mostly diarrheal. During the American Civil War, 95,000 soldiers died from diarrhea or dysentery. During the Vietnam War, hospital admissions for diarrheal diseases outnumbered those for malaria by nearly four to one.

—Mary Roach, from *Grunt*

. . .

A 122-millimeter rocket is seventy-five inches long and carries one hundred pounds of explosives. This one had been so close to the bunker that we hadn't heard it come the way you heard the ones that pass. They sound like a train you might hear in your sleep, or like a storm in the dark. We didn't hear it come but we heard it hit, an explosion that shattered my hearing for weeks to come. By the time we got to him he was drowning in his own blood. He had one boot on and his eyes were so wide I wanted to close them. He's taken a large piece of rocket shrapnel in his throat and the artery there was gushing. He was trying to cough up his own blood that was drowning him and that his whole body heaved against. The medic was too far away to help and the rockets still roared in around us. One boy with me in the bunker tried to press against the Captain's throat to make the bleeding stop, but the shirt he held there quickly soaked through with blood. I tried to hold Captain Carter down; he heaved so powerfully we were afraid he'd tear his heart out. We didn't know what to do. His eyes looked back and forth frantically at each of us, looking for an answer we didn't know. When his coughing and gurgling got loud and sounded like it came from deep in his chest, I suddenly put my mouth over his neck where the shrapnel had torn a hole. I hadn't thought about it. I found myself trying to suck the blood from his throat and lungs before I realized what I was doing. I remember that the other boys looked at me with such a great sadness that I thought they wanted me to stop. I know now that they knew it was too late and they were sad because they saw I didn't know. I began to suck the blood out of the Captain's throat. I thought if he could breathe again, he'd have a chance.

—Bruce Weigl, from *The Circle of Hanh*

. . .

With a large artery bleed, it can take less than two minutes for the human heart to hemorrhage three liters: a fatal loss. The human body holds five liters of blood, but with three gone, electrolyte balance falls gravely out of whack, and there's not enough circulating blood to keep vital organs up and running. Hemorrhagic shock—"bleeding out"—is the most common cause of death in combat.

—Mary Roach, from *Grunt*

. . .

When you're a kid, you don't know the brain is the sexy thing. When you're grown up, you may know.

. . .

Desire is like licking honey off a blade.

—Buddhist sentiment

. . .

Bees are weird. The peculiar mating rituals, the doomed drones who wait all their lives for a single sexual encounter with an omnipotent queen, leading to immediate death. As humans, we find them fascinating: perhaps the only species whose gender politics are more screwed up than our own.

—Jennifer Haigh, review of *The Honey Farm*,
by Harriet Alida Lye

· · ·

Would you have guessed that North Dakota is the nation's largest honey-producing state?

· · ·

It's nearly impossible to write well about sex and fistfights without making both activities sound like instructions for changing flat tires.

· · ·

During the American war, General Giap—who had helped defeat the French at Dien Bien Phu and, later, led the North Vietnamese Army against the Americans—had assigned Duat, a soldier for over ten years, the task of writing and reading poems for North Vietnamese Army soldiers as they traveled up and down the Ho Chi Minh Trail. To inspire them in their long struggle and to help them endure the enormous hardships of battle, the North Vietnamese Army relied on poetry.

I can't speak for other American military outfits, but the 1st Air Cavalry, the division that I served with during my year in the war, did not have a designated poet. We had *Playboy* and USO shows that featured starlets with bad voices, flashing cleavage and dancing in miniskirts.

—Bruce Weigl, from *The Circle of Hanh*

. . .

My daughter's pet hamster injured one of its legs. Elective knee surgery on a hamster not an option, I suggested a bit of aspirin. The hamster bled out.

. . .

Happiness? Your kids wearing their new sunglasses while making their beds. A new flea collar for your dog…There are people who have no clue how to be happy.

. . .

To daily drive a car you must work up an unfounded belief in mutual trust or you'd never leave your driveway.

. . .

The next morning we got up, brushed ourselves off, cleared away the air-strike garbage—the firefight junk and jungle junk—and dusted off the walking wounded and the litter wounded and the body bags. And the morning after that, just as right as rain, James, we saddled up our rucksacks and slugged off into the deepest, baddest part of the Goongone Forest north of our base camp at Phuc Luc, looking to kick some ass—anybody's ass (can you dig it, James?)—and take some names. Yessiree! We hacked and humped our way from one end of that goddamned woods to the other—crisscrossing wherever our whim took us—no more sophisticated or complicated or elegant than an organized gang; looking to nail any and all of that goddamned giggling slime we came across to the barn door. Then one bright and cheery morning when our month was up, Private First Class Elijah Raintree George Washington Carver Jones (Jonesy for short, James) had thirty-nine pairs of blackened, leathery, wrinkly ears strung on a bit of black commo wire and wrapped like a garland around that bit of turned-out brim of his steel helmet. He had snipped the ears off with a pearl-handled straight razor just as quick and slick as you'd lance a boil the size of a baseball—snicker-snack—the way he bragged his uncle could skin a poached deer. He cured the ears a couple of days by tucking them under that bit of turned-out brim of his steel helmet, then toted them crammed in a spare sock.... Jonesy sat up way after dark stringing those ears on that bit of black wire and sucking snips of C-ration beefsteak through his teeth.

—Larry Heineman, from *Paco's Story*

. . .

"Don't get killed," my parents used to say as I left home. I thought they were just lining things up to not be responsible if something happened, but now I say, "Who doesn't worry their children might die before them?"

. . .

Kien knows the area well. It was here, at the end of the dry season of 1969, that his 27th Battalion was surrounded and almost totally wiped out. Ten men survived from the Lost Battalion after fierce, horrible, barbarous fighting.

That was the dry season when the sun burned harshly, the wind blew fiercely, and the enemy sent napalm spraying through the jungle and a sea of fire enveloped them, spreading like the fires of hell. Troops in the fragmented companies tried to regroup, only to be blown out of their shelters again as they went mad, became disoriented, and threw themselves into nets of bullets, dying in the flaming inferno. Above them the helicopters flew at treetop height and shot them almost one by one, the blood spreading out, spraying from their backs, flowing like red mud.

The diamond-shaped grass clearing was piled high with bodies killed by helicopter gunships. Broken bodies, bodies blown apart, bodies vaporized.

No jungle grew again in this clearing. No grass. No plants.

—Bao Ninh, from *The Sorrow of War*

. . .

"Better to die than surrender, my brothers! Better to die!" the battalion commander yelled insanely; waving his pistol in front of Kien he blew his own brains out through his ear. Kien screamed soundlessly in his throat at the sight, as the Americans attacked with submachine guns, sending bullets buzzing like deadly bees around him. Then Kien lowered his machine gun, grasped his side, and fell, rolling slowly down the bank of a shallow stream, hot blood trailing down the slope after him.

In the days that followed, crows and eagles darkened the sky. After the Americans withdrew, the rainy season came, flooding the jungle floor, turning the battlefield into a marsh whose surface water turned rust-colored from the blood. Bloated human corpses, floating alongside the bodies of incinerated jungle animals, mixed with branches and trunks cut down by artillery, all drifting in a stinking marsh. When the flood receded everything dried in the heat of the sun into thick mud and stinking rotting meat.

—Bao Ninh, from *The Sorrow of War*

· · ·

I walk the aisles of the sporting goods store where the killer bought the gun, the same place where we buy our kids sneakers and baseballs. Between the fishing poles and compound bows, AR and AK assault rifle accessories fill the shelves—30-round mags ($12.99), 42-round mags ($14.99), rail grips ($18.99), red laser sight ($29.99). Cases of AR ammo—420 rounds of 5.56mm for $189.99—fill the next aisle. The Ruger AR-556 semiautomatic rifle, the kind the shooter used, costs $649.00, plus tax.

"CSM to the gun bar for a gun sale," the intercom announces. The gun bar runs along one side of the store under a red, white, and blue FIREARMS sign. Long guns fill a rack on the wall, and handguns fill glass display cases. Customers take numbers and wait. I look on as a dozen middle-aged men and women from San Antonio's sub-urban sprawl stand in line, waiting to buy weapons. They listen for their numbers to be called as, overhead, store speakers play "Stairway to Heaven."

—Brandon Lingle, from "Remembering Sutherland Springs"

Entr'acte

During the sixties at eighteen, I signed up for the Selective Service. I'd also waited until the required eighteen to work underground in the Anaconda Company copper mines in my hometown of Butte, Montana.

On my first day at the mines I stood at the headframe in my clean clothes and hard hat, my rubber steel-toed boots. My gloves were clean. If only I'd scratched my hard hat with a rock or screwdriver before presenting myself before the experienced miners with whom I waited for the hoist cage to be lowered into the earth. This first day, I was dropped to the 5200 level (one mile deep) at the Mountain Con Mine. The mine wasn't named as a prison—Con was the first name of one of Butte's first mining superintendents. I don't know what he was famous for.

Early in my first shift, during some shovel and pick work, one of the older crew tapped my shoulder: "Slow the fuck down, college boy! You're making us look bad." I hadn't yet started college, but I slowed the fuck down and it wasn't many days until my clothes were as dirty as anyone's around me. I'd planned to work a few months, to save money for school and, mostly, to buy a car. I worked three months and started attending the Montana School of Mines just after Labor Day. I either walked to school or had my father drop me off on his way to his work at the mines. On and off during the school year, on weekends and holidays, I worked underground for what was the town's best pay—21 dollars a day.

I got assigned to clear grizzlies—a greenhorn's job. The grizzlies lidded a hundred-foot shaft with a grid of spaced iron bars, like railroad rails. There was enough room between the rails to fall through, which was why it was a rule to wear a safety belt connected by rope to a rock bolt. Ore had been mucked into a smaller shaft (called a raise) to tumble by gravity from mining above to the grizzlies below. This happened on each level of the mine. If ore didn't fit between rails, my job was to break it into suitable size with a double jack—a sledge with a head weighing in at twenty or so pounds and forged from heat-treated high-carbon steel. The two rounded striking faces minimized chipping and provided blunt force. Sometimes the ore was just too dense to break with a hammer and you would resort to dynamite. All this to reduce the mined ore to a size that would fit between the rails and, thus, into a motor car to be taken to the main shaft to be hoisted to the surface.

My education in dynamite was (1) pack a stick (or two) onto the block of ore with handfuls of mud; (2) insert an electric blasting cap into one of the sticks; (3) run out your wires until you could find what felt to you to be adequate cover; (4) expose the wires to the terminals of your wet cell battery (that powered your headlamp) and attend the immediate blast. Before touching the wires, shout FIRE ON THE GRIZZLIES! If that didn't break the ore, you repeated the process, using additional sticks. I once used six sticks and nearly blew the place up. The blast rattled my teeth and rib cage. It pushed on the air in my lungs. In the time it took for the concussed dust to settle, I worried I'd loosened the grid. I double-checked my safety belt before stepping onto the grizzlies, where, with a steel pry bar, I maneuvered the broken ore to fall betwixt the rails. Thereafter assigned to the grizzlies, I never exceeded four sticks.

I had no notion then, and none now, why the grids of spaced iron bars are called "grizzlies." I found no explanation online, only confirmation of the term "grizzly." What

I did know is that ore the size of a hay bale can weigh as much as your car and is hard to disassemble with a hammer.

The bomb dropped on Hiroshima was the equivalent of 12,000–15,000 tons of TNT, which terrifies when you know what six sticks can do.

The largest bomb in service in the U.S. nuclear arsenal has a yield of 1.2 megatons. A megaton is a unit of explosive power equivalent to one million tons of TNT.

I worked in the mines, on and off, during the first years of the war in Vietnam. I was told that the copper being mined was being used mostly as shell casings for that war. I've wondered if that were true. Of course, it certainly could be.

Years after my stint in the mines, I managed to buy my first car, a 1970 Chevrolet Chevelle two-door two-tone (gold and white), which I purchased using my Air Force orders as collateral. I drove it from Salt Lake City to Biloxi, Mississippi, where within the month, I took it to Sears to have it retrofitted for air-conditioning—hands down the best money I ever spent.

Butte, Montana, still holds the record for the lowest recorded temperature in the contiguous United States: −61°F.

I showed up at Keesler Air Force Base in Biloxi on Bastille Day, July 14, 1971. Immediate first thought: Why had we fought for the South?

Have you been to Mississippi? What did you think?

Castle Bravo, the largest thermonuclear detonation by the United States, set off in Bikini Atoll, Marshall Islands, on March 1, 1954, produced twice the energy expected from eight million tons of TNT—an explosion equivalent to some fifteen million tons of TNT.

It's common knowledge—isn't it?—that the prizes Alfred Nobel funded, benefiting science, culture, and peace, were (and are) made possible by his manufacture and sale of TNT?

The world's most powerful hydrogen bomb detonated on October 30, 1961, over the Novaya Zemlya archipelago in the Soviet Union. The bomb had an explosive force of fifty-eight megatons, six thousand times more powerful than the Hiroshima bomb. Dropped by an aircraft, and detonated twelve hundred feet above the earth's surface, the Novaya Zemlya bomb emitted a shock wave that circled the planet three times, the mushroom cloud extending thirty-eight miles into the atmosphere.

The Soviets labeled the experiment Tsar Bomba. Tsar can be translated as (1) Russian emperor, (2) tyrant, or (3) somebody in authority.

Alfred Nobel's father manufactured land mines.

Many think a mine, like a cave you might enter in summer, would be cool, but a mine is not cool—it is hot and humid, like Mississippi.

There were crates of dynamite and blasting caps scattered throughout the mine I worked in. The amounts were restocked constantly, like an armory for munitions training.

What I think of now is that a blasting cap—never mind a dynamite stick—is enough to blow your hands off. How was I permitted use? I was a teenager in a hard hat. I felt conscripted, ready for deployment.

. . .

1968: Memphis
Portrait of a Dangerous Man
The Reverend Martin Luther King preaches against the Vietnam War. He protests that twice as many blacks as whites are dying there, cannon fodder for an imperial adventure comparable to the Nazi crimes. The poisoning of water and land, the destruction of people and harvests are part of a plan of extermination. Of the million Vietnamese dead, says the preacher, the majority are children. The United States, he claims, is suffering from the infection of the soul; and any autopsy would show that the name of that infection is Vietnam.

Six years ago the FBI put this man in Section A of the Reserved List, among those dangerous individuals who must be watched and jailed in case of emergency. Since then the police hound him, spying on him day and night, threatening and provoking him.

Martin Luther King collapses on the balcony of a Memphis hotel. A bullet full in the face puts an end to this nuisance.

—Eduardo Galeano, from *Century of the Wind*

. . .

I write to establish the reality of things. It's as if I'm afraid they aren't there unless substantiated by language, and consubstantiated. I need the confidence of a street preacher who can go on shouting to oblivious traffic. American poets have written both the country and the city, but no one seems to know what to do with the suburbs and bedroom towns. There must be something so unreal about spending huge chunks of our days commuting in a kind of limbo that we are inarticulate. Perhaps the true location of the suburbs is television, not any terrain.

—Robert Morgan, from *Good Measure*

. . .

Fear of failure and fear of success—the same?

. . .

It has been recently reported that the melting of the ice sheet in Antarctica over the last quarter century has released enough water to cover the state of Texas to a depth of thirteen feet. The ice melt raised *global* oceans three-tenths of an inch. From 1992 to 2011, Antarctica lost 84 billion tons of ice a year. During 2012–17 the melt rate increased to 241 billion tons a year.

. . .

EPA changes during the first year of the Trump administration have caused Harvard social scientists to estimate an additional eighty thousand more American deaths each decade due to environmental damage—dirtier air and more exposure to toxic chemicals. The scientists called it "an extremely conservative estimate." The EPA dismisses the claims.

. . .

They carried all the emotional baggage of men who might die. Grief, terror, love, longing—these were intangibles, but the intangibles had their own mass and specific gravity, they had tangible weight. They carried shameful memories. They carried the common secret of cowardice barely restrained, the instinct to run or freeze or hide, and in many respects this was the heaviest burden of all, for it could never be put down, it required perfect balance and posture. They carried their reputations. They carried the soldier's greatest fear, which was the fear of blushing. Men killed, and died, because they were embarrassed not to. It was what had brought them to the war in the first place, nothing positive, no dreams of glory or honor, just to avoid the blush of dishonor. They died so as not to die of embarrassment. They crawled into tunnels and walked point and advanced under fire. Each morning, despite the unknowns, they made their legs move. They endured. They kept humping.... It was not courage, exactly; the object was not valor. Rather, they were too frightened to be cowards.

—Tim O'Brien, from *The Things They Carried*

. . .

**re: If you could require the President
to read one book, what would it be?**
If this person who can't make it through his abbreviated daily briefing could make it all the way through a book, he'd be somebody else, which would be a very nice thing for all the living things on earth now and yet to come.

—Rebecca Solnit

. . .

We learn from history and repeat it cheerfully. History does not caution, it sanctions.

> —Don Paterson, from *The Book of Shadows*

. . .

Who said when Fascism comes to America, it will be called anti-Fascism?

. . .

We had only one lad that deserted. He did it twice and he got sentenced to death. They stripped him of his medal—he had a medal—and he was sentenced to be shot. We all had to go and see it, every one of us. That was as good as to say, "Now you know!" That's about what it was. The whole battalion was on parade, whether you shut your eyes was up to you, but we were all there. We were all up the hill, down below they'd got like a little stage. I just watched it. It took only a minute or two. There was a chair in the middle of the stage, and he was brought out, sat on the chair. He was in just a shirt and his trousers. His identification was there dangling on his chest. He must have asked about being blindfolded, and they did blindfold him. They had to take the firing squad out of his own platoon. They took eight of them. One of them was his mate and he refused to take part in it. He was told that if he didn't he would be court-martialed and get a really bad sentence. They told him, "There's nothing to worry about because you won't shoot him!" The thing was there were eight rifles and one had a dummy bullet, but none of the eight men knew which one of them had got the dummy bullet. So as the officer said, "Each one of you have got it there that you didn't shoot him!" As a matter of fact some of them must have missed deliberately, but that was unfortunate because he just slumped forward, but he wasn't dead. That's when the Provost Marshal had his revolver and he shot him.... I was relieving as company clerk and I had to send a telegram home to his people. The procedure was that if anybody was killed I used to send this telegram, "We regret to inform you that your son was killed in action." With him I had to send a telegram just "Killed." The words in action were not in the telegram.

—Private John Grainger, 1/7th Lancashire Fusiliers, in Peter Hart, *Voices from the Front: An Oral History of the Great War*

. . .

My first shot had missed him, embedding itself in the straw wall, but the second caught him dead-on in the femoral artery. His left thigh blossomed, swiftly turning to mush. A wave of blood gushed from the wound; then another boiled out, sheeting across his legs, pooling on the earthen floor. Mutely, he looked down at it. He dipped a hand in it and listlessly smeared his cheek red. His shoulders gave a little spasmodic jerk, as though someone had whacked him on the back; he then emitted a tremendous, raspy fart, slumped down, and died. I kept firing, wasting government property. Already I thought I detected the dark brown effluvium of the freshly slain, a sour, pervasive emanation which is different from anything you have known. Yet seeing death at this range, like smelling it, requires no previous experience. You instantly recognize it in the spastic convulsion and the rattle, which in his case was not loud, but deprecating and conciliatory, like the manners of the civilian Japanese. He continued to sink and he reached the earthen floor. His eyes glazed over. Almost immediately, a fly landed on his left eyeball.

—William Manchester, from *Goodbye Darkness*

. . .

Shakespeare: "hard-favored death"—what does that mean?

. . .

Who said being dead is like being asleep except you don't have to get up in the middle of the night to pee?

. . .

When I was going to college, the quickest route to culture was a beard, a book of Rod McKuen poetry (*Listen to the Warm*), desert boots, a backpack, flannel shirts, khakis, a twelve-speed bike...

. . .

They have mandatory boxing at the U.S. Air Force Academy where I teach. Makes sense to me. If you are going to drop things on people's heads from the sky, remaining unscathed, you should, at least once in your life, get hit in the face. Agree?

. . .

re: So starts an Orwell essay, dated 1941
As I write, highly civilized human beings are flying overhead, trying to kill me.

. . .

I worked for a while at a publishing house. Applying to be an editor, one applicant misspelled "proofreader" in his paperwork. His application was thumbtacked to the bulletin board in the breakroom.

. . .

Is "snooked" a word?

. . .

Frank Lloyd Wright, considered a modern architect, was born two years after the Civil War.

. . .

Ninety percent of cheetah cubs die within three months.

. . .

History isn't what happened, history is just what historians tell us.

—Julian Barnes

. . .

The trenches bounded the horizons of the infantry, restricting them to a worm's eye view glimpsed over the sandbags. The classic configuration had a wide sandbag and earth parapet measuring about 3 feet high and 6 feet thick in front of the trench, which was at least 3 feet 6 inches wide, with behind it a similar parados. The trench would be over 6 feet deep, so it had to have a fire step 2 feet high and around 18 inches wide for the soldier to stand on when firing over the parapet at an approaching enemy. Where possible the walls were revetted with wire, timber or corrugated iron to prevent collapse, while drains and duckboards attempted to hold back the water. A further

sophistication was a system of "fire-bays" with interven-
ing traverses of solid earth which minimised the impact
of shells bursting directly in the trench and reduced the
occupying troops' vulnerability to enfilading fire. As the
war wore on there were a variety of developments: early
on, barbed wire was erected to prevent a "rush" attack,
communication trenches were carved out to allow safe
approach and a plethora of support and reserve lines
appeared. In the end there would be a complex trench system layered back for several miles, all defended by rifles,
machine guns and massed artillery fire—the most deadly
form of military hardware, responsible for over 60 per
cent of total casualties.

—Peter Hart, from *Voices from the Front*

. . .

There were six in my bay. It was my turn on duty for a couple of hours. They said, "Let's go to the next bay; they've got
some cards in there—we can have a game of cards." Away
these other five went. That made about twelve in their bay
and only me in this one. All of a sudden there's one—God,
honestly and truly I'll never know what happened—it was
such a bloody explosion and it blew me, the sandbags, the
barbed wire all in a bloody heap. I just don't know what
happened, it must have fallen quite near me. While I was
trying to get myself together a young officer came along, he
says, "You all right?" I said, "Yes." I was a bit dazed. I said,
"Where did that shell fall, then?" He said, "You should see
the next bay, all dead, all of them!" He said, "Can you help
me dig them out?" I was half dazed myself. He got another
man, but when we got round the bay he put his hand to
his forehead and said, "Oh Sir, I can't look at them, I can't
touch them! It makes me ill to see them!" We got down to

it and did the best we could. Pulling bits and pieces out.
We got hold of a fellow's neck bone—his head was off—to
pull him out of the loose earth and all it was his two legs
and his backbone. Next one the shell had scalped him, so
that all his skull was peeled white, a hole in the skull. As I
tried to get my hand under his chin, all his brains shot out
all over my arm…. The officer got his water bottle out, got
some rum, and we had a good sip.

—Private William Holbrook, Fourth Royal Fusiliers,
in Peter Hart, *Voices from the Front*

. . .

*The fiction is that we're all equally responsible for what our
government does.*

—William Stafford, from *Sound of the Ax*

. . .

Doc Bryan cuts away the cast. The girl screams. Her mother
climbs in on the driver's side and wraps her arms around
her daughter's head and chest, holding her in place as she
writhes in agony. Whatever hit the girl's leg ripped chunks
of flesh from her calf to her thigh. The bones were broken
as well. Whoever treated her stuffed the wounds with cotton, which Doc Bryan now must rip out. Pus oozes out.
She has a high fever, a bad septic infection. On top of this,
her foot was set in the cast with the toes pointing down, so
if she lives and her bones heal, she'll walk with a lame foot.

"We've got to get her to a hospital," Doc Bryan says.
"This infection is going to kill her."

Fick radios the battalion, requesting permission to
medevac the girl. It's denied. The platoon delays its mission
for two hours, while Doc Bryan does his best to clean the

wounds out. The girl wails and sobs most of the time. Her mother holds her head. Doc Bryan curses softly.

Fick walks away, turning his back on the girl. "This is fucking up our mission," he says, pissed off at the girl for showing up with her horrific wounds. "A week after liberating this city, the American military can't provide aid to a girl probably hit by one of our bombs," he says, pissed off at the war.

—Evan Wright, from *Generation Kill*

. . .

Following the invasion, some Iraqis complained that under Saddam Hussein they at least had electricity and water.

. . .

As the garbage truck is backing up, one of the garbagemen is absorbed
    watching a pretty girl pass
and a sleeve of protruding steel catches him hard enough on the bicep to
    knock him down.
He clutches at his arm, limping heavily across the sidewalk, obviously in
    quite serious discomfort,
but the guy who works with him and who's seen the whole thing abso-
    lutely refuses to acknowledge
that his partner might be hurt, instead he bursts out laughing.

—C. K. Williams, from "Men"

. . .

re: If You Were a Roofer

How many weather-perfect days do you think you would get?

. . .

As an undergraduate, I took an anatomy class. I remember looking forward to it each time it met, but all I remember today is *peristaltic rush* and *hemostasis*. The course was taught by a crippled man.

. . .

It's another Iraqi town, nameless to the Marines racing down the main drag in Humvees, blowing it to pieces. We're flanked on both sides by a jumble of walled, two-story mud-brick buildings with Iraqi gunmen concealed behind windows, on rooftops and in alleyways, shooting at us with machineguns, AK rifles and the odd rocket-propelled grenade (RPG). Though it's nearly five in the afternoon, a sandstorm has plunged the town into a hellish twilight of murky red dust. Winds howl at fifty miles per hour. The town stinks. Sewers, shattered from a Marine artillery bombardment that ceased moments before we entered, have overflowed, filling the streets with lagoons of human excrement. Flames and smoke pour out of holes blasted through walls of homes and apartment blocks by the Marines' heavy weapons. Bullets, bricks, chunks of buildings, pieces of blown-up light poles and shattered donkey carts splash into the flooded road ahead.

The ambush started when the lead vehicle of Second Platoon—the one I ride in—rounded the first corner into town. There was a mosque on the left, with a brilliant, cobalt-blue dome. Across from this, in the upper window of a three-story building, a machine gun had opened up.

Nearly two dozen rounds ripped into our Humvee almost immediately. Nobody was hit; none of the Marines panicked. They responded by speeding into the gunfire and attacking with their weapons. The four Marines crammed into this Humvee—among the first troops to cross the border into Iraq—had spent the past week wired on a combination of caffeine, sleep deprivation, tedium and anticipation. For some of them, rolling into an ambush was almost an answered prayer.

—Evan Wright, from *Generation Kill*

. . .

"Man, I'm glad I didn't see any dead little children," Garza says.

"How do you think we would feel if someone came into our country and lit us up like this?" Carazales says. "South of Al Gharraf I know I shot a building with a bunch of civilians in it. Everyone else was lighting it up. Then we found out there were civilians in there. It's fucked up." Carazales works himself into a rage. "I think it's bullshit how these fucking civilians are dying! They're worse off than the guys that are shooting at us. They don't even have a chance. Do you think people at home are going to see this—all these women and children we're killing? Fuck no. Back home they're glorifying this motherfucker, I guarantee you. Saying our president is a fucking hero for getting us into this bitch. He ain't even a real Texan."

—Evan Wright, from *Generation Kill*

. . .

The strength of the pack is the wolf.

. . .

A few years back, selected for jury duty, I was ensconced, as it turned out, for a weeklong affair, having to do with a lawnmower repair shop that burned down and an insurance company that was laboring to not pony up. The insurance tribe's angle was that gasoline had been stored at the repair shop. I can still hear the fancy lawyer for the insurance folks asking where we (the jury) stored the gasoline for our own lawnmowers at home. He seemed surprised when we each reported that we kept gasoline with the lawnmowers in our garages. Where did he think we'd store it?

. . .

One of the jurors, a just-turned eighteen-year-old, rail-thin black kid, informed us that his life's ambition was to become a monster truck driver. I've wondered if this has turned out. It seemed something he really wanted.

. . .

re: Overheard, various locations
Ninety percent of trout in rivers lie within three feet of the banks.

Have you seen *Cats*? It's people in cat suits on roller skates and there's only one good song.

Having your cake just in case you might want to eat it?

She had a baby, but it took a while for her to realize she needed diapers. She was that kind of mother.

Calm down.

If you are born blind, what are you missing really?

How long do parrots live for?

Like stealing light from the sun, then falling to earth. That's what she said, but what does it mean?

How is white chocolate made?

Is it love?

Dumber than a bucket of hammers.

Is "erotopath" a word?

The place was too small to swing a cat without getting hair in your mouth.

It's because you're stupid and make bad decisions.

Darkness waits.

What has Jesus ever done for Santa on his birthday?

If you're the HVAC guy…in the winter, you're cold, installing furnaces you never use, and in the summer, you're hot, installing AC that's flipped on once you leave.

…"cancer free" is like "recovering alcoholic"—you need to pay attention.

Pornography is just the same thing over and over.

. . .

Lovers are the most hideously selfish aberrations in any given territory. They are not nice, and careless to the degree of blind metal-hided rhinoceroses run amok. Multitudes of them cause wrecks and die in them. Ask the locals how sweet the wreckage of damned near everybody was around that little pube-rioting Juliet and her moon-whelp Romeo. Tornado in a razor factory, that's what sweetness.

—Barry Hannah, from "Through Sunset into the Raccoon Night"

. . .

Saying something is "on the blink" makes its own kind of sense, doesn't it?

. . .

Marie Curie won a Nobel Prize for physics *and* for chemistry. Her death by cancer was probably brought on by her exposure to radioactivity. To this day her professional papers are housed in a lead-lined box.

. . .

Robert Penn Warren won a Pulitzer Prize for fiction *and* for poetry (for poetry twice!).

. . .

For most of his life, Beethoven changed addresses on an average of more than twice a year. And was more than once sued by landlords for having scribbled notations all over his walls.

—David Markson, from *Reader's Block*

. . .

Wolfsbane is a poisonous Eurasian perennial flowering plant. Its name refers to its use as a weapon against werewolves. Compounded with bait, infused in tea, applied to arrowheads, slathered on swords, it can, in a pinch, be used against vampires too.

. . .

Art is here to prove, and to help one bear, the fact that all safety is an illusion.

    —James Baldwin, from "The Artist's Struggle for Integrity"

. . .

It looked as if a night of dark intent
Was coming, and not only a night, an age.
Someone had better be prepared for rage.
There would be more than ocean-water broken
Before God's last Put out the Light was spoken.

    —Robert Frost, from "Once by the Pacific"

. . .

We are all a conduit for heredity—*all* the assets and liabilities of *all* forbearers. Are you spooked?

. . .

Go ahead, excavate the family line. See if you don't find kings and queens, drunks and addicts, bigamists, bigots, priests, bankers, forgers, rustlers, pirates. Did you find someone from Africa or Iran? Do you contain some Apache blood?

. . .

My grandfather taught my father how to stack wood to look like a cord when it was not, stretching the profit on sales. When my father was younger, my grandfather taught him to cast sand in open fields near stills to locate hidden glass jars of moonshine to steal, then sell. These are not things a kid should know, but then neither should my father have been driving a truck hawking wood when he was twelve.

. . .

During the Depression, consumers were converting to more efficient coal. My father, having parked his loaded truck atop a hill, had been going door-to-door offering wood. The truck, without the brake properly set—if it had brakes—began its descent down the hill, obeying all the laws of physics until impaling the side of a house. My father ran home crying. He eventually found his father in a bar. My grandfather, accompanied by equally drunk and curious cronies, made their way to the house and the truck. My father said he never knew what deal was struck, but his father was kind to him about the event. My father taught me how to chock the tires of a parked truck. He carried blocks in the truck bed.

. . .

Who's your designated texter?

. . .

He is teaching her how to break bottles against the side of the house. A whiskey bottle works best, he tells her. She thinks this is very lucky because that is what they have the most of—he has spent the last few weeks emptying them. So whiskey bottles are what they are using. Now, he says.

Like this. Crack. So that you get something like a shiv, not just a fistful of glass and stitches. Like this, he says. Crack. And she feels a great swell of pride in her sparrow chest— he gets it perfect, every time. Now you, he says, and he hands her the next bottle. Because a father can't always be there, he says, and she nods and tries to look solemn, to make him believe she understands. The bottle does not break on the first try. She swings harder on the second try and gets it, but it is a bad break. Her father does not say this, but she knows. Too close to the neck. Shards of glass from other afternoons shine dully in the dry earth at their feet. He hands her another bottle and the second break is better, the glass jutting out like the snaggled teeth of some prehistoric fish.

—Josephine Rowe, from "Love"

. . .

"Paul West," wrote the *Baltimore Sun* some years back, "is a master of the word. He uses language as a scalpel, as an axe handle, a periscope, a trumpet, a flute, a cattle prod, a stiletto, a feather, a bludgeon." And William Gass, a master himself, wrote, "West is an extraterrestrial, and while he flies over he sometimes looks down on us poor word-birds pecking at our corn."

. . .

re: Moscow 2018
Burger King has apologized for offering a lifetime supply of Whoppers to Russian women who get pregnant by World Cup players. Critics assailed the offer, announced on Russian social media, as sexist and demeaning. The announcement was removed Tuesday from Burger King's

social media accounts but was still circulating among Russian social network users. It promised a reward of free burgers to women who get "the best football genes" and "ensure the success of the Russian team for generations to come."

—Associated Press, June 20, 2018

. . .

Who invented the mirror? And when was that?

. . .

Portrait painting and sculpture were early mirrors, as was, we must suppose, the still surface of a pond. And the regarding of another's face regarding yours is a sort of a reflection, is it not?

. . .

As it turns out, the invention of the silvered-glass mirror is credited to German chemist Justus von Liebig. This was in the year 1835. His process, still maintained, involves the deposition of a thin layer of metallic silver onto the back of glass through the chemical reduction of silver nitrate.

. . .

Anyone's death always releases something like an aura of stupefaction, so difficult is it to grasp this irruption of nothingness and to believe that it has actually taken place.

—Gustave Flaubert

. . .

Mirror, Mirror, on the Wall, Who Is the Fairest of Them All?

. . .

We are at the Bargello in Florence, and she says,
what are you thinking? *And I say,* beauty, *thinking*
of how very far we are now from the machine shop
and the dry fields of Kansas, the treeless horizons
of slate skies and the muted passions of roughnecks
and scrabble farmers drunk and romantic enough
to weep more or less silently at the darkened end
of the bar, out of, what else, loneliness, meaning
the ache of thwarted desire, of, in a word, beauty,
or rather its absence, and it occurs to me again
that no male member of my family has ever used
this word in my hearing or anyone else's except
in reference, perhaps, to a new pickup or dead deer.

—B. H. Fairchild, from "Beauty"

. . .

The face that launch'd a thousand ships…

. . .

One time my Uncle Ross from California called my mom's
Sunday dinner centerpiece "lovely," and my father
left the room, clearly troubled by the word "lovely"
coupled probably with the very idea of California
and the fact that my Uncle Ross liked to tap-dance.

—B. H. Fairchild, from "Beauty"

. . .

And burnt the topless towers of Ilium…

. . .

On Christmas Eve 1865, the Ku Klux Klan is formed in
Pulaski, Tennessee. The name for the secret social fraternity was derived from the Greek word *kyklos*, meaning

"circle," and the Sottish-Gaelic word "clan." The organization's intention was to reverse the federal government's progressive activities in the South, especially policies that elevated the rights of the African American population.

. . .

Suicide: a form of criticism?

. . .

It took fourteen years to sculpt Mount Rushmore. The granite composing the presidents' faces is, at least, 1.6 billion years old.

. . .

The Crazy Horse sculpture, also in the Black Hills of South Dakota, dwarfs the carved portraits of Mount Rushmore. Korczak Ziolkowski began the work in 1948, continuing until his death in 1982. The monumental work persists through the sculptor's ten children and the Crazy Horse Memorial Foundation. Ziolkowski had worked as a sculptor's assistant to Gutzon Borglum on the Mount Rushmore project. He was fired after a fistfight with Borglum's primary assistant, Lincoln Borglum, the head sculptor's son. Orphaned at the age of one, Ziolkowski was raised in a series of foster homes in Boston. Before his sculpting work, he volunteered for service in the U.S. Army and was wounded in 1944 at Omaha Beach in Normandy.

. . .

The world is what you see outside your window plus what you think of.

—William Stafford, from *Sound of the Ax*

. . .

At least at night, a streetlight
Is better than a star.
And better good shoes on a
Long walk, than a good friend.

—William Stafford, from "So Long"

. . .

Geico using a gecko in its insurance advertising is not the genius of the ploy, the genius is in assigning the lizard an Australian accent.

. . .

If you want to talk to your kids, text them.

. . .

Nuclear Fission and Nuclear Fusion. Do you know the difference?

. . .

If your father dies and he's always worn a mustache, do not allow the mortician to trim it. The mortuary professional will make your father look like a cheap private eye in a pressed suit. And you won't know if he's wearing shoes—gumshoes, or not.

. . .

If somehow, perhaps blindfolded with plugs in your ears, you can attune to it without recoiling, one inhalation of combined burning rubber, scorched beef and baby caca will last you a lifetime. They call it Ground Zero, though there is nothing zero-like about it except the absence of human life. It is the ground gruesomely fed and fostered, upheaved and manured, with, deep down, blocks of gold odorless amid the debris of plundered bodies. Smoke wafts and spirals from the lower depths as from an inexhaustible supply. What is on fire beneath? You may well ask. It is as if corpses develop into a new fodder they never knew in life. And there are hundreds of them as in some ancient Scandinavian burial zone where bog people reign, and you wonder how in years to come the diggers of the day will construe the jumbled carnage that reposes here, crammed together in an instant as if an instant were some kind of creative maestro, devising fresh combinations of human limbs and trunks undreamed of in Japanese sex manuals or the *Kama-sutra*. No voices to be heard among the hisses and creaks. Nothing much to be seen in the rump of sludge that lids the cenotaph around which an increasing circle of sightseers gathers, in the fashion of villagers who grouped around the actual cenotaphs of older wars, envisioning if they could the twigs of humanity buried there in clinical disorder, they presumably having propelled the world to a humaner understanding as their relentless, heroic gift. The war artist, Paul Nash, visiting the trenches of 1914–18, reconjured the fetid scene in a canvas he called *Totes Meer*, Death's Sea, in which the stochastic waves of rippled linseed are the remains of folks, the remains, elongated and contorted tunnels for surfing through. Even the title is German, as if English were too chicken a language for this, and of course you try *Zero Grund* or something such, but this master work of depravity is the result of Meccanization.

—Paul West, from *The Immensity of the Here and Now*

. . .

The blind woman, writing her memoir, page after page, not knowing the pen has run out of ink.

. . .

Ah, words are poor receipts for what time hath stole away...

—John Clare

. . .

Between the idea
And the reality
Between the motion
And the act
Falls the Shadow.

—T. S. Eliot, from "The Hollow Men"

. . .

The sure extinction that we travel to
And shall be lost in always. Not to be here,
Not to be anywhere,
And soon; nothing more terrible, nothing more true...
And specious stuff that says No rational being
Can fear a thing it will not feel, *not seeing*
That this is what we fear...

—Philip Larkin, from "Aubade"

. . .

re: April 1940
Land, sea, and air forces are sent by Germany to "protect Danish neutrality." These forces overrun Denmark in less than a day. Treated as "fellow Aryans," the population remained mostly acquiescent for half the war. But in 1943,

when the Germans take absolute control and target the nation's Jews, members of the Danish resistance ferry more than 90 percent of the country's nearly eight thousand Jews to safety in neutral Sweden almost overnight. And of more than four hundred Danish Jews who did fall into the hands of the Nazis, most were released through Danish governmental negotiations with Heinrich Himmler.

With the surrender of German forces in Denmark, a quarter million prisoners fall into Allied hands. Unrepatriated, some twenty-five hundred are kept in Denmark in captivity to clear land mines from the Danish coasts. These mine-clearing teams suffer an aggregate of 20 percent casualties by the time the operation ends early in 1946. The use of prisoners for such a "dangerous and unhealthy" operation was in violation of Article 32 of the 1929 Geneva Convention, to which Denmark was a signatory.

. . .

Everybody suffers: War, sickness, poverty, hunger, oppression, prison, exile, bigotry, loss, madness, rape, addiction, age, loneliness. We suffer, depending on our religions or ideological convictions, because we are born in sin; because God has chosen us; because he is punishing us; because we are bound by craving and illusion; because suffering makes us better. We suffer because some of our cells are programmed, when exposed to certain biological stressors, to turn cancerous. We suffer because some of us have nothing and others have everything and those with everything want even more. We suffer because some reptilian portion of the brain delights in murder and sways not only individuals but entire nations to its purposes. We suffer because at a very early age we learn that we are going to die and spend the rest of our lives in dread of it.

Everybody suffers, but Americans have the peculiar delusion that they're exempt from suffering. In support of that statement one might cite everything from the rate of medical malpractice claims to the national epidemic of incomprehension and rage that followed the terrorist attacks of 9/11, when in a matter of moments the distant, negligible world was revealed to be no longer *there* but *here*, its breath hot in our faces.

—Peter Trachtenberg, from *The Book of Calamities*

. . .

How I loved those spiky suns,
rooted stubborn as childhood
in the grass, tough as the farmer's
big-headed children—the mats
of yellow hair, the bowl-cut fringe.

—Jean Nordhaus, from "A Dandelion for My Mother"

. . .

My father didn't understand my training for and running marathons. To him, it was excessive and, essentially, nonproductive work. No money.

. . .

If you've just spent ten hours digging ditches on a hot summer day you don't enter the tavern and begin to talk about the virtue of hard work and thrift, the beauty of Calvinism as a moral system. You want several mugs of beer.

—Jim Harrison, from *Off to the Side: A Memoir*

. . .

Doubtless people have felt religious ecstasy since the Pleistocene though now it is largely ridiculed, mostly because of the charlatan behavior of the leaders. I certainly don't view fundamentalists as more threatening than the somewhat fascist monoethic of our surging, prosperous young middle class who were educated with the usually politically correct fodder to the point that they seem to keep totally to their own kind. Blacks, Latinos, and Native Americans are well out of their purview. They live in a consensus world of day care, Little League, stock portfolios, healing, closure, ergonomics, with pablum concerns about air pollution and smoking (in their immediate areas.) It is a version of life much closer to Huxley's prophecies than those of George Orwell. Imagine a serious discussion of whether thirty-five hours is too much television for the little nitwits they are breeding.

—Harrison, from *Off to the Side*

. . .

I'd rather be named Thelonious than Chip. Or: Aeschylus, not Biff. You?

. . .

The best name for a football player I've yet encountered is Thane Gash. He played for the Cleveland Browns. His middle name was Alvin.

. . .

The worst boss I ever had in the Air Force was Colonel Richard Head. This is true.

. . .

"Send in the Clowns," written by Stephen Sondheim for Broadway and famously sung by Judy Collins, Frank Sinatra, and Barbara Streisand, is purported to be a love song, but an old family friend and former carnival worker said that it was what a circus manager says when there is a glitch or accident during the night's high-wire acts: *Send in the Clowns.*

. . .

A good friend, Bill Wallisch, tells me one of his life's goals is to direct a Shakespeare tragedy wherein all actors are attired in different clown suits. The idea is to do the play straight, but never mention the outfits. I'd like to see that play. Wouldn't you?

. . .

I'm guessing a lot of rich people have AAA Roadside Assistance, which is a good thing for AAA because rich people have functioning cars.

. . .

Turns out there is little medical evidence that flossing is effective. With any luck, that's true.

. . .

Basically, in the Black Hills, Custer was killing Indians for gold.

. . .

Multitasking: you cannot, in fact, do two things at once.

. . .

The bomb had hit Auntie. Helene Harnisch was dead. Born 1885, died January 1945, unmarried. Two months before her sixtieth birthday. It had smashed her chest open.

Traffic was building up into a jam behind the coach. Other carts were lying on their sides, and lamentations filled the air. At last men came along to push the wrecked vehicles off the road and make way for the great trek that wanted to get past them.

Women laid the dead, including the body of Auntie, in the ditches at the roadside. Now, for heaven's sake, the other carts could go on....

After a while a man arrived from the village, the local pastor coming to take the dead away. He helped Peter to roll Auntie into a blanket, and put the arm that had been torn off, her left arm, into the blanket with her. It had come right away from her shoulder joint, and was broken as well.

They carried the old woman into the church and laid her in the vestibule, beside the offertory box and the frame that held the numbers of hymns to be sung. On the wall was a plaque bearing the names of the dead who had fallen in the wars of 1870–71 and 1914–18.

—Walter Kempowski, from *All for Nothing*

. . .

re: Overheard, various locations
She looks like Biafra. But I don't think she thinks so.

The Singing Cowboy. Who came up with that?

Following the reception, my first wife's mother boxed up the stainless steel and copper-bottomed pan and skillet set, returned it to the store and exchanged it for the cheaper avocado green aluminum. I still have one skillet.

Big hat, no cattle.

TV doctors are as bad as TV evangelists. The last fucking thing I want to hear when I walk in the door is "On Dr. Phil today..."

I took calculus, but I can't for the life of me remember what a derivative is.

Recovering addicts have to embrace all their free time. It's an adjustment.

One of my sisters has spent her life looking for something to pray about: a kid's earache, a fender bender, a roof leak, clogged plumbing. *Dear Heavenly Father.* Do you have a sister like that?

It's not about being strong, it's about having no options.

Do you know if it's not good to feed your dog pork bones?

Just another reminder that we are all temporary.

You *know*: those nasty shakes workout people make, then drink?

If a bird shits on your head, it's a sign of good luck? Who said?

One sheep for every ten people in New Zealand.

Figure it out.

It's like getting excited about mixed doubles in bowling.

Bitcoin?

My granddaughter carries a stainless steel straw for use in restaurants. She says plastic straws can get stuck in a porpoise's nose...a turtle's.

Why do you lie to yourself?

Is it possible our mind is more aware of us than we are of it?

We must learn to articulate death's banality, mustn't we?

What is paper but a thin slice of tree?

Disappointments come straight from expectations.

Well, I'm not sitting at a bus stop, wondering if I can see a doctor.

Nefertiti. *Nefertiti.* Why did I wake up with that on my tongue?

. . .

When I found out that waxing is the opposite of waning as it applies to the fullness of the moon, I understood, in new light, the meaning of "waxing poetic" or "waxing philo-sophical." Did you always know?

. . .

Retired guys and their yards...

．．．

Don't you like the word "dumbbells," featuring metal that hasn't been hollowed out and fitted with a clapper?

．．．

When you discover that the word "bolt" is a noun designating the "arrow" for a crossbow, you begin to understand its function as a verb.

．．．

Anyone who buys into their own mythology is destined to become a clumsy human being. We all know people like that. Don't we?

．．．

Don't carry identification, so if you die it will be inconvenient for someone, which it should be, right?

．．．

I have no problem with stories about prostitutes, if they are written by prostitutes wanting to tell their story.

— Bao Phi, from "War Before Memory: A Vietnamese American Protest Organizer's History Against *Miss Saigon*"

．．．

Once heading into church, my wife and I stepped aside for a family to enter the large front entrance. A father and mother were lifting a wheelchair in which was strapped one of their children. He looked twelve or so, sporting a white shirt and tie and khaki shorts. He was without arms and legs. He looked like a dressed-up bullet. His hair was barbered. He had the look of a dog guilty of biting. We waited again while he was wheeled up to the forward pews. The father unstrapped him from the chair, then propped him upright at the end of one of the center rows. As the father was pushing the chair (it was like an airplane wheelchair, tall and narrow) up the aisle of that pew to the side of the church, the boy squirmed on his little hams to the edge of the bench to drop to the floor. On the floor, he toppled to his side and began rolling back up the aisle to the front entry through which he'd just passed. The speed at which he rolled was flabbergasting, and he maneuvered like a floor-boarded and drifting NASCAR car around people who had entered the church and were milling in his direction. He was moving so fast that his father, hearing gasps, then racing for him, barely caught him before he was about to bounce down the stone church steps to either enter the road into traffic or turn to roll up the sidewalk. Either way, it was an honest-to-god escape attempt—a full-fledged *break*—and he almost pulled it off. It was as if we all should have stood to applaud to give him credit. We should have.

. . .

...the transcendent *weirdness* of the primary experience.
—Thomas Pynchon

. . .

A deaf friend said that lip reading depends on context and that deaf friends of hers who sign for others find Donald

Trump nearly impossible to follow because he doesn't operate in complete thoughts.

. . .

Boxing fans resemble the wives of fighter pilots.
—Jim Harrison, from *Just Before Dark*

. . .

"El Chapo" (Joaquin Guzmán, the Mexican drug lord, heading the Sinaloa Cartel) was captured because he was reaching out to movie producers concerning the making of a movie about his life.

. . .

When my children were small, I escorted them to a Muppets show at Universal Studios in California. Following the show, there was an available tour of the backstage setup to see just how Kermit, Miss Piggy, and the others worked. This seemed to me a terrible suggestion, so I saw to it that we skipped it. My children are now middle-aged. I'm still proud of my decision.

. . .

A boxing trainer and friend justifies it thus: *Boxing teaches you to face danger with courage, to shun pain, and to return violence rather than just passively accepting it.* If you put it that way...

. . .

re: Soldier Talk
Why take Sexual Assault Training so long as he's Commander-in-Chief? No, tell me.

. . .

a sleuth of bears
a mob of emus
a memory of elephants
an array of hedgehogs
a plague of rats
a gaze of raccoons
a trip of rabbits
a shrewdness of apes
a pride of lions
an obstinacy of buffalo
a caravan of camels
a bed of scorpions
a business of ferrets
a crash of hippos
a nest of vipers
a dazzle of zebras
a lounge of lizards
a rout of wolves
a convocation of eagles
a charm of goldfinches

a band of coyotes
a leap of leopards
an exaltation of larks
a parliament of owls
a cloud of bats
a burden of mules
a murder of crows
a quarrel of sparrows
a wake of vultures
a watch of nightingales
a shiver of sharks
a richness of martens
a fever of stingrays
a skulk of foxes
a down of hares
a smack of jellyfish
a bask of crocodiles
a quiver of cobras
a harem of seals
etc.

. . .

"Dumb Bunny" and "Birdbrain." Does this seem fair to you?

. . .

The boys liked to watch pigs being born. Drying them off in the straw. Putting them next to the sow's teats. Watching them discover the little world of the farrowing pen. But after a while the boys would get tired of this and go off to do something else.

Except for the youngest boy. He liked to stick around by himself. When the other boys left, he leaned down and put his face close to the sow. Now that there was no one there to laugh at him. This way he could hear the pig coming, and when it was born his face was right over the newborn. He quickly put his eye over the eye of the little pig. When it opened its eye, the first thing it saw was the boy's eye, only an inch or two away from its own.

The boy stared into the pig's eye and the pig stared into the boy's. What the boy liked to see was the expression on the pig's face. It was a look of surprise. But not a big surprise. Not the startled look of seeing something you didn't expect to see—like a ghost or a creature from Mars. More like the look of somebody waking up in the back seat of a car who doesn't realize how far he's gone since he fell asleep. The look that says, *Oh, I didn't know we'd gone this far, but okay.*

The boy lifted his head so the pig could notice everything else. The pig knew what to do. Stand up, breathe, look around for a nipple. The boy didn't try to keep the pig from its business. He knew they both had their own worlds to live in. That didn't change the fact that for a few seconds they had been somewhere that nobody else would have to know about.

—Jim Heynen, "Eye to Eye"

· · ·

Morning and night, I pitched hay into a manger over my head for our cows. I would then toss the pitchfork over the manger into the covered part of the barn where the cows slept. I impaled a calf. I pulled myself up to see over the manger, the pitchfork quivering in the back of the calf. The bellowing animal reminded me of a speared oryx or gazelle like I'd seen on *Mutual of Omaha's Wild Kingdom*. When I cornered the calf and extracted the tool, the tine holes geysered blood. I was worried because I also used the pitchfork to muck manure. Maybe the wounds would self-disinfect? Then I had the additional thought of any teenager: *Maybe no one will notice*. But I worried about infection and death. We raised our own calves for food. And: didn't open wounds and manure have something to do with lockjaw or something? I told my father. He was pretty nice to me about it.

. . .

re: Good Pet Names
Archimedes, Cervantes, Dante, Copernicus. Better than *Rover*, or *Pal*, or *Princess*. Why would you name your pig *Gordon* when you can name him *Prometheus* or *Hamlet*?

. . .

My first assignment in the Air Force was in Biloxi, Mississippi. My report date was Bastille Day, July 14, 1971. Two years earlier, the Mississippi coast had been devoured by Hurricane Camille. Peak winds of 175 mph had blown all asunder and had caused a storm tide of twenty-five feet. In the summer of 1971 you could still smell the damage, and imagine children's toys, mattresses, fan belts, dead pets, and washers and dryers on the beach.

. . .

When we were kids, at the beginning of each school year, my mother would sit us down with the Sears Roebuck catalog to pick one new item of clothing. I selected a pair of red slacks. The first day I wore them, I was heckled and came home so humiliated I never wore them again. Somewhere in the world today there's a new pair of red slacks. I'd wear them.

. . .

In Minneapolis, in 1886, Richard Warren Sears inaugurated a mail-order watch business, calling it "R. W. Sears Watch Company." He met Alvah C. Roebuck, a watch repairman. By the next year, they'd relocated the business to Chicago and published their first mail-order catalog—in this case, offering watches, diamonds, and jewelry. Later the company expanded to offer sewing machines, bicycles, sporting goods, even automobiles. In time, Sears offered virtually anything a consumer in any outlying area could desire. For instance, red slacks in the 1950s in Butte, Montana, a state in which there were more cows than people and laws suggesting hanging for rustlers but not for murderers.

. . .

Sears sold more than seventy thousand mail-order prefab *houses* in North America between 1908 and 1940.

. . .

Some vehicle names make sense. The large SUVs, for instance: Armada, Sequoia, Explorer, Expedition, Pathfinder, Land Cruiser, Pilot, Navigator. Naming cars for animals seems modestly legitimate: Cougar, Mustang, Viper, Beetle, Stingray, Impala, Cobra, Ram, Colt, Rabbit. But: Valiant, Renegade, Diablo, Impact, Volt, Leaf, Probe, Thing, Citation, Gremlin, Aspire, Mirage, Charade, LeCar, Brat, Hummer, Esteem, Golf, Q? These are names that you, at least, know are bad. Some names come in as so nonsensical, though, that you don't even know why they're bad: Camaro, Prius, Camry, Tiguan, Touareg, Yaris, Celica, Azera, Avalon, RAV4, Edge, Murano, Insight, Venza, Miata, STS, RXD? What's a CR-V? For that matter, what the fuck is Honda?

. . .

It feels acceptable, of course, that Porsche and Ford are two known and accepted surnames of cars. Who do you know named Buick? Oldsmobile?

. . .

How to account for so many big-tired, 4WD, dusky-glassed, black Cadillac Escalades in Miami?

. . .

Some peasants were blocking the road up ahead. I honked the horn but they chose not to hear. They were standing around under their pointed hats, watching a man and a woman yell at each other. When I got closer I saw two bicycles tangled up, a busted wicker basket, and vegetables all over the road. It looked like an accident.

Benet reached over in front of me and sounded the horn again. It made a sheepish bleat, ridiculous coming from this armor-plated truck with its camouflage paint. The peasants turned their heads but they still didn't get out of the way. I was bearing down on them. Sergeant Benet slid low in the seat so nobody could get a look at him, which was prudent on his part, since he was probably the biggest man in this part of the province and certainly the only black man.

I kept honking the horn as I came on. The peasants held their ground longer than I thought they would, almost long enough to make me lose my nerve, then they jumped out of the way. I could hear them shouting and then I couldn't hear anything but the clang and grind of metal as the wheels of the truck passed over the bicycles. Awful sound. When I looked in the rear-view most of the peasants were staring after the truck while a few others inspected the wreckage in the road.

Sergeant Benet sat up again. He said, without reproach, "That's a shame, sir. That's just a real shame."

I didn't say anything. What could I say? I hadn't done it for fun. Seven months back, at the beginning of my tour, when I was still calling them people instead of peasants, I wouldn't have run over their bikes. I would have slowed down or even stopped until they decided to move their argument to the side of the road, if it was a real argument and not a setup. But I didn't stop anymore. Neither did Sergeant Benet. Nobody did, as these peasants—these people—should have known.

—Tobias Wolff, from *In Pharaoh's Army*

. . .

Guarding the supply train through Baghdad, we stuck to our Rules of Engagement. These included denying civilian vehicles access into our convoys. They'd have to wait for us to pass, which forced Iraqi drivers to sit idling in traffic. They'd often try to pull in and drive to wherever they were headed, but our Strykers would slam into them and push them out of the convoy's path. Nineteen tons of metal, armament, intention. Our drivers and vehicle commanders kept a kind of informal daily count of the cars they'd hit during each convoy. The highest number I heard from one of the drivers was eight. During one of these hits, Sgt. Zapata was up in the hatch. A Stryker in front of us had just slammed into a vehicle trying to enter the roadway at a busy marketplace with pedestrians milling around. He saw the car flipped onto its passenger side, pinning one or more people underneath it. He saw the crowd rush to pull the car off. And he watched as a man with distant expression leaned against a nearby wall, part of his scalp peeled back from his forehead, skin and hair dangling behind him. And, as we drove on, Zapata saw the man reach to smooth the flap back into place.

—Brian Turner, from *My Life as a Foreign Country*

. . .

While the drivers used our vehicles to dominate the roadway, those of us standing in the rear hatches warned off civilians by other means. When a car began to approach us as if it meant to pass, I'd raise my M4 up in the air, the barrel towards Mars. If the car continued , I'd step up onto the troop seat below to make myself as visible as possible to the driver, before lowering the barrel of my weapon and training it on the car.

We'd use multiple hand gestures to warn the driver to slow down. But if they kept coming, I'd fire. I'd lean into the weapon and fire two shots into the radiator. The car would then slow and pull over to the shoulder of the road, or decelerate rapidly, then disappear as we drove on. I stopped counting the cars we shot at each day. I got tired of counting.

—Brian Turner, from *My Life as a Foreign Country*

. . .

In the stories that Vietnam narrators tell, the killing, which was the point of the strategy, appears to be random, accidental, arbitrary, often brutal. The army printed up rules of engagement and distributed them among the troops; but in the field there were no rules. The enemy was invisible, or indistinguishable among civilians, and all Vietnamese looked alike to the young short-timers; how could he avoid killing wrongfully? Robert Mason tells of a training question that was asked of all prospective grunts: What would you do if you were the driver of a truck loaded with soldiers, traveling very fast down a muddy road, flanked on both sides by steep drop-offs, and a child suddenly walked into your path? Would you try to avoid the child, and drive off the road to certain death? Or would you run over it? Everybody knew the right answer: kill the kid. Mason tells the story to illuminate his account of flying his helicopter over a village where an innocent-looking crowd of Vietnamese is bunched around a man with a machine gun. What do you do? You kill the kid. Mason's gunner machine-gunned the whole crowd.

—Samuel Hynes, from *The Soldiers' Tale*

. . .

To yield to force is an act of necessity, not of will; it is at best an act of prudence.

—Jean-Jacques Rousseau

. . .

I heard a woman: "I want to get back to my life of paper cuts and hangnails. Enough of this cancer." I wanted to look. She was behind me. I never saw her face.

. . .

The bottom line is this: You write in order to change the world, knowing perfectly well that you probably can't, but also knowing that literature is indispensable to the world. In some way, your aspirations and concern for a single man in fact do begin to change the world. The world changes according to the way people see it, and if you alter, even by a millimeter, the way a person looks or people look at reality, then you can change it.

—James Baldwin, from a 1979 interview

. . .

The clock is punched for war in Mesopotamia. Six hours until midnight, the day before the sudden flourish of air combat. I am suited, armed, and briefed for a 20,000 mile flight. The middle 208 seconds of the journey will be over Baghdad. Tomorrow's strikes will compose the first salvos of "shock and awe."

Our war-birds are carbon-fiber and titanium Stealth Bombers. They idle, topped with fuel, pre-flight crews tending aircraft systems on the rain-damp tarmac of Whiteman Air Force Base. In the course of the next two days, I will stiffen my backbone against exhaustion and battle with Air Force-issued amphetamines, a half-case of canned espresso drinks, and 40,000 pounds of steel and high-explosive. And books.

The Northrop Grumman B-2A "Spirit" is a flying wing—a 60-year old concept writ lethal in composites and computers. In profile, it is racy—a falcon stooping on distant prey. From the front—a menacing winged whale; from overhead—a wedge-shaped Euclidean study in parallel form. The plane carries aloft a crew of two pilots with the necessary life-support systems—oxygen, heating, air-conditioning, and cockpit pressurization. The pilots sit next to each other in twin ejection seats. The running joke is that the seats don't work because you'd rather be dead than face an accident board having crashed a $2,140,000,000.00 national asset.

Satiny charcoal in composition with a smooth, blended body, the B-2 is simultaneously rounded and angular. The skin is exotic and TOP-SECRET. Wing span is 172', two-and-a-half times the length of 69' nose-to-tail. It is rare—only 21 were built—but not endangered. It threads the 3-D envelopes of missile defense networks. Stealth has the same effect on defenses as speed, rendering reactions ineffective because they are too little, too late, if at all. This plane will bring us home.

The payload consists of 16 weapons mounted on two, eight-position, rotating launchers in each of the three aircraft of our flight. My primary weapons are 13 one-ton penetrator bombs for hardened targets and runways. The three remaining launcher stations carry the 4617 pound GBU-37 "Bunker Buster." These two-and-a-half-ton monstrosities are targeted against deeply buried, steel-reinforced, concrete command centers in a planned effort to "decapitate" Iraq's leadership. In the lingo of combat aviators, these bombs will "prosecute" targets. Rarely—unless talking about Saddam or his sons—is killing mentioned. We are distanced. We make "inputs" into a network of flying computers. I manage the ghost in the machine.

Our enemies label us the "Great Satan"—moral descendants of the Paladins of Charlemagne, Protector of the One Church. I don't know if those we aim to liberate call us anything at all. We are armed to strike from the air, over the land, between the two rivers.

I have brought a bag of books and journals to pass the hours of tedium. I am bound for desert places.

—Jason Armagost, from
"Things to Pack When You're Bound for Baghdad"

. . .

If temporality were held to be invalidating, then nothing real ever succeeds.

—John Updike

. . .

It wasn't so much a marriage of true minds as a fusion of two libraries.

—Olivia Laing on finding love later in life
with the poet Ian Patterson

. . .

What did I know, what did I know
of love's austere and lonely offices?

—Robert Hayden, from "Those Winter Sundays"

. . .

When I learned I might have cancer,
I bought fifteen white lilies. Easter was gone:
the trumpets were wilted, plants crooked with roots
bound in pots. I dug them into the garden,
knowing they would not bloom for another year.
All summer, the stalks stood like ramshackle posts
while I waited for results. By autumn, the stalks
had flopped down. More biopsies, laser incisions,
the cancer in my tongue a sprawling mass. Outside,
the earth remained bare, rhizomes shrunken
below the frost line. Spring shoots appeared

in bright green skins, and lilies bloomed
in July, their waxed trumpets pure white,
dusting gold pollen to the ground.

—Karenne Wood, from "The Lilies"

· · ·

It's unprofitable to monetize peace.

· · ·

Tomahawk cruise missiles come at a cost of $1.5 million apiece. This is not unprofitable for Raytheon.

· · ·

In 1592, the London theaters closed for sixteen months due to an epidemic of bubonic plague.

· · ·

I attended an AA meeting near Austin, Texas. It was hot in the tin-sided building with only fans to cool. People were drinking hot coffee. In the parking lot was the usual array of luxury sedans, dusty pickups, ATVs, and bicycles. A woman, who could have weighed four hundred pounds, waddled in to plop onto the concrete floor. When it came her turn, she announced her name, pointed to one of the flimsy folding chairs, and said, "I know I'm fat, but I haven't had a drink in two months." We applauded for her. We wanted to.

· · ·

Are we really the only developed country still debating climate change?

· · ·

20 May 2002

In today's *New York Times*, reading of schoolchildren in lower Manhattan said to be "more deeply saddened" by the devastation of the World Trade Center Towers, but for many of these children, sadness, if not actual clinical depression, had in fact preceded the devastation. The principal of an elementary school on the edge of Chinatown tells a reporter, "We have kids in trauma all the time. Some come to school hurt. Some have housing problems. Our kids were fragile before. Are they more fragile now? I don't know. I can't make that leap."

—Joyce Carol Oates, from
"A Fragmented Diary in a Fragmented Time"

. . .

. . . nothing works like clockwork, not even clocks.

—Robert Urquhart, from "Toy"

. . .

To hold a pen is to be at war.

—Voltaire

. . .

re: The Internet

Whose idea was it to put all the idiots on earth in touch with each other?

—P. J. O'Rourke

. . .

Forty million Chinese children take piano lessons.

. . .

Ezra Pound once suggested Homer was an army doctor because of his keen descriptions of the honor displayed and the horror rendered in combat deaths. I seek honor in my posthistorical air war, but it is difficult to match deeds with the ancients. I am cloaked in the conceit of technology.

I look down at a map and figure angles and distances in my head based on our current heading. The Greek Peloponnese is off our nose, out of sight, over the horizon. Ancient Sparta. I look up and left, past the wingtip. Honor is, at best, diluted in the binary code of the most advanced airplane in the world. I place maps and mission papers in a lidded case behind the throttles to my left and pull out the *Norton Book of Classical Literature.* I linger on a highlighted section of Hesiod. By his description, the Olympian gods were petulant, arrogant, inhuman. When brilliant—yet inevitably flawed—mortal heroes approached the gods in deeds, their deaths were tragically orchestrated. But they lived on in myth. They reflected great truths, truths that were refined with the first spoken art—an art that began around campfires, in caves, in halls, on wooden ships: the poems and stories we have always needed to bring meaning to the random acts of man and nature that thwart our best plans.

Tonight, I will shoot Apollo's silver bow, which never misses. I will be miles above the Olympian mountaintops. The skin of the airplane that shields me from my enemies' eyes also shields me from renown. Popular stories of pilots are more often about machines pushing the limits of human capacity and endurance than about the nature of the individuals who fly them. Technology trumps our shared human nature. I tell myself that my actions will help save the lives of soldiers who are racing north out of Kuwait. This is honorable. It is not honor.

> —Jason Armagost, from
> "Things to Pack When You're Bound for Baghdad"

. . .

Do you know what long-range bomber pilots worry about?—kidney stones.

. . .

It took until 1992 for the Roman Catholic Church to formally proclaim that it had erred in condemning Galileo for holding that the earth was not the center of the universe.

. . .

re: High-end Travelers
The more stars in your itinerary, the less likely you are to find the real life of another country.

> —Ruth Reichl

. . .

The war occurred half a lifetime ago, and yet remembering makes it now. And sometimes remembering will lead to a story, which makes it forever. That's what stories are for.... Stories are for eternity, when memory is erased, when there is nothing to remember except the story.

> —Tim O'Brien, from *The Things They Carried*

. . .

...let us not talk falsely now, the hour is getting late.

> —Bob Dylan

. . .

The human race needs stories. We need all the experience we can get.

. . .

We read to know that we are not alone.

—C. S. Lewis

. . .

Watch the pretty woman in a group of women. She *knows* she's the pretty one. She *likes* her surroundings.

. . .

Because we both drive Porsches he thinks we're friends?

. . .

America: a country where everything is done to prove life isn't tragic.

—Albert Camus

. . .

Is it useful to know that our hearts beat about three billion times between birth and death? That the amount of blood that passes through an adult heart every week is enough to fill a swimming pool?

. . .

Difficulty, even suffering, lands on everyone. It is not a sign of personal failure.

. . .

Ordinary life is more dangerous than war because *nobody* survives.

—Janet Burroway

. . .

Memory makes things more than they were. This isn't a problem, is it?

. . .

Wreckage: a word that sounds like what it is. Say it.

. . .

Humans—despite their artistic pretensions, their sophistication, and their many accomplishments—owe their existence to a six-inch layer of topsoil and the fact that it rains.

. . .

This morning I have been trying to think about heaven, but without much success.

—Marilynne Robinson

. . .

re: Common Sense
The governor of Washington State has signed legislation to permit composting as an alternative to burying or cremating human remains.

. . .

Supporters say the method is an environmentally friendly alternative to cremations, which releases carbon dioxide and particulates into the air, and conventional burial, in which people are drained of their blood, and pumped full of formaldehyde and other chemicals that can pollute groundwater.

. . .

Licensed facilities offer "natural organic reduction," which turns a body, mixed with wood chips and straw, into about two wheelbarrows' worth of soil in a span of several weeks.

. . .

What man of you, if his son asked for bread, would give him a stone?

. . .

The graveyards are full of indispensable men.

—Charles de Gaulle

. . .

All sins are attempts to fill voids.

—Simone Weil

. . .

Is that true?

. . .

re: Enlarged prostate
How does it feel? If someone handed you a stick and said *Shove this up your dick*, you'd probably say, *I'll pass*. But if you shoved it up—that's how it feels...

. . .

re: Removal of Catheter (after several weeks)
You don't want part of any procedure that begins with "Take a deep breath."

. . .

re: Or a Subsequent Procedure That Begins
"You can leave your socks on."

. . .

Our love a difficult instrument we are learning to play. Practice, practice.

—C. D. Wright, from "Living"

. . .

Sisyphus, exhausted,
left his rock for us…

—Dunya Mikhail, from "N"

. . .

I learned late to focus on the ridiculously fortunate moments that have occurred for me, rather than on how I wish my life were. Also: These many moments of ridiculous luck have, for the most part, it must be said, been undeserved. *You?*

. . .

…all I can think of is how terrifying spring is, in its tireless, mindless replications.

—Kim Addonizio, from "Onset"

. . .

re: What to Put on Your Tombstone
I knew this would happen.

—Dan Jenkins

. . .

I ache in the places where I used to play.

—Leonard Cohen

. . .

When does empathy actually reinforce the pain it wants to console? Does giving people a space to talk about their disease—probe it, gaze at it, share it—help them move through it, or simply sharpen its hold?

—Leslie Jamison, from *The Empathy Exams*

. . .

Science is the only honest means man possesses for turning the world around him to account, but it is a material means; however disinterested science may be, it is justified only by the establishment, sooner or later, of utilitarian techniques. Literature has other goals.

—Alain Robbe-Grillet, from "Nature, Humanism, Tragedy"

. . .

Painting from Nature is not copying the object; it is realizing one's sensations.

—Paul Cézanne

. . .

Most of us rail against injustice from a position of personal safety. It is not that this is not admirable, but it's right to understand it for what it is.

. . .

The emperor who ordered construction of the Great Wall of China also ordered the burning of all the books in his kingdom.

. . .

When you find out root canals aren't permanent.

. . .

The claws of time…

. . .

That Leonardo da Vinci was the illegitimate child of a fifteen-year-old orphan from the Tuscan town of Vinci…

. . .

We forget we have blood in us until it starts coming out.
—Jim Harrison, from *Just Before Dark*

. . .

The Kindness of Strangers? How iffy is that?

. . .

re: What my father would say
You see a frog atop a fence post, do you know what you know? I will tell you: He didn't get there himself.

. . .

re: What I should have said to my colleagues in the English Department before I retired
Remember how you used to read before you became so smart?

. . .

People who don't read have only the experience of their lives.

. . .

Life is not a spectacle or a feast; it is a predicament.

—George Santayana

. . .

...and your device of comprehension—a book?

. . .

There is a crack, a crack in everything.
That's how the light gets in.

—Leonard Cohen

. . .

When I got the diagnosis—the tumor and all—my wife said, "Brush your teeth like you are going to live another twenty years. The last thing you need during all of this is a toothache."

. . .

Does the very act of thinking about the Holocaust... diminish its horror by refusing to treat it as unthinkable?

—James Carroll, from *Constantine's Sword*

. . .

H. L. Mencken re: Puritanism
The haunting fear that someone, somewhere may be happy...

. . .

Fritz Haber, the inventor of Zyklon B, was a Jew?

. . .

Books, once written, what further need of their authors?

. . .

re: A Note to Writers
An author is responsible for everything that appears in his books. If he claims that reality requires his depiction of the sexual, in addition to having a misguided aesthetic, he is a liar, since we shall surely see how few of his precious passages are devoted to chewing cabbage, hand-washing, sneezing, sitting on the stool, or, if you prefer, filling out forms, washing floors, cheering teams.

—William Gass, from *On Being Blue*

. . .

Why does it sadden Reader to realize he will almost certainly never know what book will turn out to be the last he ever read?

—David Markson, from *Reader's Block*

. . .

re: Just Saying…
It was like going from a Mini Cooper to a white 1982 Impala with blown shocks.

—Nicholson Baker, from *The Way the World Works*

. . .

What is literature but words that bear repeating?

. . .

Myths are things that never happened, but always are.

                    —Sallustius, Roman philosopher, fourth century

                        . . .

Books do furnish a room.

                                    —Anthony Powell

Entr'acte
My birthday surfaced as draft lottery "Number One" in the 1970 drawings. A college senior, I rushed to join Air Force ROTC. My immediate plan was to avoid the walking tour of Southeast Asia. Not lost on me was that more soldiers were being buried than airmen. But what I failed to grasp, when, in my panic, I contracted with the Air Force, was that the draft lottery dates applied to that year's newly turned nineteen-year-old males. I turned twenty-four that summer and could have completed school, and soon, with the war seemingly winding down, moved past the specified draft-age window (nineteen-to-twenty-five-year-olds). I'd been born on July 9 all right but July 9, 1946, not 1951. I entered military active duty because I misinterpreted what the lottery meant for me.

Two years before—1968—the USS *Pueblo* had been seized by the North Koreans. Martin Luther King Jr. was removed. Robert Kennedy. Riots and fires—DC, Baltimore, Chicago—exceeding, eventually, one hundred cities: a Tet Offensive at home. Fear and peril felt yeasty.

All the while I was enrolled in ROTC, I believed I had, in an acceptable way, dodged war. But when I received my first ROTC check ($100 a month), I felt bothered enough to donate the sum to the American Red Cross. But I needed the money, so after giving away the first check, I kept them. I did, though, donate blood every six weeks or so when the Red Cross set up to collect in the gym. All-Service ROTC classrooms were housed in the same building as the gym, and everyone knew the blood collected was being shipped to Southeast Asia. I donated the blood (drank the Tang, ate the Oreos), and tried not to chafe at the aspiring Marine ROTC midshipmen who would arrive in noisy squads, an enthusiastic arrangement that allowed for competition as to who could fill his blood bag soonest. These embryo Marines brought handballs to squeeze and clipboards and charts and stopwatches. I worried for the Marine midshipmen then, as I would worry for them now: they could hardly wait to give blood.

The average age of a soldier in Vietnam was 19. The average age of the 58,148 killed in Vietnam was 23.11 years.

I joined the Air Force to avoid Vietnam, then spent the next twenty-two years in the service. My military service wasn't, I believe, a mistake for me, though it would have hardly surfaced as a career choice without the undeclared fifteen-year war in southeastern Asia. In 1970, besides confusing the rules of the lottery draft, I also managed to select the single service willing to commission color-blind officers—or, as the government puts it, color-vision-deficient persons. I'm color-blind, but that's not what kept me out of war. It wasn't ROTC or the Air Force either. It was luck.

· · ·

re: What happened eleven months before my birth
At 8:16 AM on August 6, 1945, a fission weapon containing sixty-four kilograms of uranium detonated 580 meters above the Japanese city of Hiroshima, and Einstein's equation proved mercilessly accurate. The bomb itself was extremely inefficient: just one kilogram of the uranium underwent fission, and only seven hundred milligrams of mass—the weight of a butterfly—was converted into energy. But it was enough to obliterate an entire city in a fraction of a second. Some seventy-eight thousand people died instantly, or immediately afterward—vaporized, crushed, or incinerated...

> —Adam Higginbotham, from *Midnight in Chernobyl*

. . .

re: What happened seventy-four years later
Malignant neoplasm. That's what the doctor called the tumor. He showed me. With the camera up my dick and into the bladder, I was able to take in the view. "Turn the screen for him," the doctor said to his assistant. What I saw looked vegetative, like something you might see in the ocean, near coral, say, but it reminded me that Mussolini said watching bombs from the air was like watching flowers bloom.

. . .

Where did I get the idea that I could go to the doctor once and it would be over?

. . .

A close friend explained that his mother had penned a letter to be read to her children upon her death. Fearing she would die young, she wrote it in 1962. She lived an additional thirty-six years, dying at ninety-three. One of eleven children, Paul sat at the Thanksgiving Day table (yes, she died on Thanksgiving!) to hear the newly opened letter's content. The oldest son stood to read, starting with the inscribed name of each child. Paul told me his mother forgot to list one of her sons.

Coda
Fragments, indeed. As if there were anything to break.

—Don Paterson, from *The Book of Shadows*

Sources and Further Reading

Abbott, Lee K. *All Things, All at Once*. New York: W. W. Norton, 2006.

Abrams, David. "Roll Call." In *Fire and Forget*, ed. Roy Scranton and Matt Gallagher. Philadelphia: Da Capo, 2012.

Ackerman, Diane. *An Alchemy of Mind: The Marvel and Mystery of the Brain*. New York: Scribner, 2005.

——. *The Zookeeper's Wife*. New York: W. W. Norton, 2007.

Addonizio, Kim. "Onset." https://www.poetryfoundation.org/poems/42519/onset.

Altfeld, Heather. "Obituary for Dead Languages." *Conjunctions* 70 (Spring 2018).

Anderson, Donald, ed. *Aftermath: An Anthology of Post-Vietnam Fiction*. New York: Henry Holt, 1995.

——. *Fire Road*. Iowa City: University of Iowa Press, 2001.

——. *Gathering Noise from My Life: A Camouflaged Memoir*. Iowa City: University of Iowa Press, 2012.

——. "How Do Wars Begin?" *WWrite* (blog). The United States World War I Centennial Commission. https://www.worldwar1centennial.org/index.php/articles-posts/5578-how-do-wars-begin.html?utm_medium=email&utm_source=govdelivery.

——. "Memorandum for Record." In *Letters to J. D. Salinger*, ed. Chris Kubica and Will Hochman. Madison: University of Wisconsin Press, 2002.

——. "TNT." *The Gravity of the Thing*, Summer 2019. http://thegravityofthething.com/catalog/summer-2019/.

——, ed. *When War Becomes Personal: Soldiers' Accounts from the Civil War to Iraq*. Iowa City: University of Iowa Press, 2008.

Anderson, Doug. *Keep Your Head Down*. New York: W. W. Norton, 2009.

Armagost, Jason. "Things to Pack When You're Bound for Baghdad." In *When War Becomes Personal: Soldiers' Accounts from the Civil War to Iraq*, ed. Donald Anderson. Iowa City: University of Iowa Press, 2008.

Atwood, Margaret. https://www.goodreads.com/quotes/8332258 -that-is-how-we-writers-all-started-by-reading-we.

Auden, W. H. "Musée des Beaux Arts." http://www.poetrybyheart .org.uk/poems/musee-des-beaux-arts/.

Baker, Nicholson. *Human Smoke: The Beginnings of World War II, the End of Civilization*. New York: Simon & Schuster, 2008.

———. *The Way the World Works: Essays*. New York: Simon & Schuster, 2012.

Balaban, John. *Locusts at the Edge of Summer*. 2nd ed. Port Townsend, WA: Copper Canyon Press, 2003.

Baldwin, James. "The Artist's Struggle for Integrity." *The Cross of Redemption: Uncollected Writings*. New York: Vintage, 2010.

———. "James Baldwin Writing and Talking." See Romano, John. https://www.nytimes.com/1979/09/23/archives/james -baldwin-writing-and-talking-baldwin-baldwin-authors-query .html.

Barnes, Julian. *A History of the World in 10½ Chapters*. 1989. London: Vintage, 2016.

Berry, Wendell. *Jayber Crow*. Washington, DC: Counterpoint, 2000.

Biss, Eula. *Notes from No Man's Land: American Essays*. Minneapolis: Graywolf, 2009.

Bourdain, Anthony. "Don't Eat Before Reading This." *New Yorker*, April 19, 1999. https://www.newyorker.com/magazine/1999/04 /19/dont-eat-before-reading-this.

Bowden, Mark. *Black Hawk Down*. New York: Grove, 1999.

———. *Hue 1968*. New York: Atlantic Monthly, 2017.

Brown, D. F. *Ghost of a Person Passing in Front of the Flag*. Houston: Bloomsday, 2018.

Bryson, Bill. *A Short History of Nearly Everything*. New York: Broadway, 2005.

Burroway, Janet. *Embalming Mom: Essays in Life*. Iowa City: University of Iowa Press, 2002.

Busch, Benjamin. *Dust to Dust*. New York: Ecco, 2012.

Busch, Frederick. *A Memory of War*. New York: Ballantine, 2004.

Campbell, SueEllen. *The Face of the Earth: Natural Landscapes, Science, and Culture*. Berkeley: University of California Press, 2011.

Camus, Albert. http://quodid.com/quotes/3105/albert-camus/in-the -depth-of-winter-i-finally-learned.

Caputo, Philip. *A Rumor of War*. New York: Holt, Rinehart and Winston, 1977.

Carroll, James. *Constantine's Sword*. New York: Houghton Mifflin, 2001.

Cézanne, Paul. https://www.paulcezanne.org/quotes.jsp.

Cheever, John. *The Stories of John Cheever*. New York: Knopf, 1979.

Chitwood, Michael. "Practicum." In *The Best of the Prose Poem: An International Journal*, ed. Peter Johnson. Buffalo, NY: White Pine Press, 2000.

Clare, John. "Remembrances." *Poems*. London: Faber & Faber, 2007.

Cochrane, Mick. "Stage Four." *The Sun*, December 2017.

Connell, Evan. *Deus lo Volt: Chronicle of the Crusades*. Washington, DC: Counterpoint, 2000.

Crane, Stephen. *The Black Riders and Other Lines*. 1895. http://www .theotherpages.org/poems/crane02.html#12.

Crews, Harry. *A Childhood: The Biography of a Place*. Athens: University of Georgia Press, 1995.

Cummings, E. E. https://quotepark.com/quotes/1894636-ee -cummings-when-you-confuse-art-with-propaganda-you -confuse/.

De Gaulle, Charles. https://www.brainyquote.com/quotes/charles _de_gaulle_103672.

De la O, Marsha. "Nobody Knows." https://www.poetryfoundation .org/poems/58744/nobody-knows.

Diamond, John. *Because Cowards Get Cancer Too: A Hypochondriac Confronts His Nemesis*. New York: Times Books, 1999.

Dickinson, Emily. "Hope is the thing with feathers." https://www .poetryfoundation.org/poems/42889/hope-is-the-thing-with -feathers-314.

Diderot, Denis. https://www.brainyquote.com/quotes/denis_diderot _105429.

Dillard, Annie. "Eclipse." In *Teaching a Stone to Talk: Expeditions and Encounters*. New York: HarperCollins, 1982.

———. *For the Time Being*. New York: Vintage, 2000.

Doerr, Harriet. *Stones for Ibarra*. New York: Penguin, 1984.

Dunnigan, James F. *How to Make War: A Comprehensive Guide to Modern Warfare*. 3rd ed. New York: HarperCollins, 1993.

Egan, Timothy. *The Worst Hard Time*. Boston: Houghton Mifflin, 2006.

Ehrhart, W. D. *Vietnam-Perkasie*. Amherst: University of Massachusetts Press, 1995.

Einstein, Albert. https://www.goodreads.com/quotes/14977-i-know-not-with-what-weapons-world-war-iii-will.

Eliot, T. S. "The Hollow Men." https://allpoetry.com/the-hollow-men.

———. *The Three Voices of Poetry*. New York: Cambridge University Press, 1954.

Elkins, James. *The Object Stares Back: On the Nature of Seeing*. San Diego: Harcourt, 1996.

Emerson, Ralph Waldo. https://www.azquotes.com/quote/611478.

Fairchild, B. H. *The Art of the Lathe*. Farmington, ME: Alice James, 1998.

Filkins, Dexter. *The Forever War*. New York: Vintage, 2008.

Finnegan, William. "California Burning." *New York Review of Books*, August 16, 2018.

Flaubert, Gustave. *Madame Bovary*. 1856. New York: Knopf, 1993.

Fountain, Ben. *Billy Lynn's Long Halftime Walk*. New York: Ecco, 2012.

Frost, Robert. *The Poetry of Robert Frost*. New York: Henry Holt, 1979.

Fussell, Paul. "My War." https://harpers.org/archive/1982/01/my-war/.

———. *Thank God for the Atom Bomb*. New York: Ballantine, 1990.

Gajdusek, Robert E. *Resurrection: A War Journey*. South Bend, IN: University of Notre Dame Press, 1997.

Galeano, Eduardo. *Century of the Wind*. Vol. 3 of *Memory of Fire*. New York: Pantheon, 1988.

———. *Children of the Days: A Calendar of Human History*. New York: Nation Books, 2013.

Gardner, Phillip. "Election Return." *North American Review* 303,
    no. 2 (Spring 2018).

Garnett, David. *War in the Air: September 1939–May 1941.* 1st Ameri-
    can ed. New York: Doubleday, Doran, 1941.

Gass, William. *On Being Blue: A Philosophical Inquiry.* Boston:
    Godine, 1976.

Gatling, Richard. https://www.goodreads.com/quotes/1068038
    -it-occurred-to-me-that-if-i-could-invent-a.

Gioia, Dana. *Can Poetry Matter?* Saint Paul, MN: Graywolf, 1992.

Giraldi, William. *American Audacity: In Defense of Literary Daring.*
    New York: Liveright, 2018.

Glück, Louise. "Nostos." https://www.poemhunter.com/poem
    /nostos/.

Goldbarth, Albert. "Untitled." https://twitter.com/nipponhamz
    /status/1050531046595469314.

Goluboff, Benjamin. *Ho Chi Minh.* Windsor, ON: Urban Farmhouse
    Press, 2017.

Gourley, Jim. "Yes Marcus. They Did Die in Vain." *Foreign Policy,*
    January 15, 2014. https://foreignpolicy.com/2014/12/31/yes
    -marcus-they-did-die-in-vain-2/.

Greene, Jonathan. *Inventions of Necessity: Selected Poems.* Frankfort,
    KY: Gnomon Press, 1998.

Groff, Lauren. *Florida.* New York: Riverhead, 2018.

Grossman, Dave. *On Killing.* New York: Back Bay, 2009.

Gwynne, S. C. *Empire of the Summer Moon.* New York: Scribner, 2010.

Haigh, Jennifer. "A Buzzworthy Debut about a Mysterious and
    Secluded Artists' Retreat." Review of *The Honey Farm,* by Harriet
    Alida Lye. *New York Times,* June 29, 2018. https://www.nytimes
    .com/2018/06/29/books/review/honey-farm-harriet-alida-lye
    .html.

Hannah, Barry. *High Lonesome.* New York: Grove, 1996.

Harrison, Jim. *Just Before Dark.* New York: Grove, 1991.

———. *Off to the Side: A Memoir.* New York: Atlantic Monthly, 2002.

Hart, Peter, ed. *Voices from the Front: An Oral History of the Great
    War.* New York: Oxford University Press, 2016.

Hayden, Robert. "Those Winter Sundays." https://www.poetry
    foundation.org/poems/46461/those-winter-sundays.

Hedges, Chris. *War Is a Force That Gives Us Meaning*. New York: Public Affairs, 2002.

Heineman, Larry. *Paco's Story*. New York: Penguin, 1987.

Hemingway, Ernest. *A Farewell to Arms*. 1929. New York: Scribner, 2014.

Heynen, Jim. *The One-Room Schoolhouse: Stories about the Boys*. New York: Vintage, 1994.

Hicok, Bob. "The semantics of flowers on Memorial Day." https://www.poetryfoundation.org/poems/50808/the-semantics-of-flowers-on-memorial-day.

Higginbotham, Adam. *Midnight in Chernobyl: The Untold Story of the World's Greatest Nuclear Disaster*. New York: Simon & Schuster, 2019.

Hitchens, Christopher. *God Is Not Great: How Religion Poisons Everything*. New York: Twelve, 2009.

Hobbes, Thomas. *Leviathan*. 1651. New York: Penguin Classics, 1982.

Hochschild, Adam. *King Leopold's Ghost*. Boston: Houghton Mifflin, 1998.

Hutchinson, George. "Why You Should Want Me on the Life Raft." http://english.cornell.edu/sites/english/files/fa13_english_cu.pdf.

Huxley, Aldous. *Ends and Means*. New York: Routledge, 2017.

Huxley, Thomas Henry. https://www.goodreads.com/quotes/75429-sit-down-before-fact-like-a-little-child-and-be.

Hynes, Samuel. *The Soldiers' Tale: Bearing Witness to Modern War*. New York: Penguin, 1997.

Jamison, Leslie. *The Empathy Exams*. Minneapolis: Graywolf, 2014.

Jeffers, Robinson. *The Collected Poetry of Robinson Jeffers*. Palo Alto, CA: Stanford University Press, 2002.

Jenkins, Dan. https://www.golfdigest.com/story/his-ownself-dan-jenkins-1929-2019-tribute-dies-at-age-89.

Johnson, Denis. *The Throne of the Third Heaven of the Nations Millennium General Assembly: Poems Collected and New*. New York: Harper Perennial, 1996.

Junger, Sebastian. *Tribe*. New York: Twelve, 2016.

——. *War*. New York: Twelve, 2010.

Kafer, Krista. "Facts Should Matter More Than Feelings in Public Policy." https://www.denverpost.com/2018/05/17/facts-should-matter-more-than-feelings-in-public-policy/.

Kastan, David Scott, with Stephen Farthing. *On Color*. New Haven, CT: Yale University Press, 2018.

Kempowski, Walter. *All for Nothing*. London: Granta Books, 2015.

Kooser, Ted. *The Poetry Home Repair Manual*. Lincoln: University of Nebraska Press, 2005.

Krauthammer, Charles. "Pelosi's Armenian Gambit." *Washington Post*, October 19, 2007. https://www.goodreads.com/quotes /672506-krauthammer-s-razor-with-apologies-to-occam-in -explaining-any-puzzling.

Lanzmann, Claude. *Shoah*. New York: Pantheon, 1985.

Larkin, Philip. "Aubade." https://www.poetryfoundation.org/poems /48422/aubade-56d229a6e2f07.

Larson, Greg. "Plague." *North American Review* 303, no. 2 (Spring 2018).

Lears, Jackson. "How a War Became a Crusade." *New York Times*, March 11, 2003.

Lepore, Jill. *These Truths: A History of the United States*. New York: W. W. Norton, 2019.

Levi, Primo. *The Complete Works*. New York: Liveright, 2015.

———. *Survival in Auschwitz*. New York: Simon & Schuster, 1996.

Lewis, C. S. https://www.goodreads.com/quotes/1034489-we-read -to-know-we-are-not-alone.

Lincoln, Abraham. http://www.abrahamlincolnonline.org/lincoln /speeches/liberty.htm.

Lingle, Brandon. "I Thought You Were in Afghanistan." *Zone 3* 29, no. 2 (Fall 2014).

———. "Remembering Sutherland Springs." *American Scholar*, April 9, 2018. https://theamericanscholar.org/remembering -sutherland-springs-/#.XeiKtihKg2x.

Lohnes, Kate. "How Rye Bread May Have Caused the Salem Witch Trials." Britannica. https://www.britannica.com/story/how-rye -bread-may-have-caused-the-salem-witch-trials.

Lowell, Robert. *Interviews and Memoirs*. Ann Arbor: University of Michigan Press, 1988.

Loyd, Anthony. *My War Gone By, I Miss It So*. New York: Penguin, 1999.

MacLeish, Archibald. "Ars Poetica." https://www.poetryfoundation .org/poetrymagazine/poems/17168/ars-poetica.

Mahoney, Donal. "Analyzing the Election." https://www.poem
    hunter.com/poem/analyzing-the-election/.
Manchester, William. *Goodbye Darkness*. New York: Back Bay, 2002.
Markson, David. *Reader's Block*. Chicago: Dalkey Archive, 1996.
———. *This Is Not a Novel: And Other Novels*. Berkeley, CA: Counter-
    point, 2016.
———. *Vanishing Point*. Washington, DC: Shoemaker & Hoard, 2004.
Marlantes, Karl. *What It Is Like to Go to War*. New York: Atlantic
    Monthly, 2011.
Marlowe, Christopher. *Four Plays*. London: Bloomsbury, 2011.
Matthews, William. *After All: Last Poems*. Boston: Houghton Mifflin,
    1998.
———. *Rising and Falling*. New York: Little, Brown, 1979.
———. *Time and Money: New Poems*. Boston: Houghton Mifflin, 1995.
McCarthy, Cormac. *Blood Meridian*. New York: Vintage, 1985.
McDaniel, Jeffrey. "Disasterology." In *Last Call: Poems on Alcohol-
    ism, Addiction, and Deliverance*, ed. Sarah Gorham and Jeffrey
    Skinner. Louisville, KY: Sarabande Books, 1997.
McPherson, Sandra. https://www.robert-morgan.com/published
    -works.
Melville, Herman. https://www.brainyquote.com/quotes/herman
    _melville_157727.
Mencken, H. L. https://www.brainyquote.com/quotes/h_l_mencken
    _125197.
Menzies, Robert. https://www.bloomberg.com/opinion/articles
    /2019–02–16/churchill-was-more-villain-than-hero-in-britain
    -s-colonies.
Mikhail, Dunya. *In Her Feminine Sign*. New York: New Directions,
    2019.
Momaday, N. Scott. https://www.sfreporter.com/news/interviews
    /2010/01/20/writing-his-world/.
Montaigne, Michel de. https://www.goodreads.com/quotes
    /620766-if-i-had-even-the-slightest-grasp-upon-my-own.
Morgan, Robert. *Good Measure: Essays, Interviews, and Notes on
    Poetry*. Baton Rouge: LSU Press, 1993.
———. *Green River: New and Selected Poems*. Hanover, NH: Wesleyan
    University Press, 1991.

Morris, Wright. *A Bill of Rites, a Bill of Wrongs, a Bill of Goods.* Lincoln: University of Nebraska Press, 1980.

———. *Love Among the Cannibals.* New York: Harcourt, Brace, 1957.

Munro, Alice. *Friend of My Youth.* New York: Vintage, 1991.

———. *The Progress of Love.* New York: Knopf, 1985.

Nadelson, Theodore. *Trained to Kill: Soldiers at War.* Baltimore: Johns Hopkins University Press, 2005.

Newton, Peter. https://haiku.mannlib.cornell.edu/2010/08/10/2126/.

Ninh, Bao. *The Sorrow of War.* New York: Riverhead, 1996.

Nordhaus, Jean. "A Dandelion for My Mother." https://www.poetry foundation.org/poems/49847/a-dandelion-for-my-mother.

Nye, Naomi Shihab. "Trying to Name What Doesn't Change." https://www.poetryfoundation.org/poems/48599/trying-to -name-what-doesnt-change.

Oates, Joyce Carol. "A Fragmented Diary in a Fragmented Time." https://www.narrativemagazine.com/issues/fall-2003/non fiction/fragmented-diary-fragmented-time-joyce-carol-oates.

O'Brien, Tim. *The Things They Carried.* New York: Broadway, 1990.

O'Rouke, P. J. *None of My Business.* New York: Atlantic Monthly, 2018.

Orwell, George. "England Your England." *The Collected Essays, Journalism, and Letters.* Vol. 2, *My Country Right or Left,* ed. Sonia Orwell and Ian Angus. Harmondsworth: Penguin Books, 1984.

Paterson, Don. *The Book of Shadows.* London: Picador, 2004.

Phi, Bao. "War Before Memory." https://18millionrising.org/2013/09 /war-before-memory.html.

Picasso, Pablo. https://www.brainyquote.com/quotes/pablo _picasso_384494.

Pisor, Robert. *The Siege of Khe Sanh.* 2002. New York: W. W. Norton, 2018.

Plath, Sylvia. *The Bell Jar.* 1963. New York: Harper Perennial, 2005.

Pollan, Michael. https://www.nytimes.com › review › psychedelics -how-to-change-your-mind.

Pritchett, V. S. *A Cab at the Door.* New York: Random House, 1968.

Puller, Lewis, Jr. *Fortunate Son.* New York: Grove, 2000.

Pynchon, Thomas. https://labyrinthbooks.com/product/9781619 029996.

Reichl, Ruth. *Save Me the Plums: My Gourmet Memoir*. New York: Random House, 2019.

Ritterbusch, Dale. *Far from the Temple of Heaven*. Windsor, ON: Black Moss, 2005.

Roach, Mary. *Grunt: The Curious Science of Humans at War*. New York: W. W. Norton, 2016.

Robbe-Grillet, Alain. "Nature, Humanism, Tragedy." *New Left Review*, May–June 1965.

Robinson, Marilynne. *Gilead*. New York: Picador, 2006.

Robison, Mary. *Why Did I Ever*. Berkeley, CA: Counterpoint, 2001.

Romano, John. "James Baldwin Writing and Talking." *New York Times*, September 23, 1979. https://www.nytimes.com /1979/09/23/archives/james-baldwin-writing-and-talking -baldwin-baldwin-authors-query.html.

Rousseau, Jean-Jacques. *The Social Contract*. 1762. New York: Penguin Classics, 1968.

Rowe, Josephine. "Love." https://iwp.uiowa.edu/sites/iwp/files /Rowe_excerpt_0.pdf.

Salinger, J. D. *Catcher in the Rye*. New York: Little, Brown, 2010.

Santayana, George. https://www.goodreads.com/quotes/189995 -memory-is-an-internal-rumor. https://www.goodreads.com /quotes/1143939-life-is-not-a-spectacle-or-a-feast-it-is.

Sean, Alison. "Sand Key." *Dunes Review* 15, no. 1 (Summer 2010).

Shields, David. *Reality Hunger: A Manifesto*. New York: Vintage, 2011.

Simic, Charles. *The Unemployed Fortune Tellers*. Ann Arbor: University of Michigan Press, 1994.

Smith, William Loren. "Sole of Dover." In *Last Call: Poems on Alcoholism, Addiction, and Deliverance*, ed. Sarah Gorham and Jeffrey Skinner. Louisville, KY: Sarabande Books, 1997.

Solnit, Rebecca. "Rebecca Solnit: By the Book." *New York Times Book Review*, August 16, 2018. https://www.nytimes.com/2018 /08/16/books/review/rebecca-solnit-by-the-book.html.

Stafford, William. *Sound of the Ax: Aphorisms and Poems*. Pittsburgh, PA: University of Pittsburgh Press, 2014.

Sukach, M. K. *Hypothetically Speaking*. Farmington, ME: Encircle, 2017.

Tea, Michelle. *Against Memoir: Complaints, Confessions, and Criticisms*. New York: Feminist Press, 2018.

Tennis, Cary. "That's What Experience Is All About." *The Sun*, March 2018.

Tolkien, J. R. R. https://www.goodreads.com/quotes/352936-never -laugh-at-live-dragons-bilbo-you-fool.

Trachtenberg, Peter. *The Book of Calamities*. New York: Little, Brown, 2008.

Turner, Brian. *My Life as a Foreign Country*. New York: W. W. Norton, 2014.

———. *Phantom Noise*. Farmington, ME: Alice James, 2014.

Twain, Mark. https://www.brainyquote.com/quotes/mark_twain _134518.

Tyler, Anne. *Clock Dance*. New York: Vintage, 2019.

Updike, John. Foreword to *Too Far to Go: The Maples Stories*. https://www.brainyquote.com/quotes/john_updike_399775.

Urquhart, Robert. "Toy." *Paris Review* 162 (Summer 2002).

Van Reet, Brian. "Big Two-Hearted Hunting Creek." In *Fire and Forget*, ed. Roy Scranton and Matt Gallagher. Philadelphia: Da Capo, 2012.

Vegetius Renatus, Flavius. http://www.digitalattic.org/home/war /vegetius/index.php.

Voltaire. https://www.brainyquote.com/quotes/voltaire_125630.

Vonnegut, Kurt. *Wampeters, Foma, and Granfalloons*. New York: Dial, 1999.

Weigl, Bruce. *The Circle of Hanh*. New York: Grove, 2000.

Weil, Simone. https://www.goodreads.com/quotes/27774-all-sins -are-attempts-to-fill-voids.

West, Paul. *The Immensity of the Here and Now*. Rutherford, NJ: Voyant, 2003.

———. "In Defense of Purple Prose." *New York Times*, December 15, 1985.

———. *Sheer Fiction*. New Paltz, NY: McPherson, 1987.

Will, George. https://www.washingtonpost.com/opinions /trump-is-no-longer-the-worst-person-in-government/2018 /05/09/10e59eba-52f1-11e8-a551-5b648abe29ef_story.html.

Willard, Nick. "How I'll End the War: My First Week Back in Afghanistan." May 1, 2014. https://www.thedailybeast.com /how-ill-end-the-war-my-first-week-back-in-afghanistan.

Williams, C. K. *Flesh and Blood*. New York: Farrar, Straus and Giroux, 1987.

Williams, Terry Tempest. "Ground Truthing." *The Open Space of Democracy*. Eugene, OR: Wipf and Stock, 2004.

Wolfe, John. "A Different Species of Time." In *When War Becomes Personal: Soldiers' Accounts from the Civil War to Iraq*, ed. Donald Anderson. Iowa City: University of Iowa Press, 2008.

Wolff, Tobias. *In Pharaoh's Army*. New York: Knopf, 1994.

———. "The Liar." *In the Garden of the North American Martyrs*. New York: Ecco, 1981.

Wood, Karenne. "The Lilies." https://www.poetryfoundation.org /poems/147118/the-lilies.

Wright, C. D. "Living." https://www.poetryfoundation.org/poems /47843/living-56d2289b5783f.

Wright, Evan. *Generation Kill*. New York: Penguin, 2004.

Permissions Credits

About the Author

DONALD ANDERSON (MFA, Cornell University) is professor of English and writer-in-residence at the U.S. Air Force Academy and serves as the editor for *War, Literature & the Arts: An International Journal of the Humanities.* His previous book publications include *Below Freezing: Elegy for the Melting Planet* (University of New Mexico Press), *Gathering Noise from My Life: A Camouflaged Memoir* (University of Iowa Press), *When War Becomes Personal: Soldiers' Accounts from the Civil War to Iraq* (University of Iowa Press), *Fire Road* (University of Iowa Press), *Aftermath: An Anthology of Post-Vietnam Fiction* (Henry Holt), and others.